WATER WALKER

THE OUTLAW CHRONICLES

TED DEKkER

WORTHY®
PUBLISHING

Copyright © 2014 by Ted Dekker
Published by Worthy Publishing, a division of Worthy Media, Inc., 134 Franklin Road, Suite 200,
Brentwood, Tennessee 37027.

Worthy is a registered trademark of Worthy Media, Inc.
HELPING PEOPLE EXPERIENCE THE HEART OF GOD

Library of Congress Control Number: 2013954261

ISBN: 978-1-61795-274-6 (trade paper)

This book is a work of fiction. Names, characters, places, and incidents are the product of the
author's imagination or are used fictitiously. Any resemblance to actual events, locales, or persons,
living or dead, is coincidental.

Published in association with Creative Trust, 5141 Virginia Way, Brentwood, TN 37027.
www.creativetrust.com.

For foreign and subsidiary rights, contact rights@worthypublishing.com

Cover Art and Photography: Pixel Peach Studio
Interior Design and Typesetting: Kimberly Sagmiller, Fudge Creative

Printed in The United States of America
14 15 16 17 18 LBM 8 7 6 5 4 3 2 1

EPISODE ONE

PROLOGUE

MY NAME is Eden and this is my story. I know that on the surface it may seem different from your own, and on one level that's true. After all, you may not be a blond-haired girl like me and I doubt very many people have faced or will ever face the particular trials that I have.

And yet when you get right down to it, we're all the same—rich, poor, old, young, fat, skinny, white, brown, or purple—pick your costume, none of it really matters too much. What does matter is whether or not we take offense when we think we've been wronged, regardless of who we think we are or what costume we're wearing.

That's what I learned. The way I learned it might shock you a bit. You might laugh at some of it or cry at times . . . it all depends on who you think *you* are, which may not be the real you at all. You can only learn who you really are by getting to the end of who you think you are; I learned that too.

So don't feel sorry for me, or cry too much because it was the only way for me. And the same goes for you.

My story began the night I discovered that I wasn't me.

Day One
7:34 PM

"YOU CAN'T wait any longer." Wyatt heard Kathryn take a deep, controlled breath on the other end of the line. He imagined her standing in their small kitchen, phone pressed to her ear, hand trembling by her side. "You've been watching the house for two days—they're bound to see you if they haven't already. You go in there and you get my daughter, you hear me?"

"I hear you, sugar." He stared through the truck's window at the brick house. "But I can't just walk in and take her without—"

"Yes you can! And you won't have to take her. She'll come. You tell her who you are and she'll come. Tell her that she doesn't need to live in a foster home one more day because her mother's been looking for her for thirteen years and she'll come."

"What if she doesn't remember right away?"

"I'm her *mother*, Wyatt! Her mother! Blood doesn't forget blood. And you're her father, don't you forget that. Maybe not by blood, but she'll know the moment she sees you. There's nobody in the world that loves that child the way we do. One look in your eyes and she'll see that."

"She's not alone in there. The mother's home and the father will be home soon."

"Which is why you have to go in there and *get* her alone!" Kathryn snapped. "And don't use that word—that woman in there's an imposter, not a mother. Don't you dare use that word."

"I know, sugar." He felt her anxiety work through his own bones. "This isn't how it was supposed to go."

"How it's supposed to go is for you to rescue my daughter and bring her home to me. We always knew she wouldn't just walk out and get in the truck with you—the poor girl's been subjected to only God knows what."

"I was supposed to get her alone and talk to her first."

"And that's exactly what you're going to do. You're going to walk up to that front door and tell whoever answers that you have an important message for Alice—remember to call her Alice because she won't know her real name. And you make sure no one else hears what you tell her. No one can know that her birth mother came to save her."

Kathryn sniffed.

"I don't care what it takes, Wyatt." She was on the verge of tears, voice strained and weak. "We talked about this. If those snakes find you out, we may never get another chance. You have to get her before the man gets home. Now, Wyatt. Go tell her that her mother's waiting. She'll come."

She'd been obsessed with finding her daughter for years, and that need had risen to a fever pitch a month earlier when they'd discovered that Eden was alive and living in South Carolina with foster parents. She'd been taken against Kathryn's will by the legal system, so recovering her had proven to be a matter of careful planning, and it all rested squarely on his shoulders now. Problem was getting her out of that house without causing a fuss.

And the problem with getting her out without causing a fuss was that Eden wouldn't come without some convincing, no matter what Kathryn said. In her desperation, she wasn't thinking clearly now. Not that he blamed her—he was nearly as eager as she was, if only to make things right for all of them, most of all Kathryn.

He'd spent the last two days looking for any opportunity to catch Eden alone without any success. Kathryn had a point—sooner or later the neighbors would call in the blue pickup truck with a camper shell. He'd been careful to duck down behind the steering wheel when cars approached and he'd spent a good amount of time in the back among all the blankets he'd brought, so he was sure he hadn't been seen. But there was no way to hide the truck, not if he wanted to be close enough to intercept her if she ever left the house alone. Which she hadn't.

"Zeke went to a lot of trouble to set this up, Wyatt. All you have to do is get to her. I lost my daughter once, I'm not about to lose her again."

"Okay, sugar. I'll go."

"Tell her that her mother's waiting."

"I will."

"Make sure no one hears you."

"I will."

"Hurry before the man returns. Do it now and call me the minute you're back in the truck."

"Of course."

"Promise me."

"I promise, sugar."

Wyatt waited for the line to click off before removing the phone from his ear. He gave the cab a once-over. The old Ford had a black vinyl-covered bench seat, worn shiny and cracked in a couple places. At Kathryn's direction he'd cleaned the interior when he'd collected the truck and taken care not to leave any junk on the floor.

He turned the rearview mirror for a look at his face . . . two day's growth—not too shabby. Ran his fingers through his hair. Wavy blond, maybe could use a wash. Blue eyes. A kind face, Kathryn said—the kind any girl would find comforting. The thought of Eden seeing him for the first time was a bit unsettling, only because she would see a stranger when in reality he was her father.

He slipped the keys into the front pocket of his tan work pants—cleaned proper. Blue shirt tucked in neat.

Had to get this right. Had to or Kathryn would likely die of grief. And Zeke wouldn't approve.

With a quick look up and down the quiet street, he stepped out of the truck and eased the door shut. The man of the house had come home between seven thirty and eight both nights . . . it was seven thirty-five now.

He crossed the street, angled up the sidewalk, and headed for the front door, heart thumping like a fist in his chest. He'd seen Eden six times in the last two days. Twice through binoculars when she'd had the curtains to her room on the second floor pulled open. Thin, with pale skin and straight blond hair that fell past her shoulders. A spitting image of Kathryn at that age, he imagined. And when he'd described Eden to her, his wife had wept for joy over the phone.

Had to get this right.

Never mind how crazy rescuing Eden like this felt . . . right was right, and God made it so.

Wyatt dried the palms of his hands on his pants as he stepped up to the concrete landing, took one last look down the street, drew a deep breath to calm his nerves, and lifted his finger to the doorbell, aware that he wasn't as steady as he could be. And there was a thin line of dirt under his nail.

He thought about cleaning it, but now his jitters were getting worse and he knew he was stalling. If he didn't do this now, it might not happen. So he pressed the button and stepped back when he heard the chime inside.

Had to get this right and now he had. It was now out of his hands.

It all came down to—

The door swung in and Wyatt found himself facing a girl with long blond hair, dressed in a light-blue hoodie and a pair of jeans.

Eden.

"Can I help you?"

He was so surprised at seeing her—and only her—right there in front of him, that he didn't know what to say.

She stared up at him with brown eyes, as innocent as a dove, one hand on the doorknob, at a loss.

Tell her, Wyatt. Just tell her.

He glanced over her head to be sure the woman wasn't close by, then said it.

"Your mother wants to see you. She wants you to come. She loves you. No one can know that I'm here."

Not smooth enough. His voice was too raspy. He quickly cleared his throat.

"I'm your father. Please, you have to come with me. Your mother has been looking for you for thirteen years." Then, "Your real name is Eden."

"Alice?" The call came from down the hall.

He quickly reached out a hand so that she could take it and they could run before it was too late. "Please . . ."

The foster parent, a woman in her forties or fifties with short, curled blond hair stepped out into the hall with a dishtowel, drying her hands.

"Who is it, dear?"

Wyatt froze, eyes locked on the woman's. He should be thinking fast on his feet and saying something, but he wasn't always good in that way and at the moment his mind was blank.

The woman started down the hall toward them. All Wyatt could think to do was grab Eden and run, but he couldn't just grab her without her knowing what was going on—the poor girl would be frightened.

Maybe scream. Might even get hurt.

"How can we help you?" the woman asked.

"I . . ."

But he didn't know what to say. And before he could figure any-thing out, Eden moved to her left out of sight and vanished into the house, leaving him alone with the woman down the hall. The foster parent took one look in the direction Eden had gone and must have seen something that frightened her, because when she looked back at him, her jaw was set.

"I think you should leave."

She stepped up to the door and pushed it closed. The lock snapped into place.

Wyatt stood unmoving, staring at the door, stunned. Just like that?

This wasn't good. An image of Kathryn's face, sagging with dread, strung through his mind. And with it, the sickening awareness of his failure.

And then the realization that standing on the landing looking dumbstruck might be seen by either someone in the house or a neigh-bor as creepy. Which he wasn't.

So he turned and headed back to the truck, walking on feet that felt like lead. Mind blank. A knot in his throat. But he knew what he would do. What he always did. She would know . . . She always did.

Kathryn answered his call on the first ring.

"Do you have her?"

He took a deep breath. "The mother was there . . . Not at first but as soon as—"

"What do you mean 'not at first'?" she interrupted. "Did you talk to her?"

"No. Not to the mother—"

"To *Eden!* Did you do what I told you to do? Please tell me you didn't mess this up!"

"No, sugar, I swear." He told her what had happened in short order, exactly as it had, because she would insist and he had long learned it was better that way. Integrity was important if you wanted any peace of mind.

The phone remained silent for a few seconds after he finished. She was reeling and he didn't blame her.

"Kathryn?"

"We're running out of time."

"I know. But I—"

"You go back in there, Wyatt." Her voice was lower now, unnervingly intense but calm at the same time. "I don't care how you do it but you get me my daughter and you get her now. Break the door down if you have to. Take her. She may not understand now but she will when she learns the whole story."

"Break the door down?" His mind spun with what that might mean. "What if she won't come?"

"Then *take* her!" The receiver went silent for a few seconds. Kathryn continued with unmistakable clarity. "You don't harm a hair on her head, but you make her come with you. You understand what I'm saying, Wyatt?"

He hesitated only a second.

"Yes, sugar."

The phone went dead.

He returned it to his pocket with a trembling hand, mind gone on fear. He honestly didn't see how he could do what she insisted, not without raising an alarm. Not without risking injury to one or both of them. Not without getting caught and blowing any further chances of ever getting Eden back home.

Then again, he'd probably already blown any further chances. Eden would tell the woman that her birth mother was trying to get to her and the authorities would seal her up tight. God had provided a way for them to find Eden, hadn't he? Then God would also now make a way for her to come with him, and this was the only way Kathryn could see it. She had faith—it was now only a matter of his own faith. Eden had to be rescued—sometimes doing good required taking risks.

Wyatt thought about Eden's plight all of these years, having been thrown away into an orphanage as an infant against her mother's will. And about the hole in Kathryn's soul since that day, searching in vain for her lost daughter.

And with those thoughts drumming through his mind, he got out of the pickup truck, walked calmly to the back of the camper shell, opened the lift gate, withdrew his gloves, the hammer, and the duct tape, and headed across the street.

Day One
7:42 PM

WHY? I suppose that's a question the runs through every thirteen-year-old's mind, but judging by the way most other kids talked, I doubt the question was as prevalent in their minds as it was in mine.

Why? Why me? Why am I so different? Why can't I quite figure out where I belong? Why do I speak differently than most people my age? Why does everyone keep saying that I'm so smart when I feel mostly clueless? Why is my IQ so high and my learning so advanced and my knowledge so low? Why do people look at me strangely?

But for me there were even more questions, most of which I kept hidden because I didn't know anyone I felt comfortable asking. Like *who?* Who am I, really? Who made me this way? Who are all these other people? Who is my mother, who is my father?

And *what?* What am I? What am I supposed to do now? What am I supposed to even *think* now?

The counselor I see once a week, Amy Treadwell, tells me that all of the testing they've done on me shows that parts of my mind work much more like an adult than a thirteen-year-old, like the parts that absorb new information and the way I speak.

On the other hand, she says that I'm quite naïve. Too trusting.

Evidently something terrible happened to me when I was younger.

I don't know what happened. I don't remember, and either no one knows, or no one wants to tell me. In fact, all I do know is what I've learned during the last six months of my life. Everything before that is gone from my mind.

Think of my mind like a perfectly tuned, powerful computer. When I awoke from whatever happened to me six months ago, my operating system was still there, humming along, so I had good command of language and I could process information perfectly, but the hard drive that held all of my memory had been wiped clean.

So I had to learn everything from scratch. And having the kind of circuits that I had, I learned quickly. Many things came to me automatically, like survival reflexes—knowing to step out of the way of a speeding car to avoid being crushed, for example. But I had to learn most things by being fed information, not unlike downloading data onto a computer.

My intuition, however, was much less advanced. My way of being in the world. The complexities of relationships and proper etiquette. Things like trusting and not trusting, believing and not believing, judging and not judging. In this way, they said I was like a young child. While I saw the world as full of wonder, most people had developed strange reactions to it. Anger, worry, and fear were strange things to me at first. Naturally, I eventually began to learn them, but slowly, like a naïve child.

Or so they said. Made sense.

One of the intuitive leanings I learned very quickly was a simple longing to know my real mother and father. For several months, I felt certain that being with them would somehow offer a kind of wholeness that I couldn't otherwise find. But when it became clear that I never would meet them, much less know them, I began to set this idea aside and embrace the prospect of being perfectly happy with John and Louise Clark, the generous and loving foster parents who'd taken me in four months earlier.

So when I answered the door that night and stared up into the blue eyes of a strange man who claimed to be my father, my world suddenly felt flipped on its end. I didn't know what to say. I didn't even know what to think.

"Do you want to talk about it?" Louise said.

I sat next to her on the sofa with my hands in my lap as the man's words whispered through my mind like ghosts.

Your mother wants to see you. She wants you to come. She loves you. Your mother has been looking for you for thirteen years.

Louise put her hand on my knee. "It's important that I know what happened. This world is full of predators and if there's anything, anything at all, that might present a threat, I need to know. Please, Alice, you have to tell me. What did he say?"

Your real name is Eden.

My mind was still spinning. I didn't want to open up a can of worms for Louise—she was a sensitive woman and had taken a great liking to me, as had John. What would it mean for her to learn that my real mother wanted me back, assuming that was true?

No one can know that I'm here.

Was I afraid? Yes and no. Yes, because I got the distinct impression that the man who claimed to be my father was afraid of being found out. Why was that? And he didn't appear to be the put together father I had imagined. His blue shirt had a few smudges on it and his hair looked like it could use a wash. But his eyes were kind, weren't they?

So, no, I wasn't afraid. More like confused. What if the man really was my father? What if they really had been looking for me for thirteen years? What if I belonged with my real mother instead of with John and Louise?

"Sweetheart, you have to talk to me."

A loud crash of glass from the back of the house cut my thoughts short. Louise twisted and stared at the hall, which ran to the kitchen.

For a moment neither of us moved, me frozen by curiosity, she by fear—I could see it on her face.

The sound of the back door closing made me wonder if John had come in through the back, but that didn't explain the shattering of glass.

Louise gasped and instinctively grabbed my arm.

The padding of heavy feet sounded down the hall.

Louise spun to me, frantic. "Get behind the couch!" she whispered. "Hurry! Hide."

But it was too late to hide. He was there again. The man who claimed to be my father. Standing at the entrance to the living room, dressed in the same blue shirt tucked into light-brown slacks, this time wearing leather work gloves. He had a hammer in one hand and a roll of duct tape in the other and he stared at us as if he was as surprised to see us as we were to see him.

For a few long seconds, none of us moved. I could feel Louise's hand trembling as she gripped my arm, and her fear spread to me. The thought that my father had come to get me was chased away by the notion that he planned on doing it using a hammer and duct tape.

But then there was the way he looked at us, almost apologetically, and I couldn't help thinking that he didn't want to harm us.

The man half-lifted his right arm. "I'm not going to hurt you." He saw that Louise was staring at the hammer, so he lowered it to the carpet and lifted an open, nonthreatening hand.

"I promise, I'm not here to hurt anyone. But I have to take her with me."

Louise still didn't seem able to speak.

"I have to take her and I don't want to cause any trouble."

Louise came off the couch like a spring. "Get out!" She shoved her finger at the door. "Get out of this house right now."

"No, no, no . . . I can't do that." He stepped forward, hand still raised to calm us, face red, but not with anger. "It's okay, I promise. I'm not going to hurt you but I have to take her. And I can't let you call the cops yet."

"You can't do this!" Louise was panicking.

"Yes, I have to. I have to."

My heart was crashing through my chest. I knew that I should be running for the door or something, but I couldn't move. And a small part of me was wondering if this really was my father. He didn't look like he had done this sort of thing before. In fact, he looked as uncomfortable as we were.

Why?

His eyes switched to me. "Stay on the couch, darling. Please don't move. I don't want to hurt anyone, but I have to do this. It's the only way. Please don't . . ."

Louise bolted toward the dining room then, but she only got three running steps before the large man leaped in front of her, grabbed her waist with one arm, and lifted her from her feet, screaming and pounding at his back.

"Sh, sh, sh . . . ." He tried to hush her, but she wasn't listening. So he grunted in frustration, dropped her to her back like a sack of grain, and shoved a gloved hand over her mouth.

"Be quiet! I told you I don't have a choice and I don't want to hurt you. But you're going to hurt yourself if you keep putting up a fight."

His eyes lifted to meet mine. "I'm so sorry, darling. I didn't want to do it this way. Stay on the couch okay? I'm not going to hurt you. Promise. Just stay right where you are."

By now I was truly afraid, but I saw no reason to make a run for it. He would only tackle me. And there was still that small voice that told me he was a good man and maybe my father. So I pulled my legs up onto the couch, hugged my knees, and stayed.

The fall seemed to have knocked the wind out of Louise, because she'd gone silent.

"Roll over."

When she hesitated, he pulled her over onto her stomach and held her down with a knee on her back.

Hands now free, he quickly tore off a long strip of tape, pulled her arms behind her, and strapped her wrists together tight.

"You can't do this." She was crying now. "Please . . . Please, she's just a little girl."

"I'm not going to hurt her, I already told you that!" He sounded as if he'd been insulted. "I would *never* hurt her. She's a very special girl."

"Please . . ."

But that was as far as she got before he twisted her head around and strapped tape to her mouth.

He jumped down to her ankles, gripped them together with a large hand and bound them so she couldn't walk.

Then he stood and stared down at her for a second, breathing hard from exertion. He looked around at the room, at the front door, then at me.

"I can't let her make a fuss after we're gone. So I'm going to put her in the closet, but she won't be hurt. Okay?"

He seemed to want my permission. I was still in too much shock to talk.

"Will you promise to stay put while I do that?" He eyed me sympathetically, unsure. Then walked up to me and sat down on the couch.

"Maybe it's best if I put some tape on your legs and wrists so that you don't try to run. I don't want to, you understand, but I know this might all be a bit frightening and you might try to run. If you do, I'll have to catch you and you might trip or something. I can't let you get hurt, you understand. I just can't do that."

He stared at me again as if looking for my approval.

"Can you hold your arms out?"

He tore off a strip of tape.

Now at a crossroads, I saw no alternative but to follow his lead. Even if I did have a scrapping bone in my body, I didn't stand a chance of either outrunning or overpowering such a strong man.

So I slowly lowered my feet to the carpet and held out both arms. They were pale and they were thin and I had no doubt that he could snap them like twigs if he wanted to.

Instead he put the tape on as if securing something delicate, like crystal tubes. After another moment's hesitation, he tore off another strip and placed it gently over my mouth.

"I'm sorry, darling. I really am. I don't want you to scream when we leave, you understand?"

I don't know why I nodded, but I did. Maybe because I knew then that I was going with him and nothing short of John coming home a few minutes early was going to change that.

"Thank you." He stroked my head with his hand, then crossed to Louise who had her head lifted as far as she could and was glaring at him, enraged.

Scooping her up in his arms, he dragged her to the small closet under the staircase, pulled the door wide, and carefully set her on the floor inside. She objected vehemently behind the tape, but she didn't struggle—she knew it was no use.

With one last apology—"Sorry"—he shut her inside. Less than thirty seconds later he had the closet door wedged shut with a chair from the dining room.

Then the large man in the blue shirt who said he was my father led me from the house on my own two feet, walked me to a blue pickup truck across the street, helped me into the front seat, and drove away into the night.

Day Two
5:43 AM

SPECIAL AGENT Olivia Strauss's mind clawed its way out of her haunting nightmare at the sound of buzzing on her nightstand. Cell phone . . .

Michelle?

Eyes blinking against the patchwork of shadows that blanketed her studio apartment, she lay still, shirt soaked through with sweat. No, it wasn't Michelle. Her daughter was dead. Had been for many years.

She leaned over, picked up her phone, and stared at the familiar name on its bright screen. Todd Benner. She thumbed the Talk button and brought it to her ear.

"Tell me you have a good reason for calling at this hour," she said.

"Sorry to drag you out of bed."

"I was up anyway. What've you got?"

"Abduction case was just called in. They've asked for the Bureau's consult."

"Who? Where?"

"Hour away, Greenville. A thirteen-year-old girl was taken from her foster home."

Silence.

"Liv?"

"What's her name?"

"Alice. Alice Ringwald."

She could feel the sudden surge of her pulse. Her own daughter would be thirteen if she were still alive.

"Liv?"

"I'm still here." Her mind shifted. She was already on her feet and halfway across the room, snatching a robe from the back of a chair. "When did it happen?"

"Between seven and eight o'clock last night. I'm still waiting on the full report so details are sketchy. The abductor, a single, middle-aged male, fled the scene in a truck with Tennessee plates."

She glanced at the clock. "He's got ten hours on us . . . they could be halfway across the country by now."

"Which is why we're being called in."

"Any of our people on scene yet?"

"Forensics will be there at seven. I told them we'd be close on their heels."

"What else do we know?"

"The local detective talked with the mother. He'll be on scene when we arrive."

"She was there?"

"She's the only witness." A beat. "Liv?"

"Yeah," she said, swapping the phone from one hand to the other.

"Listen, if you're not up for this . . . I know this week is tough for you every year."

"Come on, Todd. You know me better than anyone else."

"Which is why I'm saying it."

"It's also what makes me one of the best."

"I'm just concerned about you. That's all."

"Just get what you can from Murphy. We'll brief on the way. I'm headed out the door in twenty. I'll swing by and pick you up."

Olivia ended the call and sat in silence. Glanced at a framed picture of her daughter that hung on the wall.

It's what makes me one of the best.

It was the truth. Her passion bordered on personal obsession. If her superiors knew how close she stood to the brink they might rethink her assignment.

Seven years had passed and the wound was still raw. It had been a perfect afternoon. Her husband, Derek, was away on a business trip so she'd taken off work for a girls' day out, just like the old days when Michelle had been younger—pancakes at Dominy's, then to the zoo, then a Disney movie marathon at the local dollar theater.

At six o'clock that night Michelle had fallen asleep on the couch while Olivia set about whipping up a batch of her daughter's favorite: peanut butter cookies. But a quick look in the fridge revealed that they were out of milk to go with the cookies.

Milk. Just a quick trip to the store down the street to buy a quart of milk. Five minutes tops. Problem was, she'd been in such a rush to get there, get the milk, and get back that she'd forgotten to lock the door on her way out.

When she returned, the door was ajar and Michelle was gone.

After three days of frantic searching, the detective delivered the news she'd dreaded. A utility worker had stumbled across Michelle's dead body in a field three miles from their house.

The life Olivia had known ended that day. Her daughter was forever gone and within six months, so was everything else. Sleep was the first to go. Then her job. Then her friends. Then her husband, who might have coped with his own loss if not for her unrelenting depression.

Why? Because of her. Because she, and no one else, had left the door open.

Three years later, she'd found a new home with the FBI. Michelle's case had gone cold and remained so to this day, but there were a thousand Michelles out there, and Olivia made every one of them her own.

Olivia snatched the bottle of Xanax that perched on the nightstand, emptied one into her hand, and grabbed the half-filled water bottle that was next to the Xanax to wash it down.

The clock was ticking.

Forensics was already processing the house when Olivia arrived at the Clarks' residence. They'd been briefed by the local supervisory detective, Randy Smith, on the drive. A dozen protocols were already in full motion, teams of people already engaged in the search—dispatchers, patrol officers responding to the Amber Alert, detectives, CSI, citizens now being informed of the abduction on the news. Evidence was being compiled, a case would be quickly built based on that evidence, searches would be made. What could be done was being done by caring, very capable investigators.

But for Olivia, only one question really mattered now: *Why?*

"I want to talk to them alone," she said, staring at the front door, now open. Benner knew both her penchant for connecting emotionally to a case, and her preferences for how to do so.

"I'll join you in a bit. Smith is with the witness who saw the vehicle."

She nodded, watched him depart, and stared up at the house. They were all the same, really. Every crime scene would offer up its evidence: the where, the when, the what, the process, the means. But it was the *why* that kept Olivia awake at nights.

Why do you take children?

Why did you choose her?

Why did you take her?

Her mind skipped tracks.

Why did I leave the door open?

Why did you kill my daughter?

Alice wasn't Michelle and there was no evidence that she'd been killed, but Alice *was* a Michelle and if they didn't find her in time . . .

Why? To understand that single question, Olivia had to connect with Alice's parents and to her environment.

She took a deep breath and walked up the sidewalk, through the front door, and into the home from which Alice had been taken.

A middle-aged couple stood in the center of the dining room, watching two technicians combing for fibers. Neither looked like they'd slept.

She approached them and extended her hand to the mother.

"John and Louise Clark?"

Louise took her hand.

"My name's Olivia Strauss. I'm the special agent in charge of the FBI's investigation." She offered Louise a smile as she looked into her swollen eyes. "I'm sorry, sweetie. I'm so sorry you're going through this. I know it's hard."

"Thank you." A fresh tear slid down the mother's face.

Olivia took a tissue from her pocket and offered it to Louise. "Do you mind if I ask you some questions?"

John cleared his throat. "We've been asked a lot of questions. Truthfully, we could use some answers."

"I understand. You can be assured that we're doing everything we can. A whole set of procedures were set in motion last night."

"What procedures?"

"Local authorities sealed off the immediate area and issued a statewide Amber Alert within an hour of the abduction. That turned a lot of eyes—local and state police, as well as the public—our way. The National Center for Missing and Exploited Children was immediately notified and Alice's information was entered into the National Crime Information Center's database. A leads management system is in place—every tip will be followed up. The team has already processed more than two dozen. It may not look like it, but the search for Alice is in full swing out there."

Louise softened. "They asked for some of her clothes."

"For the scent. The local K-9 unit established an active search grid of a half-mile in every direction and detectives started working door-to-door last night, talking with anyone who might've seen anything out of place. They'll pick it up again this morning. We've also cross-checked criminal and sex-offender databases to determine if any might be principal suspects or possible participants in the crime."

"They said our neighbor reported the truck," John said.

"Yes and she got the plate number too. We already know that the truck was reported stolen several weeks ago in Nashville. We'll find it."

They stared at her, no less concerned, but at least she'd given them something to hold on to.

"We're going to do everything we can to find Alice, I promise you. This isn't just my job. It's my life."

"Thank you," John said.

She gave him a nod and turned to Louise. "I understand you were here when he took her."

"Yes."

"I know you've already told the detective everything you remember, but I need to hear it from you. Walk me through it. Beginning with the first encounter at the front door."

"Alice answered the door first."

"Show me where you were standing when you first saw him."

Louise walked to a spot about eight feet from the front door and stopped. "Here."

Olivia sized up the door from Louise's vantage point. "The report said the man was wearing gloves when he entered the house. What about when he first came to the door? Did you notice whether or not he wore gloves?"

Louise thought a moment then shook her head. "No, I don't

think he was. I would've remembered."

"You're certain?"

She nodded. "Yes."

No gloves the first time. Why?

Because he didn't expect to have to use force.

Olivia caught the attention of a CSI tech in a blue windbreaker. "We need to double check the work-up for this area, especially the doorbell—prints, fibers, skin. The abductor had exposed hands."

"Will do."

Back to Louise: "What happened next?"

Louise led her through the house, starting at the living room and ending at the closet. She recounted in detail the terror she and Alice had experienced. The man. The way he forced her to the ground. Everything she could remember.

Olivia stood at the foot of the stairs, mind churning. Why come into the house? Why not wait for a better opportunity, when Alice was away from the house? Why risk a home invasion in daylight, and while the mother was home?

He was desperate. Inexperienced. He hadn't come for a girl; he'd come specifically for Alice.

"Can you show me her room?"

Louise led her upstairs. Four doors flanked the short hallway. To the right, a hall bathroom and the entry to the master bedroom. To the left, two other bedrooms.

Olivia angled into the bathroom. "This is the bathroom Alice used?"

"Yes. John and I have our own."

She scanned the countertop. A pair of hairbrushes sat on top of a neatly folded hand towel. A pump bottle of Burt's Bees hand soap. A red toothbrush next to a half-used tube of toothpaste.

Alice's, but in Olivia's mind they were as much Michelle's.

She turned to Louise. "Can you show me her room?"

The woman led her directly across the hall and nudged the door open. To her right, rays of sunshine highlighted yellow-painted walls the color of daffodils. A full size bed with a lavender comforter sat against the far wall, and a small desk nestled beneath the window was stacked with books. Several framed pictures, black-and-white landscapes of the desert, were laid out on the bed.

Olivia stepped deeper into the room. Picked up one of the pictures.

"She was going to hang those up last night," Louise said. "She picked them out herself. She was beginning to feel like this was her home too."

"Tell me about Alice. What is she like?"

"Quiet. Curious. She's unusual for her age, we saw that the first week she was with us."

"How so?"

"John and I have raised two so we're used to the turmoil that comes with this age." Her face lightened. "But Alice is different. She's more like an adult trapped in a young person's body. Unusually quick-minded, but naïve to the ways of the world. She trusts too much. That scares me the most. When the man broke in, she just sat there on the couch. She did what he told her. She didn't say a thing."

"And the man? How did he react to her?"

"That's the thing. He seemed apologetic. Scared even. It was so strange. He forced me down only because I tried to run. I know it sounds crazy, but when he said he wouldn't hurt us, I believed him."

"Did he say anything else? Anything unusual that sticks out?"

Louise thought for a moment then shook her head. "Not that I can think of."

"The detective who interviewed you last night wrote in his report that Alice suffered from amnesia. That she couldn't remember anything beyond six months ago. There's nothing in the file that explains why."

"They say her amnesia probably came from trauma she suffered at some point. Her brain's way of protecting her, like post-traumatic stress disorder."

"What do you know about her parents?"

"Nothing. They said the documents are confidential. Do you think someone from her past took her?"

Yes.

Everything pointed to an abductor who valued Alice for who she was and his connection to her. It was why he'd come to the front door first. Why he hadn't worn gloves when he'd come. Why he'd been apologetic. Why he hadn't harmed either of them. It was always in the *whys*.

But she didn't say yes. Not yet.

"Half of all children who're abducted are taken by family members. It's a possibility that we can't rule out."

Louise blinked. "Actually, now that you say that, there was something else. He said Alice was a special girl. He made a point of saying it."

"Special?"

"Yes. No . . . Very special. He said she was very special." She paused. "What do you think he meant?"

Olivia's thoughts spun back to Michelle's abduction. A monster that could not fathom the meaning of *special* had crushed their lives.

Five minutes. That was the time difference between saving Michelle and allowing her to be taken. Time. In Alice's case, it wasn't the time it took to get a quart of milk; it was the time she'd lived prior to her amnesia.

"It means we have hope," she said, reaching for her phone. "It means he values her. It means we may have more time. It means the key to her abductor probably lies in her past."

"A past she doesn't remember."

"But someone else does. Whoever that is, I have to find them."

She dialed the field office on her cell phone and got her lead analyst.

"Get me Alice Ringwald's adoption files. I want everything, as far back as you can go. And find out who's running the orphanage that handled her adoption. I want them on the phone ASAP."

Day Two
10:23 *AM*

I DON'T know how long it had taken us to reach the cabin in the woods—maybe two hours after we left the city—but it felt much longer because all I could think was that at any second the police were going to pull up with flashing red-and-blue lights behind the truck and take me back. Each minute it didn't happen felt like an hour; every mile farther felt like the distance between the earth and the moon.

Back in the house I'd been in too much shock to fully realize what was happening, but the moment we pulled onto the highway with me sitting in the cab, gray duct tape over my mouth, I realized that everything I knew might be changed forever. I really was being taken. Stolen. Driven away into the darkness without a clue about what would happen to me.

I might end up a slave. I might end up dead. I didn't think the man would kill me—my thoughts were more about suddenly feeling totally lost. For six months I had carefully constructed my world from nothing, and now that nothing seemed to be coming back to me.

There on the highway I began to cry silently.

The man had been focused on getting away as quickly as possible and the sight of tears on my cheeks so surprised him that he swerved. He reached over and took the tape off my mouth, apologizing profusely:

"I'm so sorry. Are you okay? I promise I'll take the tape off your hands as soon as I can pull over, but I have to get to a safer place. Please don't cry . . . It's going to be okay. You'll see . . . you'll see . . . .Please don't cry, sweetheart."

He told me that his name was Wyatt; that he was my father; that everything was going to be okay. That my mother's name was Kathryn and that she was going to be out of her mind with excitement when she heard that he'd rescued me.

But I kept crying.

Worried, he pulled out his cell phone and called her. On one hand, I could hear the enthusiasm in his voice when he told her he'd rescued me, but his face went flat when he told her that I was crying. He listened intently for a while.

"I will, sugar. I promise." He listened again. "You're right . . . It would be too much. I will, sugar. I promise."

They spoke a little while longer and then he hung up. He glanced at me with sad eyes.

"Kathryn said just to let you feel whatever you need to feel. It's going to be okay. This is a big shock to your system and you're going to be confused for a little while. To let you sleep and tell you more when you wake up. You just need to know that she loves you very much. You're going to be so much happier now. You'll see, sweetheart . . . you'll see."

"Why are you doing this?" I asked. I think those were my first words to him.

"Because you're our daughter. You deserve to belong to your own family. It's the way it should be. I can't tell you everything right now; Kathryn said you should go ahead and cry if you want to. It's okay. I promise."

By the time we left the highway maybe an hour later, my mind was numb and my tears had stopped. We followed a few paved roads then turned onto a dirt road that wound up into the hills to an old cabin hidden in tall trees. It was dark so I couldn't see much as he led me into the house and to a bedroom at the back.

He lit a small oil lamp and brought me some pickles, a glass of milk, and two Snickers bars with a plate of crackers. The small bed had been neatly made and the room looked tidy. A brown teddy bear sat on the white pillow, smiling at me with one white eye.

We'd hardly spoken during the ride—him because Kathryn had told him to leave me alone, I suspected; me because I felt too lost to voice any of my thoughts. Every time I thought of a question or wanted to say how I felt, I would realize that it was pointless. But when I sat down on the bed, I looked up at him and told him that I was afraid.

He stood at the end of the bed, looking at me awkwardly, at a loss for words. So I told him I wanted to go back home.

"I *am* taking you home, Eden," he said. He meant his home, where he thought I belonged. "I know you're afraid. And I'm sorry. But please don't be. I'm going to be right outside on the couch. There's bears in the woods up here, so don't go outside. No one can hurt you here, I promise." He looked around uncomfortably. "Okay, get some rest, okay? Okay . . . I'll be right outside if you need anything. It's going to be okay, I promise."

My first thought was that he was telling me about the bears because he didn't want me to run away. But after he left, it occurred to me that he could just as easily, and probably had, locked all the doors and windows to keep me in, so he probably was serious about the bears, for my own safety.

I only had to leave the room once—to use the bathroom, which he quickly showed me to. Then I returned to the room, ate one of the Snickers bars, drank some of the milk, lay down, and stared at the ceiling. It took me a long time, but I finally fell into a numb sleep.

It was late morning when I awoke and my first thought was that I'd had a terrible nightmare. That Louise was downstairs setting the table with eggs and bacon, because I could smell it. But it only took a few seconds for the events from the night before to come crashing into my mind.

I was in a cabin. In the woods. With a man named Wyatt who'd kidnapped me. I was still alive. He hadn't threatened or hurt me. He claimed to be my father and was taking me to my mother.

It took me a few minutes to work up the courage to get out of bed and open the door, and when I did, to my left I had a direct line of sight down a small hall into the kitchen. He was there, leaning over a skillet, dressed in the same clothes from last night, humming softly to himself.

My fear eased a little as I watched him, thinking that he didn't look like a man who'd committed a terrible crime. I glanced to my right and saw that the hall ended at the bathroom I'd used last night. The window in there was too small to climb out, I remembered that.

But it was day now—what if I could climb out the bedroom window? Once outside, I could sneak to the road and make a run for it. Maybe find someone who could help me. Hide in the forest if Wyatt came after me.

I slowly backed into the room and closed the door, then rushed to the window, grabbed the two handles at the bottom, and yanked up.

It didn't budge. I immediately saw why. The edges were painted shut. Staring beyond the smudged glass, I saw that rusted nails pinned the window to the frame. And there would be no way to break out through the glass because metal bars blocked the way, maybe to keep bears out.

Or maybe to keep me in.

No, the bars looked too old. The cabin had been sealed shut a long time ago to keep robbers or animals from entering while it was vacant. The only way out was probably through the front door.

A knock startled me and I spun around.

"Eden?"

"Yes?" I slid back onto the bed.

The door opened and Wyatt stood there, smiling awkwardly. "You're up. Did you sleep well?"

I blinked at him, wondering if he could tell by the guilty look on my face that I'd just tried to climb out the window.

"Yes."

"That's good. Are you hungry? I made up some eggs and bacon. You like eggs?"

It felt strange, him asking me the kinds of questions someone would ask if nothing at all was out of place.

"Yes."

"I thought you would. Want to come eat?"

I was too nervous to be hungry, but I saw no choice but to follow him into the main room. An old brown sofa and two wooden chairs sat around a large crate in front of a fireplace on the left; the kitchen and a small table stood on the right.

"Go on, sit at the table."

I crossed to it, carefully pulled out one of the chairs, and sat with my hands in my lap.

He set in front of me a green metal plate loaded with more scrambled eggs than I could eat. Five strips of bacon. Then he carefully laid an aluminum fork to the right of the plate and finished the setting off with a glass of milk. His hands were thick and his nails could have used a cleaning, but he moved with care, as if he was performing a very special task for a queen.

He beamed at me, proud of his accomplishment. Maybe fixing breakfast wasn't so common for him.

Wyatt sat across from me and put his hands on the table, palms down. "Go ahead and eat. I've already had mine."

I stared down at the large helping. "I don't think I can eat all of this."

He smiled. "I guess I did overdo it a bit. You eat as little or as much as you want. It's okay, we're only gonna be here three days and I have plenty to last us that long."

"Three days?" I looked around, unnerved by the idea of spending so much time away from John and Louise. But it could be much longer than that.

He looked at me sympathetically, then nodded. "I'm sure you have lots of questions. You have no idea how much trouble we went to, tracking you down and rescuing you. We've been looking for years. It was Zeke who finally found you—contact of his came across your name a couple months ago. Alice Ringwald. But that's not the name your mother gave you. She named you Eden because you're the place of perfect new beginnings," he patted his chest, "in here, where it counts."

I didn't know how much to believe, but not knowing my own past, I had no reason not to believe anything he said either. Which only meant that I didn't know what to think.

"Go ahead, sweetheart—you can ask me anything you want."

"Anything?"

"Anything. I'll tell you everything."

WHILE ALICE searched her mind for the right questions to ask the man who'd taken her, Special Agent Olivia Strauss sat at her desk in Columbia's FBI station, reading through the thin adoption file yet again.

Far too thin. Why were the details regarding Alice's past so scarce? Still no call from the orphanage she'd left to join the Clarks. Evidence was being gathered, processed, and quickly compiled, but the whys and motivations behind abductions were the real case breakers. *Why*s led to *who*.

And *who* was what they needed to know. Who had taken Alice?

Her phone buzzed and she snatched it up. "Strauss."

"I tracked down your guy. Andrew DeVoss, from Saint Thomas Orphanage. Line two."

"Thank you."

She punched up the line.

"Mr. DeVoss?"

"Please, call me Andrew."

"Andrew. This is Olivia Strauss, special agent in charge of an active missing-persons case involving a child who left your orphanage a few months ago."

"Oh my," he said. "Who?"

"Alice Ringwald."

There was a brief moment of silence. "Oh, no."

"We've pulled our best resources, but I've run into a snag. I'm hoping you can answer a few questions for me."

"Of course. Anything."

"What can you tell me about Alice's history? We suspect that someone from her past, possibly a close relative, is involved in the abduction."

The phone went silent.

"Andrew?"

"She's . . . Oh my . . ."

"What is it?"

"You *must* find her!"

His intensity surprised her.

"We're trying. But to do that I need to know who from her past might have had any reason to take her."

"No, no, it's not that. She *has* no past outside of the orphanage."

"She had a birth mother and a birth father."

"Yes. Her father was James Paul Ringwald—"

"The senator who was killed in the plane crash a few years ago?"

"Yes. He had an affair with a woman right before his presidential bid. When he discovered she was pregnant he cut her out of his life.

Several years later, she committed suicide."

"What was her name?"

"Catherine Miller. But you see, they've both passed. As to Alice's missing years . . . I doubt any information I could give you would help you find her."

"It's my job to determine what information will help us. If I'm going to find her, I have to know more about her past."

"It's just that . . ."

"It's just what?"

She heard him take a deep breath.

"This is very sensitive information, you understand. No one must know, for Alice's sake as well as the others."

"What others?"

"The other children. Promise me that what I tell you goes no further."

She thought about his request.

"I have to file—"

"No files. Just you. Promise me."

"Okay. Just me."

"I can trust you?"

"You have my word."

Another short pause.

"A project was established in the Colorado mountains. Thirteen years ago, thirty-six orphans were legally adopted by a classified orphanage, totally isolated from the rest of the world. I'm not at liberty to reveal any specific details about the location or the project . . . It's best for the children, and there's nothing there that would help you find her."

She doubted that.

"Then tell me something that will help. What happened at this orphanage?"

"You should know that Alice isn't just any girl. She, like the others, is quite special."

Special. *Alice is a very special girl* . . .

"What do you mean?"

"Before the project was shut down, some of the children were able to affect the world in ways bordering on the paranormal. Some of it got out of hand, but it was all self-contained. It was why the project was shut down, you understand? Fortunately, none of the children has any memory of their years at the monastery."

"Monastery?"

"The orphanage was located in an ancient monastery."

"How did they lose their memory?"

He hesitated.

"They were exposed to a substance that had some side effects, one of which was to eliminate memory. It was the only way they could be reintegrated into society."

"What kind of substance?"

"A poison of sorts, produced by an extremely rare species of worm. It's no longer of relevance. Either way, you must find Alice. Beyond this, I'm afraid I can be of no further assistance."

"What about the other children? Isn't it possible that someone who worked with them is now targeting all of them?"

"Highly unlikely. We have our ways of monitoring them."

"Ways that obviously failed Alice."

He didn't respond. So she pressed.

"It could happen again."

"That's our concern. Yours is to find her."

"That's not enough."

"And yet it has to be." He paused. "Find her, Agent Strauss. Find her quickly."

WYATT, THE man who'd taken me, said that he would tell me everything and that I could ask him anything. So I did.

"Are you my real father?"

"Yes." He shifted in his chair. "Well, not by birth, no. Which is why your last name isn't Ringwald anymore either. It's Lowenstein. My name. Your birth father was James Ringwald, a senator from Nevada. He died a few years ago. He was the one who took you away from your mother because he wanted nothing to do with either of you after you were born. Sent you away to an orphanage and forced Kathryn into an institution to cover his tracks and save his career."

"Now you're doing that to me?"

"Doing what?"

"Forcing me."

He looked horrified. "No, it's not like that. Those people have no right to you by blood. You belong with your mother. And me. It's the way God designed it. Sometimes the law just isn't on God's side, is all."

"Shouldn't I have a say? I know I'm only thirteen, but I'm not a nobody that can be pushed and pulled around."

"No, sweetheart! No, of course you're not."

"What if I want to go back?"

Judging by the look on his face, this seemed like a new idea to him. So I continued.

"You frightened me and hurt Louise, who loves me very much. Why didn't Kathryn just come to the door and ask to speak with me?"

"You don't understand. They put her in an institution to get her away from you! You think they would just let her take you back?"

"Why would they want to keep my mother away from me?"

"Because James Ringwald was an evil man. He didn't want Kathryn to mess things up for him—he was married to someone else and he wanted to keep her quiet so he accused her of being crazy and sent her to an institution. When she got out, you were gone and there was no way for her to find you."

It sounded like it could be true, but I didn't know if I could believe him.

"I may be young and I may have lost all my memory from before I was thirteen, but I can still make my own decisions. If my mother loves me, she would understand that."

"You lost your memory?"

So he didn't know.

"You don't remember anything?"

I wondered if I should explain. Then thought it better not to.

"Everything up until six months ago."

"How did that happen?"

"I don't know."

"You see? You poor thing, you've been hurt. You belong with your mother. I promise, after you meet your mother and brother in a few days, you can make your own decision. Kathryn would never make you stay. That wouldn't be right."

I stared at him, confused.

"I have a brother?"

"Yes. Bobby. He's ten and I know you're going to love him. He needs his big sister, you're going to see that too. You belong with us, Eden. But you can decide for yourself. Promise."

He used that word a lot. Maybe he meant it. Maybe he didn't. But the idea of having a brother worked its way into my mind—one more thing to make my head spin.

"Then why not just take me now and let me decide?"

"I'm going to, but I can't yet. Zeke says the first two or three days are the most critical. I can't be on the roads. He set it up so we could spend three days here—it's an old 'shiner's place, empty for a couple months. Right now the FBI's all over the place hunting for my truck. It's got Tennessee plates so they'll think I've gone there, but we're right here, hidden in their backyard. We'll leave the truck here when we go. They'll eventually find it but we'll be long gone and back home. Then, if you decide not to stay, you can come back."

I could leave a note, I thought. When they did find this place, they would find the note.

"Where are you taking me?"

"A long way away. But I can't tell you where, not yet. You'll see for yourself. No one can know. If they find us, they'll put your mother in jail. Both of us. Even if you decide to leave us, you can't ever tell them where we live. You have to promise me that much. Okay?"

He was going to trust me? Maybe he really did mean everything he said. Or maybe he had no intention of ever letting me go.

"I promise," I said. But I don't know if I meant it.

"So you'll come with me?"

It was a strange question.

"Aren't you making me?"

"Not really, no."

"Then you'll take me back?"

"No. No, I can't do that. It would kill your mother. You can come with me and you'll see."

"And then I can leave if I want to?"

He hesitated a moment, then dipped his head. "Sure. But you have to come with me first, of course."

His thinking was a little upside-down, I thought. As if he wanted my participation in what he was actually forcing on me, maybe to make himself feel better. Which meant he did care. But he'd taped me up and kidnapped me.

"So you'll come?" he asked again.

I nodded.

He slapped the tabletop. "That's what I'm talking about! Kathryn will be delighted. If we had cell service up here, I'd call her now and let you talk to her. Wait here."

He stood up, hurried into the kitchen, withdrew a jar of clear liquid from the cupboard, and came back, grinning ear to ear.

"We're going to make a toast," he said, unscrewing the jar's lid. "To you. To Kathryn."

"What's that?"

"Moonshine, sweetheart. Made it myself. It's strong but it will purify you inside and out."

He took a drink and swallowed, then passed the jar to me.

"Me?"

"It's holy juice. Just take a small sip. You'll see."

I took the jar tentatively, sniffed it, then took a tiny sip.

It tasted like poison and I spewed most of it out.

He laughed. "Good, isn't it?"

"It's horrible!"

"Well, yes, at first I guess it is a bit strong. But it's the real deal, sweetheart. You're now purified. Welcome to the family."

For a moment I actually felt like part of some strange family, and I think I might have even given him a little grin.

Then I remembered where I was and I wasn't so sure.

Not at all.

Day Four
9:03 AM

OLIVIA LOOKED over downtown Greenville from the second-floor conference room as the morning sun made its undeterred journey to mark the beginning of this, the fourth day since Alice had been taken.

Four days too long.

Although her office at the FBI headquarters in Columbia was only an hour-and-a-half drive south, the local field office had become her base for the last three days because of its proximity to the crime scene.

Behind her, several caseworkers sat around the long table that filled the room, poring over the situation reports that had come in during the night from local police who were helping follow up on leads.

"You should think about getting some sleep," Benner said and passed her a steaming cup of coffee.

"I'm not tired."

"Well, you look it."

She took a sip.

"At least get a bite to eat."

She turned on her heel and walked toward the front of the room. "Not hungry."

Olivia set the coffee on the table's edge and stopped, arms crossed, in front of the flat-panel TV mounted on the wall. Multicolored markers dotted a digital map, each one indicating a lead in the case. Three days ago, the majority had been yellow and green—good, or at least viable, leads mostly reported sightings of the truck after the Amber Alert had been issued.

Now she was staring at a landscape of red.

We're losing her.

Professionalism only went so far. No one could bury their frustration forever. The energy in the room had taken a negative turn—she didn't want it to take root.

She turned to face them. "All right, people. Let's run through what we've got."

The low murmur of activity stopped. All eyes focused on Olivia.

"We've missed something. Something right in front of us. Today's the day we find it. We start at the beginning."

The beginning again. Yes, again. Always from the beginning.

"Tell me what we do know about the perpetrator."

"No positive ID on the man," Benner said as he settled into a chair. "We canvassed the whole area; the artist's sketch of the suspect didn't turn up anything."

"Kristen, anything new from forensics?" Olivia focused on the petite blonde next to Benner.

"Nothing new. We've expanded the database search for the partial print CSI lifted from the doorbell to include Canadian and UK repositories. I want to rule out all possibilities."

"Still no hits on CODIS?"

Kristen shook her head. "I've run our data set through the paces and we're oh for three on hair, fiber, and prints. Our guy's a ghost."

"Nothing on the ViCAP cross-reference?" The violent crimes database.

"No, ma'am. If our abductor's a career criminal, he knows how to stay off the grid."

A ghost. Unfortunately, Alice had also been a ghost.

Olivia's enigmatic conversation with Andrew DeVoss ran through her mind. She'd gone as high and as far as she could in an attempt to uncover more information on the project he'd referenced, but come up empty-handed. She'd also kept the information to herself, as promised.

Information from Alice's mysterious past might be helpful, or it might not, as Andrew insisted. Either way, it wasn't in play.

"Anything new from known associates? Tutors, teachers, her therapist?"

Benner: "We covered all the bases—neighbors, friends, school administrators, grocery store clerks, gas station attendants, anyone who could've had contact with the family. Local vice detectives also tapped their sources for possible child trafficking connections. Nothing."

Olivia picked up a remote from the table and pointed it at the TV. An image of a young woman filled the screen.

"Which brings us to our most likely connection. Her mother."

How far would Olivia have gone to recover her own daughter? Pretty far.

"Catherine Miller of Houston, Texas. Raised in a broken home, ended up with child services."

The screen transitioned to a headshot of a teenager. Catherine.

"She ran away from an orphanage and eventually turned up in Vegas where she got a job in Ringwald's campaign office. They hit it off and she got pregnant. Typical story. Ringwald shut her out and arranged for their daughter to enter an orphanage. Then he put Catherine in an institution to keep her quiet. Clearly, the man had some expensive lawyers."

She clicked the remote and the image shifted to a mug shot of Catherine, now staring into the camera with vacant eyes.

"Two years later, she escapes the mental facility and turns up dead.

I still think she's our best lead."

"She'd not a lead," Benner said. "A maid found her remains in a Las Vegas motel. Police report said she was seen with a local pimp that night."

"There's no conclusive evidence that she died in that room. They never found a body."

"Because it was in pieces. They found a severed finger positively identified with her fingerprint from her police record. There was enough blood to paint a small bedroom."

"We still don't have a body. And I have a missing girl who was abducted by someone who appeared desperate to get her. We can't dismiss the possibility that she faked her death and went after her daughter."

"We've chased it down," Benner said. "There's no record of a Catherine Miller meeting that description alive in the country today. If it is her, she's out of reach."

"Then chase it down again!" Olivia snapped.

They stared at her in silence.

The whole chain of evidence was disintegrating. No forensics that linked them to anyone. No witnesses. Nothing they could sink a hook into.

"What've we got on the truck? From the top."

"It's registered to a Donald Harper from Lawrenceburg, Tennessee." Jay Lee, an analyst with unruly hair, sat at the opposite end of the table. "It was swiped from long-term parking at Nashville International Airport six days ago. No helpful footage from security cameras. Metro PD in Nashville contacted the owner after we ran the plate. Apparently, he'd left the keys in a magnetic box in the wheel well."

"And no link between him and the Clarks or Alice?"

"Nothing."

"Nothing new on the contents reported stolen? Just the toolbox?"

He flipped through a copy of the police report. "Just the toolbox in the back. And a cell-phone charger."

"Cell phone charger? Why would the owner report a cell-phone charger worth twenty bucks?"

"Exactly. Worthless."

"That's not the point. *Why*?" she reiterated. "*Why* would anyone report a cell-phone charger missing? It makes no sense."

Unless . . .

"Get on the phone with the owner. Find out if he meant cell-phone charger, or cell phone *and* charger. If he had a cell phone, find out what kind. If it has GPS capabilities and was on, the wireless company may be able to track the phone's movement."

"It's been six days since the truck was taken. Even if it was on, the battery's probably dead."

"Depending on the make and model it could still have juice. Call him."

"On it," Jay said, heading for the door.

It was a long shot, but at this juncture, she'd take a long shot over no shots. She scanned the room, thinking she should say something. But there was nothing new to say. They'd covered the same ground today as they had yesterday. Nothing but dead ends.

She slid into a chair, ran a hand through her hair, and stared at the wall. The waiting was always the hardest part. Hours, days, weeks, months . . .

Years.

That was a lot of *why*s.

"No further sightings in Tennessee?" she asked absently.

"None."

"Nothing new from the DMV?"

"No."

She slammed her hand on the table and took her frustration out on no one in particular. "Come on, people! There has to be something out there that we're missing! Think!"

The door swung in. "Got a hit," Jay said, phone still plastered to his ear. "He had a smartphone in the truck for work. Said he reported it stolen with the toolbox. Cell phone *and* charger."

She felt her pulse spike.

"Did he have it on?"

"He couldn't remember."

She was out of her chair. "Phone number and carrier."

Jay asked the owner, quickly jotted down the information on a pad, and handed it to Benner.

"Call them . . ." Olivia said.

But he was already calling.

She could hear the throb of her pulse in her ears as she paced. Her lungs tightened. If the cell phone had been left on, they would be able to track its movements for as long as the phone had held its charge.

On the other hand, if the cell phone had been off, or died before Alice had been taken, they would know nothing.

It would be back to waiting. God, she hated waiting.

Benner covered the receiver with his hand. "They got it. It'll take some time for them to work it on their end, but they've got an active signal. Phone's still on."

ACCORDING TO the data provided by the carrier, the blue truck carrying Alice and her abductor had traveled north out of Greenville on US 25 on the night of the abduction. Well outside of town, the man had veered west on I-26, exited near Asheville Regional Airport and made his way onto the Blue Ridge Parkway.

Despite the difficult terrain and dense vegetation, the wireless company had been able to track the vehicle's southbound progress into the mountains to where it had angled off the main road and onto a ribbon of dirt road that disappeared into the woods. Five miles in, the truck had stopped where it had remained for the past three days.

Because the smartphone had been in standby mode, the battery life had been conserved long enough for them to determine the exact GPS coordinates of the device. And the truck.

Within hours, a tactical team had been assembled and converged on the location.

Olivia knelt in the thick shade that pooled beneath the trees at the clearing's edge and scanned the scene. Thirty yards away, the blue truck was parked next to an old cabin with a green metal roof that drooped over a covered porch. The building's darkened windows gazed out like hollow eyes at the thick forest that crowded it on every side.

Her attention lingered on the truck for a long moment.

"You okay?" Benner said at her side. He was clad in a black Kevlar vest and held a 9mm by his side.

"I'm fine."

They'd staged their operation from the main road and moved on foot to avoid drawing attention. The plan was simple: Olivia and Benner would enter the front with Asheville SWAT and secure the cabin. Local FBI assets would provide secondary support on the exterior. Speed was the key, which is why they were moving now, with the sun still high in the sky, not later. Every minute they waited was a minute wasted.

"Adam Three in position," a voice crackled in her earpiece. The backup unit was in place.

"Copy that, Adam Three," she whispered. She gave a nod to the captain of the SWAT unit. "Let's roll."

He motioned his team of five forward with Olivia and Benner bringing up the rear. Moving low and fast, they left the cover of the forest and angled toward the northeast corner of the cabin in single file, weapons raised.

Olivia's pulse quickened with each step, her nerves raw and humming with adrenaline. They reached the edge of the cabin, rounded the corner, passed beneath the front windows in a low crouch as they closed the distance to the front porch.

The SWAT leader lifted a clenched fist as they approached the front stairs, bringing everyone to a silent halt.

Olivia's eyes flicked from the door to the window. No movement that she could see. She scanned the clearing, half expecting the man to make a run for the truck. But there was no sign of the man, no sign that they'd been seen.

We have to move . . . we have to move . . .

After a breath, the man motioned forward with two fingers. One of the men broke rank and climbed the steps with a black battering ram at his side. In unison, the others followed close as he crossed the porch and, in one smooth motion, swung the metal ram.

It connected with a loud boom that rattled the cabin's front windows. The force of impact nearly knocked the door from its hinges as it swung open violently.

The man stepped aside, dropped the ram and drew his weapon as the others rushed past him and into the cabin.

Olivia entered the dimly lit cabin close on the SWAT unit's heels.

Weapon leveled, she crossed the room, eyes sweeping right to left as she went. The main room was empty. Daylight filtered through the grimy windows and the tang of woodsmoke and bacon hung on the air. Her focus clicked through the surroundings, registering every detail as she moved toward a narrow hallway straight ahead.

To the left: a dinette with two wooden chairs and a small kitchen.

To the right: a brown couch and two chairs gathered around a large crate used as a coffee table. Beyond it, a fireplace with a heap of gray ash.

She pulled up in the hallway as SWAT kicked in the door on the right and two men rushed through, weapons snugged against their shoulders. The fast rustle of bodies and gear. Boots clomping against the hardwood floor.

"Clear!" the voice came from inside the room.

The remaining officers turned their attention to the rickety door on the opposite side of the hallway. Forced their way in without hesitation. Two seconds later it too was declared clear. Empty. Then the next room: a bathroom.

Olivia angled into the first room. She stopped, eyes searching. A small bed covered with a tattered quilt. A pillow with a teddy bear, one eye missing, on top of it. A single window—bars on the exterior.

But no Alice. They were gone.

"Get forensics in here! I want every inch of this place searched. She's a smart girl, she might have left something behind for us."

Benner stood in the doorway with his gun at his side. "You got it."

"And gather the others. Our guy's made a run for it."

AN INVESTIGATIVE team comprised of thirty-two local police and FBI agents gathered in front of the cabin as the whump of a circling helicopter filled the air. Two men held a large map of the area as Benner spoke.

"The only tire marks coming or leaving the cabin are the truck's. That means he didn't drive out of here. The K-9 unit picked up Alice's scent in the house and followed it to two sets of fresh tracks leading into the woods on the south side of the property. Our guy left on foot, and he may have left under cover of night. We don't know."

He drew a line with his finger from the cabin's location to the flowing green contours of the mountains. "There's nowhere else for him to go, but along this ridge or over it. Search Group Three is staged here."

He pointed to a location to the south. "They will sweep north and converge with the teams departing from here. If our perpetrator's in the area we'll box him in. We don't know how much of a head start he has, but he's got Alice in tow, so he'll be slower than us."

He looked at Olivia. "Local police has eyes in the sky providing support. If our guy's still in the area, we'll get him. Special Agent Strauss will coordinate Search Group Two and Captain Richardson with Asheville PD will oversee Group One. Any questions?"

The group was restless, but no one spoke.

Olivia scanned the team. "This is our best chance, folks. Remember, we don't know what this man is capable of or what his mindset is. We have to assume he's armed and willing to harm Alice if he gets pinned down. Be smart; I don't want her hurt."

They watched her without responding—she was saying nothing they didn't already know.

"Let's go."

The group broke up, each team forming up and setting out from the clearing with their assigned task.

Olivia stood for a long moment, studying the squat cabin, which now stood vacant and lifeless. The CSI team meticulously processed the blue truck sitting next to it.

Judging by the contents of the trash bag forensics found behind the cabin, the perpetrator had kept Alice here for several days, likely since the night of the abduction. Question was, when had they left?

She turned from the cabin and hurried to join the search.

Hold on, Alice. Just hold on a little longer.

Day Six
5:37 PM

LOUISIANA. That's all I knew. Because Wyatt had blindfolded me and asked me to lie down on the front seat for the last four hours of the drive.

He'd kept me at the cabin in the woods for three days, just as he'd said he would. I felt like I was living in a strange dream most of the time. Sometimes, like when I thought about how he'd taped Louise up and put her in the closet, it felt like a nightmare, but mostly it felt like we were just pretending. And most of that was because of Wyatt.

He was a moonshiner, he said, and being in the woods was home to him. He was perfectly happy living on a diet of eggs, bacon, sausage, white bread, peanut butter, boiled cabbage, pork, milk, an occasional Snickers bar (which was a real treat for him), and a slug of moonshine now and then, though he was careful not to drink too much. He said it could make you go silly in the head.

But it wasn't only that Wyatt was at home in the woods; he didn't seem to have a care in the world apart from making sure that I was safe and comfortable. Not once did he talk about any concern that the authorities might find and take me, or the trouble he might be in for kidnapping me. He was only thrilled that he'd succeeded in rescuing me, as he kept putting it.

Watching him, I couldn't help thinking that he actually thought he was on a vacation with his daughter, and his enthusiasm was sometimes a little infectious.

He didn't tell me much more about Kathryn and nothing about where we were going because he said Kathryn wanted it all to be a surprise. Instead he talked about moonshining and told me stories from his days in the enterprise, his successes and mishaps and avoiding the law. Evidently there were laws about selling alcohol, all of which were an abuse of rights, he said.

When he wasn't telling stories, he was trying to convince me to play one game or the other—I spy, find the pine cone, poker with an old deck of cards and pebbles as money. It took some convincing on his part to persuade me to play, but as I did I found some comfort in the distraction, particularly since I almost always won once I learned the rules. As the days passed, I began to see that Wyatt was a kind man with a good heart who rarely showed any deep concern.

In fact, the only time he became uptight at all was when he talked about Kathryn. I didn't see it at first, but I began to notice that lines sometimes formed over his brow when he spoke about her. He seemed fiercely loyal and deeply caring of her, but there might have been some fear in those lines as well.

In the middle of the second night, I scratched out a note on an old piece of paper I'd found outside. There were no pencils or pens I'd seen so I used a piece of charred wood from the fireplace. In the note I gave my name and said that Wyatt Lowenstein, a moonshiner, had kidnapped me and was taking me somewhere to meet my real mother, Kathryn. I also wrote that my real father was a senator from Nevada named James Ringwald who was now dead.

I tried to think of what else might be useful but couldn't think of anything. I didn't want John or Louise to worry about me too much so I added one more line: *Please don't worry. Wyatt is a kind man and is taking good care of me. He said I can come home soon.*

I folded the note up and hid it under the mattress. If they found it, they would at least be able to assure Louise that I wasn't being mistreated.

At dusk on the third evening, which was actually the fourth night of my kidnapping, Wyatt cleaned up the cabin, wiped the truck down with great care, and led me through the woods, south, to a small clearing. A blue car was hidden there under branches—our ride home, he said, with a big grin.

Home. The word frightened me.

Thirty minutes later we were back on a main highway, again headed south. Two days later we were in Louisiana, and I was curled up in the front seat, blindfolded.

He'd explained that I had to wear the blindfold so that I wouldn't know where they lived in the event I decided I didn't want to stay. The authorities would force me to tell them where they lived and they couldn't risk that. And I had to lie down because if anyone saw a girl wearing a blindfold in a car they might be suspicious and call the cops. They couldn't risk that either.

On one hand, that made sense to me. On the other hand, I already knew their names—wasn't that enough information for the authorities to go after them?

So why the secrecy?

But I still chose to believe that I really would be able to leave if I wanted to, so I had no problem lying down blindfolded. I didn't want anyone to hurt Wyatt, however strange that might seem. In fact, I even wondered whether I should have given his name in the note I'd left. If it led the authorities to Wyatt, they might put him in prison, like he said.

He might have been wrong in taking me the way he did, but part of me didn't blame him. He and Kathryn had only gone to terrible trouble and risked so much because they were so eager to have me back. Part of me felt desperately wanted and maybe that's what being a daughter was supposed to feel like.

"Okay, sweetheart. You can sit up and take the blindfold off."

"Now?"

"Yes, now. We're almost home."

I pushed myself up and pulled off the blindfold. The sight that greeted me through the windshield was unlike any I'd ever seen.

It was late afternoon, dusk, and a bit gloomy. We were on a narrow, gravel road with tufts of grass growing down the center. But it was the thick blanket of trees that struck me. Huge trees, with drooping branches and vines as far as I could see. The road dropped off into deep, wide ditches on either side as if they'd been dug to protect the road from the tangle of encroaching trees.

"Where are we?"

"Home."

I stared at the huge trees on my right and saw that the gravel road was built up, higher than the ground, which looked wet. No, not just wet.

Flooded with water.

"What's that?" I asked.

"The swamp," he said. "You're going to love it. Lots of water. We have lakes, rivers . . . Our house is just around the corner."

I immediately thought about what little I knew of swamps, and images of snakes and beady-eyed alligators strung through my mind. The sound of the road crunching under the tires somehow worsened the sudden fear that gripped me. I felt totally isolated and far away from anything that was familiar or safe.

And then we were around the corner and driving down a dirt driveway.

"End of the line," Wyatt said. "This is as far as the road goes. We already passed the last house half a mile back. We have all the land you could dream of down here. You'll see."

We passed a square outbuilding with a sloping tin roof. No windows that I could see. Maybe it had something to do with moonshine because barrels were stacked behind it. Three old trucks sat out front, one of which was on blocks, missing its rear wheels.

We passed a swing set—metal tubes that formed a teepee with hanging chains that held two tires. A small woodshed sat by itself just past the swing set. Maybe a toolshed. The ground was partly grassed, partly bare, without any care given to it. Bushes and trees grew up here and there, wherever seeds had happened to fall.

It was hard to believe that I was somehow connected to such a strange place hidden away in the swamps. It was all so foreign.

An old, white house with a porch loomed between the trees ahead, to our right. Windows across the front, a black roof, three steps leading up to a porch—about what I might expect in a house.

What I didn't expect was the large, paper sign with the words Welcome Home written in red that hung from the porch's roof. Nor the sight of the dark-haired woman wearing a flowered dress with long sleeves, standing under it, watching us intently. Nor the short boy who stood next to her.

"That's your mother and your brother," Wyatt said.

I don't know what I expected because up until that moment I had only thought of *mother* in terms of an idea without putting any face or body to it. But now I was looking at her and I panicked.

What if I didn't like her? What if she wasn't as kind as Wyatt? What if she was disappointed in me?

What if she *wasn't* my real mother?

"Don't be nervous, sweetheart. It's going to be just fine, you'll see."

Wyatt brought the car to a stop at the end of the driveway fifty feet from the house, put the shifter in neutral, and turned off the engine.

I stared up at the two people on the porch, mind suddenly blank.

ired boy was staring in wide-eyed wonder, and I could see
ss of him immediately. His head seemed a little large for
his body, and his face looked . . . well, I didn't know quite how to think
of it except . . . off.

I shifted my eyes and looked at the woman. Kathryn. Who was
peering at me through the windshield, looking as tense as I felt. For a
moment I thought she might be frightened.

This was the mother who'd gone to such great lengths to find me?

Maybe she was afraid . . . I was, wasn't I? Maybe a voice in her head
was saying that it was all too good to be true. Or that I was too skinny
to be her daughter. Or maybe she was afraid that I wouldn't measure up
to her expectations for the daughter she'd dreamed about for so many
years. Or maybe she was just nervous.

She was suddenly moving, rushing down the steps in her ankle-
length dress with long sleeves, then running toward us, nearly frantic.

I didn't know what was expected of me, and a glance at Wyatt told
me that neither did he. He just watched, hands on the wheel.

Kathryn flew up to the car, gripped the door handle on my side,
yanked the door open, and stared at me, speechless, lips trembling.

I was only distantly aware of the heat and humidity that rushed
into the car when she opened the door. I barely heard the chorus of
a million bugs and insects that might have otherwise convinced me to
quickly shut the door.

This was my mother?

Her hair was dark, pulled into a bun at the back of her head, and
she wore black leather flats. I wasn't terribly given to style, but hers was
like nothing I'd ever seen. She looked like she'd stepped out of the pages of an old magazine.

Tears suddenly flooded Kathryn's eyes, and her face began to re-
lax as relief washed over her. She lifted both arms and held trembling
hands out to me.

"It's really you. God has brought you home. Come to your mother, sweetie. Come into your mother's arms."

I didn't know if I really wanted to go to her because I wasn't sure she really was my mother. But I didn't know what else I could do, so I climbed out of the car.

Before I could go to her, she closed the distance between us, wrapped her arms around my body, and pulled me close to her bosom.

"Thank you, Jesus." She held me tight, with one hand behind my head, pressing me into her shoulder. "Thank you. Mommy has missed you so much." She was speaking through tears, overwhelmed. "You're here. You're really here."

Bobby walked up beside her, staring in wonder. Quiet.

Kathryn eased me back arm's length and studied my face, my hair. She brushed a gentle thumb across my cheek as if to wipe away a tear. "You're more beautiful than I could have imagined. My precious lamb." She sniffed. "So beautiful. All will be made right. All will be made right."

Then she leaned forward and placed a light kiss on my forehead.

"Welcome home, Eden."

I was too flat-footed to react. A strange mix of fear and comfort ran in circles through my mind, like a fox chasing a rabbit.

Wyatt had climbed out, rounded the car, and now rested his hand on Bobby's shoulder, smiling.

"Eden, this is your brother, Bobby." He looked at the boy. "Say hi, Bobby."

Bobby's face flushed red and he offered me a crooked grin. "Hi." He was pressing the tip of his forefinger against his thumb down by his side as he spoke—a nervous tic. Eyes peering up at me because he was a foot shorter. "You're my sister?"

I had to answer. I had to because I immediately liked Bobby. But I wasn't sure if I should say "yes, I am your sister" unless I knew for certain.

I glanced up at Kathryn who was smiling warmly.

"It's okay, sweetie. You can tell him."

So I looked at Bobby. "I think so."

He was smiling wide enough for me to see his gums. Then he did something I couldn't have anticipated. He stepped up to me and took my left hand in his.

"Bobby's been waiting for you for a long time," Kathryn said. "We all have. Haven't we, Bobby?"

"I'm your brother," he said, looking up at me.

"I'm so sorry we had to get you like that, sweetie," Kathryn said. "If there was any other way, we would have taken it. But . . ." She looked like she might break down. "I'm sorry if you were frightened."

"Are you going to stay with me?" Bobby asked, still on his own track.

I was unnerved, but I felt sorry for these people, you see? Especially Bobby. And now as I thought about it, I could see parts of my reflection on Kathryn's face. She had my nose, and my mouth, I thought.

She really must be my mother. Which meant that Bobby really was my brother. They were simply acting a bit strange because they had no more experience at reuniting with a long-lost daughter and sister than I had with finding my mother and brother.

"Of course she's going to stay with us, Bobby," Kathryn said when I didn't respond. "She's just in a little bit of shock. This is all new to her, that's all."

I still wasn't sure how to reassure Bobby, but I didn't have to because Wyatt shifted our focus.

"Zeke's here," he said, looking back down the road.

I followed his gaze and saw that a black truck, much newer than any I'd seen on the property, was headed our way up the driveway. Zeke, the man who'd helped them find me.

Bobby removed his hand from mine and pointed a stubby finger.

"That's Zeke," Bobby said. "He's the apostle."

"Hush, Bobby," Kathryn said, turning to face the truck.

We all watched as a man with dirty-blond hair and a short beard, dressed in black slacks, jacket, and boots, stepped out of the truck. For a few moments, he just stood there, staring at me, as if trying to decide if I measured up.

He walked up to us, smiling gently now, a good sign, I suppose. But like everything else, I didn't know how to feel about this man. His eyes were dark, but his face was kind, I thought.

Zeke nodded at Wyatt. "Saw you coming in. I'm assuming you got here clean or you wouldn't be here."

"He's clean," Kathryn insisted adamantly.

Zeke looked at her, brow raised. Somehow that simple expression shifted her demeanor, because she immediately softened.

"No one saw them," she said quietly. "It was just like you said it would be."

He studied her a moment longer, then turned his eyes to me.

"So you must be Eden," he said, then waited for me to respond. And I felt compelled.

"I . . . Yes, I think so."

He grinned. "But of course you are. I'm sure this must be a bit of shock to your system. But I can assure you—one look at both of you and a person would have to be a fool not to see mother and daughter, side by side. Alice has become Eden; the prodigal has finally been brought home." He hesitated. "Did you have a comfortable trip?"

"I'm okay," I said. "Wyatt was very good to me."

"Of course he was. You'll find nothing but goodness here. But it's not every day the hand of God works in such a mysterious way. I'm sure all of this has been a little confusing."

"A little."

"More than just a little, I'm sure," he said.

What could I say?

"I . . . I just don't know what to think."

"No, of course you don't, darling." He walked up to me, touched my hair, then lifted my chin in his large, warm hand. "Poor thing must be terrified. But I can promise you that will all change." He released me and smiled kindly. "You're a very fortunate girl, Eden. I've never known a mother as resolved as yours. She's moved the hand of God to bring you home and now here you are, a vision of heaven itself."

At this Kathryn moved next to me and placed her arm around my shoulders, facing him, as if to lay claim to me. Or maybe just to offer me assurance.

"She's yours Kathryn," Zeke said. "Your inheritance. The daughter God promised you. Be sure to raise her as appointed. She's one of God's children now."

"I will."

"Without wavering."

"Without wavering," she said.

I had no idea what they meant and I wasn't sure I wanted to. So I let it go. After all, everything about his place was strange to me, including all of the God talk.

Wyatt stepped up to Zeke, withdrew his hand from his pocket, and handed him a piece of folded paper. I immediately recognized the note I'd left under the mattress.

"Here's the note she wrote," Wyatt said.

Zeke palmed it and slipped into his pocket. "Thank you, Wyatt."

And that was that. My note had been discovered . . . Of course it had. They didn't want to be found. Zeke was no idiot.

I felt slightly nauseous.

Zeke wagged his head toward the outbuildings. "I need two barrels. Give me a hand." Exchanging a nod with Kathryn, he headed back to the truck, followed quickly by Wyatt.

"You want to see my room?"

I glanced down at Bobby who as staring up expectantly. "Okay."

Without waiting, he turned and headed toward the house, wobbling a little with each hurried step.

When I turned back to Kathryn, she was watching me as if I were her greatest prize. I know everyone wants to be wanted, but I couldn't help thinking that something was wrong. That she more than just wanted me. That a mother who'd gone to such lengths to find me would go to even greater lengths to keep me.

She lifted my hand and kissed it. Not once, but three times.

"You're spotless," she said. "A treasure from our loving heavenly Father to take away all the sorrow and grief I have ever known."

The swamp was alive with the unnerving shrieks of insects as dusk settled in. Trees loomed all around us, so thick and tangled that they might as well have been a solid wall.

Kathryn put her arm around me again, and guided me forward, walking carefully, not too rushed, as if leading a wounded soldier from a war.

"You must be starving. I have a casserole ready. Fresh corn on the cob. I'm going to take care of you, sweetheart. No one's going to hurt a hair on your head ever again." She glanced down my body. "We have to get you out of those filthy clothes and bathe you immediately. I'll trim your nails and scrub your feet. Fix your hair. Would you like that? Hmm?"

Not really. But I didn't say anything.

"Of course you would. You're going to be perfect." She gave me a little squeeze. "Mommy loves you, Eden. My name means pure, did you know that? But I'm not pure. Not without you. It's you who make me pure." She twisted her head down and kissed the top of my head. "I am dead without you."

A shiver raked my spine. I don't know what it was about her words that scared me so much, maybe it was the tone she used. But it was then that I first decided that I was going to leave. And the moment I thought about leaving, I also knew that Kathryn wouldn't let me.

So I had to go on my own, without her knowing.

And I had to go that night.

Day Six
5:54 PM

OLIVIA SAT alone at the close of the sixth long day since Alice's abduction, exhausted, staring blankly at the dozens of photos, notes, and leads pinned to the wall in the conference room that she'd temporarily made her office. They would all be packed up tonight and moved to Columbia in the morning. She would continue working the case from the FBI headquarters. Assuming there *was* any more to work.

The hum of a vacuum moving down the outer hallway had an air of finality. Time to wrap it up. Not just the day, the entire case.

Most of the staff had already gone home to their families and some basic normalcy. Normalcy at least for the night, enjoying the illusion that life was safe, predictable, and manageable within four walls, however untrue that was.

In reality, the world wasn't safe at all—the terrible things that only happened to "other people" eventually found their way to everyone. It was simply the way of a cruel and unfair universe that seemed unimpressed with either the good or the evil that filled it.

She glanced at the digital clock mounted over the door. *5:55.* The front doors would be locked at six.

Her head throbbed and the onset of a migraine ached behind her eyes. She'd spent the last two hours digging through the case files one last time before they were packed up for Columbia. Considering every angle, looking at every report again. But all she saw now were snapshots in time where they'd been one step behind, one hour too late, one good idea away from finding Alice.

If only they'd discovered the cell phone sooner.

If only John had come home an hour earlier.

If only the DNA had pointed to someone and given the man a face and a name.

If only the truck had shown up in one of the scores of traffic and gas-station security cameras they'd secured footage from within a hundred-mile radius.

If only they'd found the truck a day earlier.

If only . . . but they hadn't.

CSI had turned the cabin inside out and found nothing particularly useful they didn't already have or know. The bag of trash in a plastic bin behind the cabin contained mostly a mixture of candy-bar wrappers, eggshells, bacon packaging, empty milk jugs, and an assortment of other garbage. Upon further analysis of the milk's fermentation rate and the decay rates on several half-eaten pieces of fruit, forensics had determined that the last meal consumed at the cabin had been the night before they'd gone in. They'd missed them by twelve hours. Maybe eighteen, no more.

The truck and cabin had turned up plenty of fingerprint and DNA evidence, but still no match. Whoever had taken Alice didn't have a record.

The K-9 dogs had tracked their scent three-quarters of a mile southwest to a small stony clearing in the middle of the woods. The scent had ended there, presumably where another vehicle had been waiting. A useless collection of multiple tire tracks disappeared down a narrow Jeep trail.

Alice was gone. They had no leads on the vehicle they'd left in. The case was completely stalled. Until or unless they uncovered new evidence, they were dead in the water. That new evidence would likely come only at the hands of whoever had taken Alice. A mistake, carelessness which would lead to a sighting, committing a different crime that resulted in the abductor's fingerprint or DNA being entered into the system and matched to the fingerprints they now had on file.

But whoever had taken Alice, however awkward he might have appeared to Louise during the abduction itself, had enough planning in place to get out clean.

For all practical purposes, the case was dead in the water.

A thick knot of emotion cinched tight in her throat. She'd always invested herself completely in her cases, always taken a personal stake in them. But Alice . . .

Alice was different. There was something about the girl that *mattered* in a way she couldn't quite explain. Maybe it was because Alice was the age Michelle would be if she were still alive. Or maybe she'd just been at this too long and become so mired in her own guilt that she *wanted* Alice to be different. Maybe it was the private conversation she'd had with Andrew, the enigmatic caretaker who insisted that Alice was singularly unique and perhaps gifted. Dangerous even.

Maybe it was all of those things, or none of them. Either way, the chances of finding Alice alive were now statistically less than one in ten.

She slowly pushed herself back from the table and was about to stand when a soft knock interrupted her.

"Come in."

The door slowly swung open. A stranger stood in the doorframe, staring at her with blue eyes and gentle smile. Not just any stranger, she thought. The man before her was immediately arresting, not in his appearance, but in the way he carried himself, in the surety of his stare, in the fluidity of his walk as he stepped through her door.

Peering around him from behind, Susan, the receptionist, looked flustered.

"I'm sorry, Agent Strauss. I asked him to wait . . ."

"It's okay, Susan." Olivia leaned back in her chair.

The receptionist glanced between them, then nodded and backed out, offering a final apology.

"Can you shut the door, Susan?"

"Of course. Sorry."

She reached in, pulled the door closed, and was gone, leaving Olivia alone with the stranger, who was walking toward the window, staring out at the skyline. He spoke in a gentle voice without turning.

"Quite a view from up here. Amazing how the world looks so different from a new perspective."

"And you are?"

The man turned and faced her, unhurried and at ease, as if it was she who had come to see him and not the other way around.

Shocks of dark hair framed his chiseled face, which had the deep sun patina of someone who rarely spent time indoors. He wore jeans and white T-shirt beneath a black leather jacket. A round medallion hung in the center of his chest, attached to a black leather strap. His boots too were black leather with thick soles, like a biker might wear.

"A friend," he said. "Father Andrew directed me to you. He sends his regards."

"Father Andrew? Andrew DeVoss?"

He slowly dipped his head. "The same."

Her attention was now fully fixed. Over the years, she'd developed the ability to size people up quickly. Intuit their motivations. Read them not just by what they said, but by how they *were*. A person's presence always spoke more than their words.

But she'd never encountered the kind of presence carried by this man. And looking at him, she knew he was a friend. And one somehow connected to the man who knew of Alice's whitewashed past.

She stood and crossed the office, extending her hand.

"I'm Special Agent Strauss."

"Yes, I know," he said with a twinkle in his eye. He took her hand, firmly but tenderly, and then laid his left hand on top. "Olivia. It's a beautiful name."

His eyes were deep blue flecked with gray, and a strange sense of calm washed through Olivia as she held his gaze.

"And your name is?"

"Call me Stephen."

She withdrew her hand.

"Stephen . . ."

"Just Stephen. Names are like costumes, don't you think? We just make them up. Yours, for instance, symbolizes the olive branch of peace. Did you know that?"

"No."

"And yet it doesn't describe how you are right now, does it?"

He said it with a soothing tone that seemed to reach into her. So he too was a good judge of a person's disposition. Of course she wasn't at peace, but who was these days?

She was more interested in what he could tell her about the case.

"Please, have a seat." She directed him toward a chair in front of her desk and sat down.

"Thank you."

He slid into the chair, withdrew a toothpick from his pocket and slowly twirled it between his thumb and forefinger.

"I've come to help you, Olivia. And maybe you can help me as well."

"Fair enough. What do you know?"

"That no one is ever who they pretend to be. That nothing is as it first appears. Which is what Alice learned in the monastery before she lost her memory."

He was speaking in riddles. But oddly, she wasn't put off by him.

"I don't see how that helps. I have a missing girl on my hands and the trail has gone cold. Please tell me that you can help me find her."

"If Alice could be found right now, I would have already found her. I haven't, which means neither will you. Not until she's ready to be found."

"And with that attitude, she may never be found alive."

"Did I say alive?"

Olivia stared at him, caught off guard.

"Meaning what?"

"Meaning I don't know where or when we will find Alice, nor that she will be alive if or when we do. I do know that she's not what she seems to any who've met her. Her eyes were opened once, they will be opened again if she's willing."

"It's only been six days. She's a thirteen-year-old child who was abducted, not an adult who's fully responsible." She said it, thinking she should be protesting his apparent nonchalance. But he was the kind who didn't offer offense and she wasn't taking any. "She knows nothing about fatalism and frankly, I reject the idea that we are powerless to help her."

"I didn't say we were powerless," he said, tilting his head slightly down. "Locating her would be a great help to me. My reason for finding her is surely as motivated as yours. But Alice's journey is her own, not yours or mine. Do your best to find her, but don't let your search keep you in misery."

His words cut into her soul like a hot knife. She wasn't sure why.

"Is there anything you can tell me about her that will help? What about the other children?"

"I can tell you that you shouldn't worry about them. And that you shouldn't endanger them by speaking to anyone about them. I can also tell you that Alice was almost surely taken by her mother."

"How can you know that?"

"Because I do. No one else would have a reason to take her. Unfortunately, her mother seems to have vanished under the auspices of death. So you see, until Alice makes a way to be found, she won't be. If and when she does make a way to be found, we must be there to find her. Therefore, be diligent, but try not to worry."

She wasn't sure how to respond. The words coming out of Stephen's mouth seemed like nonsense, little more than the philosophical platitudes of a man who'd spent too much time alone. And yet there was something about his voice, the way he carried himself and spoke, that resonated deeply within her. Spoke to her. Made her want to believe what he was saying, however naïve it seemed.

"You came here to tell me not to worry?"

"Yes. And to assure you that if I do find her, you will be the first to know." He paused, eyes fixed on hers. When he spoke again, his voice was softer. "But mostly, I came with a message for you. And for the memories you have of Michelle."

His words stopped her cold.

Stephen placed a large hand on the desk, palm flat on the wood surface, ringed fingers spread wide.

"I see your pain, Olivia. That feeling that you're cut off from life, and that you'll never find your way back to the happiness you knew before you lost your way."

Tears began pooling in her eyes as he continued speaking in a low voice. She wanted to stand up, back away, but she couldn't move. A hurricane of emotion, terrible and wild, began to swirl deep within her.

"I've come to tell you that it's not your fault," he said. "Michelle's beyond suffering, and yet you suffer, trapped in this hell of your own making. Set yourself free, Olivia. Free to love your daughter as she is, not as you wish she could be. In this you will find more peace than you can possibly imagine."

She wanted to scream. Wanted to tell him that he didn't know what he was talking about. That he had no right to say what he was saying. He had no right. He had no idea what she'd suffered, what pain she lived with, how alone she was.

But his words moved through her like a warm breath, assuring her of their truth. How did he know? How could he know?

She closed her eyes and swallowed, aware that her pulse was pounding and that her breathing had quickened.

"You are loved, Olivia." His voice came like honey, softer now. "More than you can possibly comprehend. Forgive yourself for anything you thought you might have done or not done. Forgive the world. Let it all go. Be free now and always."

Olivia felt her emotion rise, unchecked. Felt her control begin to slip as the world blurred behind the hot tears that flowed freely from her eyes.

"It's going to be okay," he said.

The room was still, and the air thick, but with those words, a strange, comforting peace settled over her. Time seemed to stretch in the silence.

Then she heard the soft click of the door closing.

When she opened her eyes . . . he was gone. Only a black card inscribed with the word *Outlaw* remained where he'd been seated. But he'd left far more, hadn't he?

Michelle was forever gone.

Alice was now lost.

And yet Olivia couldn't help but to think that she had just found a missing part of herself.

She lowered her head to the desk, let out a long, trembling breath, and began to sob.

I'm so sorry, Alice.

EPISODE TWO

Day Seven

THE SOUNDS that came from the swamp outside chilled my bones as I lay in bed past midnight that first night in my new home, thinking I should leave then, while they were all asleep.

The problem was, I was as terrified at the prospect of escaping as I was of staying. I didn't know where I was, only that there were swamps all around. The road we'd come in led past the others' homes, I'd learned, and was guarded by Zeke's dogs to keep people away from these parts. But the idea of trying to find another way in the dark felt like an impossibility to me.

I had to try to get down that road and I had to do it while everyone else was asleep.

Kathryn had taken me into the house and proudly showed me my new home. A mud room just past the porch opened up to the main room—couch and chairs on the right and the kitchen on the left, all spic-and-span even though most of the furniture looked like it had been used for many years.

At a loss, I looked around, but Kathryn was focused on one thing: she had to get me clean. So, despite Bobby's excitement to show me his room, she led me first to the bathroom and told me to get undressed while she filled the bathtub.

Naturally I was a little embarrassed to take off my clothes in front of a stranger, even if she was my mother, but I did what she asked because there was nothing in me that suggested resisting her would be helpful. And she was only trying to help me clean up, right?

I even let her scrub my feet and clip my fingernails. To my knowledge only much younger children were cared for in such a doting fashion, but I didn't want to find out what might happen if I told her to stop. So I just went along. And in doing so I even wondered if maybe it would be best to stay. Maybe I was just overreacting because everything was so new to me.

She'd then laid out pink and yellow pajamas and told me to dress while she finished getting my celebration dinner ready. I was the prodigal daughter, as she called me, finally come home and there was great cause for rejoicing.

We ate at an old square table, a meal over which Kathryn, not Wyatt, presided. She was the master of the house—Wyatt was much quieter in her presence than he'd been on the road. Don't get me wrong, he wasn't afraid of her, but he was careful to do exactly what she wanted. I guessed that he spoke less around her because he didn't want to say the wrong thing, much like me.

Bobby, on the other hand, wasn't as discreet. Only when Kathryn warned him in a quiet but commanding voice that if he kept asking me silly questions he would have to do some silent time, did he keep quiet. He satisfied himself then by watching me intently between bites and breaking into a big, crooked-toothed smile every time I looked at him.

I liked Bobby very much. Also Wyatt. And I liked Kathryn, but there was a frantic desperation in her eyes that made me anxious. She was my mother, yes, but I think she wanted me to be the perfect something that had already formed in her mind. The spotless lamb, as she called it.

What would happen if I couldn't be what she wanted me to be?

"You're very quiet, sweetheart," Kathryn had said earlier, as I picked at the food she'd prepared. "Are you all right?"

"Yes. I'm fine."

"Call me Mother, angel."

I hesitated. "Yes, I'm fine, Mother."

"Thank you," she purred. "Do you like the goulash?"

"It's very good, thank you."

"Mother."

"It's very good, Mother."

"Is there anything you'd like to ask me? You must have questions. This has all happened so fast."

I had many questions. Could I really leave if I wanted to? Could I at least call John and Louise and tell them I was okay? Why was she so sure the authorities would never let me stay with her if they learned that she was my mother? What was the best way for me to get back home?

But I didn't want to cause any concern or raise her suspicions because I already knew that I had to leave.

So I said no. I was fine. It was all new and I just had to get used to things. And I called her Mother, which I understood—she'd gone so long without me, and hearing me call her Mother made it feel more real to her. I didn't mind that.

"Once you learn all the rules, this home will be your heaven, Eden. I promise you."

All the rules? I doubled my thoughts of getting away that very night.

So I lay in bed and stared at the dark ceiling late that night, mind spinning with thoughts of climbing out the window, and alligators, and rules, and sneaking past guard dogs—all of which chased sleep far away.

I'd thought about trying to call 911 on the house phone, but Kathryn had made it a point to tell me that the phone wouldn't work at night. Why, I had no idea, unless they disconnected it to keep me from using it. But that was probably just my fear getting the best of me.

I was home with my *real* mother. Laying in *my* bed. In *my* room, which had freshly painted pink walls, white lacy curtains, a white bedspread, and a pink lampshade on a little wooden lamp beside the bed. It was all carefully ordered, from the wall picture of Jesus inviting the little children to come sit on his knees, to the neatly hung dresses in the closet—all white, only white. The room had been immaculately prepared for my arrival, cleaner than the rest of the house, which was saying a lot, because, as I quickly learned, my birth mother was obsessive about things being neat.

What was wrong with any of that? Maybe I should have felt more grateful. But all I could think was that something was very wrong.

You have to go, Alice. Now, while you still can.

I sat up in bed and stared into the darkness. Moonlight spilled through the white curtains, just enough so that I could make out the shapes in the room. The house was quiet, but for all I knew, Kathryn was sleeping on the couch so she could stop me if I tried to leave.

Quietly as I could, I peeled back the bedspread, put my feet to the wooden floor, and tiptoed to the closet. I'd already decided that all I needed were shoes—the long pajama pants and top were otherwise clothing enough. But I had to get the black leather shoes she'd said were mine out of the closet without making noise.

I got to my knees, carefully cracked the closet door, then pulled it wide enough to reach in and feel for the shoes. My hand closed over one, then the other, and I pulled them out.

I sat back on my heels and listened for any sound beyond the heavy thump of my heart in my ears. Only the night outside, and its insect sounds.

I'd already concluded that, if I could get it open, the window was my best bet because then I wouldn't have to walk through the house.

I quickly made my way to the window, set the shoes on the floor, and reached for the two latches that held it down along the bottom sill. They came open easily and I felt a breath of hope whisper through me.

Getting the window to slide up wasn't as easy, but with considerable effort, the wood creaked and then moved. The sound of the insects doubled and the hope I'd felt was dashed by a sudden wave of fear.

I stood there for a minute working up the courage to climb out. The door to my bedroom remained closed. That was good, right? I had to at least try. I could always come back, couldn't I?

So I took the shoes, stuck my head out into the night, saw the ground only a few feet down by the light of the moon, and I climbed out, one leg after the other.

I sat down quickly and pulled on the shoes, which were made of soft black leather that laced up the front—a kind of shoe I'd never seen before.

The shoes fit a little large, but at least they protected my feet.

I stood by the window and looked around, getting my bearings. It was brighter outside than inside. I could see the driveway that led to the road clearly, just past the porch to my left.

Immediately, images of snarling guard dogs snapped at my mind.

One step at a time, Alice. Just get to the road. Just that far.

Maybe I should steal the car. But I didn't know how to drive and I didn't have the keys.

Careful not to step on a twig that might snap and give me away, I stole across the rough ground and made it to the driveway. Walking faster, headed for the road just ahead, my hope began to swell.

It was then that I heard the soft creak behind me. The sound of a door opening.

Catching my breath, I spun back and stared at the house. There, on the porch, stood a figure, and at first I thought it had to be Kathryn. But it was too small, and I realized it was Bobby. Staring at me dumbly, with his hands by his sides.

He walked down the steps and ambled toward me in his own stumbling kind of way, looking directly ahead rather than at the ground at his feet.

I could've made a run for it, but before I could make up my mind, he was there, beside me, looking up with wide eyes.

"Where are you going?" he whispered.

I wasn't sure what I should tell him, so I just said the truth.

"I'm going back."

No one else had come out of the house. But what if Kathryn woke and heard us?

"Where is back?" he asked, confused.

"Back to where I came from," I whispered.

"Can I come with you?"

"No, Bobby. You live here. You have to go back to the house."

I was suddenly certain that someone else would come out of the house and catch us standing there in plain sight, so I turned and hurried forward.

Bobby came wobbling after me, like a puppy on an invisible leash.

"Do you like eggs?" he asked, too loudly for my comfort.

Eggs?

"We're going to have eggs for breakfast. I like bacon too."

"Shhh! They're going to hear you."

He asked again, only this time in a whisper. "Do you like eggs?"

I hurried on, still fearful that we would be overheard. We reached the road and I turned back to see if anyone was following.

The porch was still empty. And by now there were a few shrubs and small trees that might hide us from plain sight if anyone looked out.

"Mommy said that I can show you the lake tomorrow. Do you like to fish?"

It was as if Bobby had no concept of what was happening. His head was caught in a simple place where problems didn't really exist.

I put my hand on his shoulder. "Listen to me, Bobby. I have to leave, okay? I have to go find out if my other parents are okay."

"Can I go with you?"

"No. You have to stay here with Kathryn."

"Where are you going?"

"I told you, I have to go back to where I came from."

He stared down the road, uncertain. "Where'd you come from?"

"Back there, down the road a long way."

"You can't go that way. The dogs'll eat you."

"They will?" I followed his stare down the road. "Are you sure?"

"There's lots of dogs. They scare me."

"What kind of dogs?"

"Black dogs. Mommy says they keep the bad people out and the good people in. If you go that way, they'll bite you."

I studied the landscape shrouded in darkness ahead, torn by indecision.

"Is there a way through the swamps?"

He looked at the foliage to our right. I could just see the moonlight glinting off the water at the base of a large tree beyond the dry ground.

"The alligators will eat you," he said. Then he looked up at me. "Will you go fishing with me tomorrow, when you get back? I can teach you how to fish."

Panic swept through me. Having tasted the little freedom I'd found by getting out of the house, I was even more desperate to get away.

"Is there any other way to get away from here?" I asked, turning around.

"I think so."

"There is?"

He grinned wide. "I can show you."

"You can?"

"Yes . . . I . . . I can show you."

With that he was already moving in his unnatural, slightly awkward gait, hurrying the opposite way, back past the house.

I wanted to ask him where we were going, but he was rushing and the house was looming against the night sky to our right and I didn't want to make any sound.

Still no sign of Kathryn. She and Wyatt were still asleep.

Bobby led me wordlessly to a wide path on the other side of the property, rushing like a trooper on a mission, barreling straight ahead. Around a small grove of trees that grew on dry ground.

"Where are we going?" I whispered. But he was too intent on his mission to respond.

He hurried around the last tree and thrust his arm forward, pointing ahead. "There."

I pulled up sharply and looked out over a large body of black water: a lake with a perfectly smooth surface that looked like oil at night.

The one phobia I had was water. A boy named Carver had pushed me into the pool at the orphanage and, not knowing how to swim, I'd nearly drowned before being pulled out, coughing and hacking up water. I'd never been in a pool since.

The last of my hope drained from me as I stared at that threatening body of dark water.

"This is the way out?" I asked.

"You can get a boat!"

"A boat? Do you have a boat?"

"No."

"Does Wyatt have one?"

"No."

"Then where would I get a boat?"

He shrugged. "Zeke's got a boat."

"Where?"

Again Bobby shrugged. "At his house."

"Where the dogs are?"

"The dogs will bite you."

I stood blinking, at a loss. Turned slowly around. There was this lake ahead of us, swamps on either side, and the one road that led past Zeke's place where a pack of Dobermans or some other breed of bloodthirsty dog waited to snarl at and bite anyone who came close.

There was no way out. I was trapped. The finality of my predicament settled over me like a lead blanket and there on the bank of the black lake, I began to panic.

"I'm trapped?" I cried in a half whisper. "I can't stay here! I have to go home! This wasn't my choice, I was forced to come here, I don't want to stay here!"

My voice had risen as my anger boiled to the surface for the first time since Wyatt had taken me.

"I can't do this!" I snapped, this time facing Bobby who watched me with wide eyes. "They can't force me to stay! They said I could leave any time I wanted. I want to leave *now*!" My hands were balled into fists and I shoved them down by my sides, as if that might make my point clearer. "Now!" Then again. "Now!"

Bobby was at a loss. He looked out at the water, confused. It occurred to me that my harsh words might have hurt him, but I couldn't just think about him now. I'd been dragged out of my home bound and gagged in duct tape, held hostage in the woods for three days, and then taken far away to a swamp, blindfolded.

Bobby was confused because he was a little slow in the head, so maybe he couldn't understand just how terrible my situation was, but that didn't make my predicament any better.

I stood there next to him for a long minute, smothered by more fear and anger than I'd felt since first waking from my amnesia, six months earlier.

Bobby had remained abnormally silent. When he turned his head and looked up at me, his eyes were swimming in tears.

"Are you my sister?" he whispered in a strained voice.

My anger softened. But only a little. I didn't want to answer because right then I didn't want to be Bobby's sister.

A soft whimpering sound broke the focus I'd placed on my misery. It grew, and I realized that Bobby had responded to my silence by crying. He stood there on the bank, staring out at the black water with tears leaking down his face. Sobbing softly, with a hitch in his cry.

"Bobby?"

He kept crying. And hearing him, a new fear rose in me. A concern for him. For Bobby. He stood before me as innocent as a dove, and yet crushed. I couldn't, in good conscience, ignore him.

I put my hand on his shoulder. "It's okay, Bobby. Please don't cry."

He responded by turning into me, mouth open and strained as he cried.

"Please don't leave me." He said it hitching through his sobs. And with those words, my heart broke for him.

And he wasn't done.

"I don't want you to go . . ." he cried, slowly pressing his head into my shoulder.

I put my arm around his shoulders and held him close. "Sh, sh . . . it's okay, Bobby."

But it wasn't going to be okay, was it? There was a deep fear in Bobby's cry that chilled me to the bone. He was hiding something behind his simple mind that reduced him to tears.

"It's going to be okay," I said, putting both arms around him. I knew that he wanted to hear me say that I wasn't going and it seemed to me that, at least for now, that was the truth, even if not by my own choosing. But still the truth.

"It's okay, Bobby. I'm not going. I promise, I'm not going anywhere."

Immediately his crying eased. Then stopped after a few sniffs. His face went blank and his eyes were closed, and I wondered what was going on in his mind.

And then, almost as suddenly as it had begun, his dark mood left him. He opened his eyes and straightened, staring up at me like a puppy.

"Can I teach you how to fish?" he asked. And then quickly, "Do you like moonshine? It makes you pure."

"I think I might like fishing," I said.

His face lit up. "I caught a big catfish! Bigger than my arm."

"You did?"

"Do you like to eat fish?"

"I think so."

"I like fish. Do you like eggs?"

I smiled at him. "Yes, I like eggs."

He laughed, delighted, snorting. It was the cutest little laugh I had ever heard and I nearly laughed aloud with him. But I was too overwhelmed with my own predicament to go that far.

"Mommy has a surprise for you tomorrow."

My mind was pulled back to the fact that Kathryn actually was my mother. *Mommy*. It sounded strange. And *Brother*. Bobby really was my brother. My own flesh and blood.

"What kind of surprise?"

He shrugged. "She said you're going to make everything perfect again."

I had no idea what that could mean.

"Bobby, can I ask you a question?"

"Sure."

"Does Mommy ever hurt you?"

He looked at me with a blank stare. "Hurt me?"

"Why are you so afraid of me going away?"

"I . . . Because you're my sister."

"That's right." I smiled at him. "And you're my brother."

He beamed like a full moon. "You're my friend."

And maybe his only friend, I thought.

"But Mommy doesn't ever hurt you? Maybe when you're naughty?"

He looked out at the lake. "No."

"Never?"

"Mommy said that if you go, there will be no one left to save me."

"Save you? From what?"

He shrugged. "From sin. I'm not perfect like you are. I was born bad."

I knew then that I couldn't leave Bobby alone, at least not until I knew that he was going to be okay without me. Or unless I could take him with me.

"No. No, that's not true, Bobby. You're perfect, just the way you are."

"I am?"

"Yes. And you're my brother too. And my best friend."

"I am?"

"You are. And I'm going to stay for a while so that I can be your friend because I think you're perfect just the way you are."

He grinned his wide, crooked-tooth smile, too overwhelmed with joy to speak, I think.

"And that will be our secret, okay?"

He nodded. "Okay."

Maybe if I had an easy way out, I would have still tried to escape that night, but I don't think so. I think I found my brother that night by the lake and suddenly I was more than just a lost girl who needed to be adopted by strangers to find a home.

In my own way, I already had a home. It was with Bobby, my brother, at least until I knew he would be okay.

We talked another half hour, mostly about things he was familiar with. Alligators and broken-down trucks and moonshine and trees and fish and eggs and bacon and the G.I. Joe that Wyatt had bought for him. He loved Wyatt.

"We should go back to the house," I finally said.

"Okay." He started up the path without waiting for me, eager to be of good use.

Kathryn was sitting on the porch when we returned, and for a moment I was sure that we were both in terrible trouble. But Bobby didn't seem worried. He walked right up to the porch and reported the good news without delay.

"I'm going to show Eden how to fish," he announced. "She's going to stay with me."

Kathryn stood from her rocking chair, smiling. "Why, that's wonderful, Bobby. I'm glad to hear that." She looked at me. "It's so good to have you back with us. Come here, darling."

I walked up the steps and she took me into her arms.

"I want you to know that it's okay, Eden," she whispered, kissing my cheek. "You'll find your way here. It's what God has planned for us all. I love you, sweetheart. You are so precious to me." Another soft kiss.

She stepped back and brushed a strand of hair off my forehead. "Now you two get some sleep. We have a big day ahead of us tomorrow."

I WAS awakened the next morning by the creaking of my door, my thoughts still caught in a dream that had haunted me throughout the night. In the dream I was Alice, and I was in a special hospital made for people who had psychological problems. There I'd met a girl named Christy who thought she was trapped. I told her she could just walk out, but she didn't believe me.

What a silly girl, I kept thinking. *Just walk out, silly.*

And that's when I woke up to the creaking, half expecting to look over and see Christy at the door. Instead, I saw a woman standing in the doorway, smiling at me.

It took me a moment to remember that she was Kathryn, my birth mother. I was in her house.

It crashed into my mind all at once, like a data download. That and the events from last night by the dark lake.

Kathryn walked in wearing a black dress that looked new, then closed the door behind her. "Good morning, Eden. Did you sleep well?" She crossed to the window and pulled back the curtain. "Hmm?"

"Yes."

"Good." She turned back to me. "Because today's a very special day." She sat down on the bed next to me. "This is the beginning of a new life for all of us. The old will pass away, behold, all things will become new."

She said it with such assurance and beauty that I thought she might be right. Maybe there was some greater good that would come out of my being brought back to her.

Or maybe I was just too naïve to see the impossibility of that. I was still too confused to know which. But I did feel better than I had the night before.

"It's time to get up," she said. "I'll help you make the bed and then I have something I want to share with you. Something very close to my heart. Okay?"

"Okay," I said.

Together we made the bed per her instructions, folding the corners just so, smoothing the bedspread with the palms of our hands, and setting the pillow squarely at the top of the bed.

She inspected the room with a satisfied smile, then asked me to kneel down on one side as she crossed to the other side.

"Kneel down here?" I asked, standing across from her.

She removed her shoes and settled down to her knees, with her elbows on the bed. "Yes, right there, Eden. Just like me."

I knelt down and rested my elbows on the bed.

"Fold your hands."

I folded them, thinking she was going to lead me in a prayer.

"That's my precious girl. Now I'm going to tell you about the old to help you understand why we need the new. Behold, the old wineskins will be made new. That's what we're going to do today, sweetheart. And you need to know why. Do you understand?"

"I think so."

"Good."

She shifted her gaze and stared at the wall behind me.

"My father's name was Byron Miller. We were wealthy. He was a religious man and served as a deacon in the church. But on the inside he was rotten to the core. He liked to gamble and run shady deals and when his sin caught up to him it was more than he could bear, so he killed himself. With his death, the blessing of God was vanquished from our lives. We went from being rich to dirt poor overnight."

A far-off look had edged into her eyes and her smile fell away. She spoke in a near monotone, and I could feel the pain and bitterness in her voice.

"My mother's name was Sarah, and she couldn't manage the guilt and shame of her loss so she turned to drinking. It destroyed her and she couldn't take care of me properly, so child services took me away from her. I ended up in an orphanage, just like you. I was eleven when they took me. It was like living in hell for me. I was a slave in Egypt and I hated it. So when I turned fourteen, I ran away."

She paused, eyes faintly misted by tears as she thought back to her childhood.

"I'm sorry," I said.

She forced a smile. "It's all right, sweetheart. All of that is going to be made whole now. Always remember that above all, one law can never fail: *you reap what you sow.* Some call it karma. But there's more. You also reap the sins of your father, until all the generational sins of your bloodline have been atoned for. That's how it works. My father brought a curse into our home and left me to suffer for his sin."

She took a deep breath.

"I had a beautiful daughter who I named Eden and she was taken away from me. That was you, darling. When I got out of the institution, I nearly lost my mind looking for you, but you were nowhere I could find. I was at the end of myself when Zeke found me. I met Wyatt, your father. More than anything I wanted another baby, so I conceived and gave birth to a baby girl named Sarah, after my mother. But Sarah was stillborn."

Her mouth had fallen, pulled down by a frown that drew deep lines in a weathered face that looked older than she'd appeared only a few minutes earlier. The weight of her burden was too much for her to bear alone, I thought. And that thought surprised me because I didn't normally arrive at those kinds of conclusions. I felt sorry for her; she was a deeply troubled soul.

"I'm sorry."

She continued as if confessing a terrible shame—maybe that's why she wanted us to kneel.

"I had failed twice, first with you and then with Sarah. I knew that I had to have a pure child that I could raise in righteousness to break the generational curse and make right what my father had made wrong. So I tried again, and when Bobby was born dumb, I knew that my womb was cursed forever. That's when Zeke helped me see that trying to have another child wasn't what God had for me. That's why Bobby was born twisted. My place wasn't to have another child; it was to rightfully reclaim the daughter who the devil stole from me. My firstborn, the pure one."

Her eyes settled back on me and she smiled. "I had to find my Eden. You're the one who will take away all of my sin and make right all of what has been made wrong. The years that the locusts have eaten, God will now restore sevenfold. You and I are one, what happens to you, happens to me. What God has made one, let no man tear asunder. Through your righteousness will come great blessing."

My righteousness?

"You don't have to understand all of it, sweetheart. I'll help you stay pure. You're a precious angel. You are my garden of Eden, my lily of the valley, the lamb without blemish. If anyone ever tries to hurt you again, it will be over my dead body." She paused. "Today, old things will pass away and all will be made new. Wyatt told me that you can't remember anything before six months ago. Is that true?"

"Yes."

"So you see. Even that's confirmation. Old things have been put away; even your mind has been made new. You are perfect. No one else on earth could be who you're called to be. You really are my spotless lamb."

It sounded terribly strange to me. But I also saw how the tenderness returned to her eyes and face, and being a person with only six months of life to recall, I wasn't in a place to find immediate fault with anything she said, however strange it sounded.

"Today is the day of your first baptism," she said. "I'll need to bathe you and scrub your hands and feet, and wash your hair, prepare you for baptism."

"I bathed last night," I said.

"That was before you went out by the lake and defiled yourself. Even if you hadn't, we will always have to take great care to make sure you're perfectly clean before we offer you in baptism. Remember, you will reap what you sow. There will be some rules. We follow only the path of our crucified Savior. In doing so, we live in resurrection, cleansed of all sin. He will turn our filthy rags into robes of righteousness."

She watched me with adoring eyes that made me feel a bit mixed up inside.

"Doesn't that sound good to you, Eden?"

When I didn't respond, she pressed gently.

"It's beautiful, isn't it?"

"It sounds a little scary," I said.

"Of course it's a little scary at first. Don't you think Jesus was scared when he went to the cross? We all feel fear, that's okay. As long as we are willing to wash it all away in obedience. Then we're made whole. All of this will become clear as you walk the path God has made for you, sweetheart."

She pushed herself off her knees and stood, then crossed to the closet, withdrew a black bathrobe, and laid it neatly on the end of the bed.

"Undress and put this on, then come to the bathroom. I've already drawn the water."

IT TOOK Kathryn over an hour and two hot baths to clean me to her satisfaction. I felt awkward at first, as I had the night before. But then I began to think of it as being cared for, like people who went to a spa, although I had never been. When I thought in those terms, I found that I wasn't bothered.

All the dead skin had to come off, she explained. Did I know that the body shed billions of flakes of skin every day? She claimed that 90 percent of all house dust came from the skin of those who lived in that house. She also said that the flesh was like an old, leather wineskin—something people used to carry wine in a long time ago. All of that old skin had to come off before I could be made new through my baptism.

So she scrubbed my feet and hands, and knees and all of my skin with different kinds of brushes, depending on how tough the skin was, because she didn't want to harm me. Some of it hurt a little, but she said that all true cleansing came with at least a little pain or there was no gain.

She had me brush my teeth twice and she washed my hair three times, so that not one hint of oil remained. Cleaned my ears out with Q-tips and rubbing alcohol. Filed and trimmed the dead skin at the base of my nails—my cuticles, only she pronounced it like "cut" icles. We had to "cut" away the "icles," she said.

When she was all done, she brought me a pair of white underwear, another black robe, this one newly washed, and some brand-new rain boots that she said had been purified. Then she asked me to sit on my bed and wait while she made sure everything was ready.

"Where are Bobby and Wyatt?" I asked. I hadn't seen them since waking.

"They're getting ready. They can't see the bride before she comes to her wedding, now can they?"

"What wedding?"

"That's you, sweetheart. I'm married to Wyatt, but God is your groom. Now you just wait right here until I come for you. Please don't touch anything; it'll defile your skin. All right?"

I didn't really have much of a choice in the matter.

"Okay."

She smiled warmly, and left, closing the door behind her.

Her comment about God being my groom was confusing, naturally, and once again I wondered if my staying might be a terrible mistake. But then I thought about Bobby. And I reminded myself that nothing bad had actually happened.

I was only playing a game, getting in costume and putting on a stage play. What harm was there in that, if it made everyone happy?

Kathryn came for me ten minutes later, put a blindfold on me because she wanted it to be a surprise, and led me out of the house, down the porch steps and across the yard, then through a door to what I assumed was one of the outbuildings I'd seen earlier.

I couldn't mistake the excitement in her voice as she stood before me and asked if I was ready.

"I guess."

Carefully, so as not to disturb my combed hair, she untied the blindfold, and withdrew it from my head.

I blinked in the dim light and looked around. We were in an old, small, wooden shed with exposed beams overhead and clean straw on the ground. Two metal candle stands each held a dozen white candles, which lit the room.

To my right sat a large porcelain bathtub with decorative iron feet. The porcelain was chipped in places but otherwise had been polished. It was filled to the brim with clean water.

Kathryn stood directly in front of me, dressed in her black dress, next to a table lit by a single candle. On the table were an open black-leather Bible, a brass bowl with some liquid in it, a clear glass with what looked like moonshine or some other clear fluid, a small golden ring, and a folded white robe.

Wyatt stood to my left, dressed in blue overalls, next to Bobby who was wearing a dark robe, but not like mine. His was old and ragged and dirty, which surprised me, considering how obsessive Kathryn was about cleanliness.

He watched me with pride, wearing that sheepish, crooked smile of his.

"Hello, Eden," he said.

"Hush, Bobby," Kathryn snapped. "Not a word from you."

Bobby hushed, but his smile remained stuck to his face. Wyatt looked on kindly, hands folded at his waist.

Kathryn gave me an encouraging nod, lifted the Bible, took a deep breath, stared directly into my eyes, and spoke without looking at the pages opened before her.

"As it is written, though having made man in his image as his children, God found man's ways wicked and intolerable. And what God had made lovely, he now detested, having no stomach for the wayward means of what he had made. Thus he hated his children and saw to confining them to a place of eternal torture without mercy. And there came into this world of hatred the Son of God, proclaiming that if those God had fashioned in his likeness bowed before God in fear and presented themselves as living sacrifices, the One who had fashioned them in love would forget his hatred of them and allow them to escape the torture awaiting them."

She took another deep breath and this time blew it out through pursed lips.

"And so it came to pass that on the morning of the seventh day of the new creation, man brought the spotless lamb, a living sacrifice, before God. And with it, a goat."

Her eyes shifted to Bobby.

"And on that goat God placed all of his hatred to satisfy his lust for vengeance."

My heart leapt with frightful worry. I had never heard of this kind of God.

She turned back to me. "The lamb was found to be pure and acceptable in his sight. He took her as his bride, to be touched by nothing impure for the length of her life. And he commanded the lowly mother of the bride to tend her well and to present her pure before him on the seventh day so that his anger might not rise up again. In this way will God's favor rest on the bride and on her household and return blessing sevenfold."

One last breath, through her nostrils.

"Selah," she said softly.

She dipped her head and set the Bible on the table.

"We present this bride to our Father to take away all of our sin, that we might be found acceptable in his sight and restored to our true birthright as the blessed children of God."

She walked up to me and slipped the black robe off my shoulders.

"In removing the black robe, we shed the stain of sin from this spotless lamb of God."

Kathryn released her grip on the robe and let it fall in a heap around my booted feet.

"Come with me, sweetheart," she whispered, taking my arm. "Please do exactly as I say."

I was wearing only my underwear and the rain boots and although it was hot outside, I suddenly found myself trembling.

"Sh . . . sh . . . sh . . . There now, it's going to be okay. I'm not going to hurt you."

She stopped at the edge of the tub.

"Step out of your boots and directly into the water without touching the ground, darling. You can't dirty your feet and defile the water."

Kathryn had said I wouldn't be hurt, and nothing she'd done so far made me think she would lie to the daughter she'd gone to such lengths to find. The words and rituals were strange, to be sure, but then everything that had happened to me during the last six months was a bit strange.

So with Kathryn's help, I pulled first one foot out of a boot and set it in the ice-cold water, and then the other. Now in the tub, gooseflesh rippled over my body and I stood shaking.

"Move closer to the front, sweetheart."

I shuffled to the middle of the tub.

"Now sit down."

I hesitated, then lowered myself into the cold water, shivering.

She smiled at me approvingly, placed her right hand gently around my throat and her left hand at my lower back.

"As God himself was lowered into the grave to appease his Father's rage, so now we offer this lamb into the grave so that she might rise and be found worthy of God's love." To me: "Don't struggle, darling."

Without further warning, Kathryn applied pressure to my throat and pushed me back. I'd heard of baptism, of course, and so I already knew that she was going to push me under. I let myself go, not wanting to upset her.

The moment the water covered my face, I felt it fill my nose and panic ripped through me. My body jerked up.

But Kathryn wasn't ready for me to come up yet. Her grasp on my throat tightened and she held me down.

For a moment, I relaxed, thinking that it would only last a second and then be over. But the second turned into two, and then four, and suddenly I wondered if she was actually going to drown me.

The instant that thought entered my mind, my survival instincts swallowed me and I began to struggle to get my head up and out of the water. But with my increased effort came increased pressure on my throat, holding me down.

I could hear Kathryn's muffled voice crying out above me, and the sound pushed my fear deeper. I began to thrash, clawing for the edge of the tub, kicking my legs, screaming underwater.

Still, my mother held me down. I thought that I was going to drown. With each passing second I became more certain.

But I didn't drown. Instead, just as my world started to go black, my head was suddenly pulled up and out of the water. I came up sputtering and gasping for breath.

Kathryn wrapped her arms around me and held me tenderly. But I was confused and I began to cry.

"It's okay, sweetheart. I'm right here. Sh, sh, sh . . . Mommy's right here to hold you. That's my girl, I'm right here for you. Sh, sh, sh . . ."

I let her hold my drenched head in her arm and slowly brought myself under control.

"It will be much easier if you don't struggle the next time," she whispered. "We're almost done."

When I had calmed, she pulled back and put her hand under my arm.

"Stand up with me."

I pushed myself up with her assistance and stood in the tub. Kathryn retrieved the folded white robe from the table, opened it wide and told me to step out of the tub. She draped the robe over me and helped me slide my arms into the sleeves.

"You see? You're perfectly whole," she assured me. "You have nothing to fear. We're almost done."

She led me to the table, picked up the brass bowl, and dipped her fingers into the liquid.

"With this virgin oil, I anoint you, Eden, the spotless lamb cleansed of all unrighteousness."

She raised her hand over my head and sprinkled some of the oil in my hair. Then retrieved the golden ring from the table and lifted my left hand.

"With this ring I do wed thee to God."

She slid the ring over my finger. Then kissed each of my cheeks.

"What was lost is now found. What was dead is now risen from the grave. What lived in transgression is now made whole, a spotless bride now loved by the God of vengeance."

She gazed lovingly at me for a long moment, then turned and walked to the wall. There was a whip with leather straps hanging from a nail. She unhooked it and walked back, face now flat, eyes on Bobby.

"And on the goat he transferred all of his anger for the goat he found unworthy of his love."

She was going to whip Bobby? My heart froze, and I almost cried out. Maybe the fear had robbed my voice, I don't know, but I watched in disbelief as Kathryn instructed Bobby to take off his robe and turn around.

He was smiling as he did it, eyes on me. Proud. Surely not aware of what horror might be headed his way.

"Bend over," she instructed.

He obediently doubled at the waist and stood ready.

Kathryn gently whipped his back with the straps once. It was a symbolic beating.

"To this unworthy flesh I transfer all of God's wrath."

She whipped him again, gently. But her words cut to my heart.

"I confer all of our sin to the defiled one . . ."

Another lash.

"So that righteousness might be found in the pure bride."

Again.

"I curse thee . . ."

Again.

"I curse thee . . ."

She laid the whip across his back seven times. On the third 'I curse thee' something in me changed. I was watching my young brother who was too naïve and innocent to fully grasp the emotional burden being placed on his back, and I realized something new.

I knew that I was home.

That I was home and I wasn't going to leave.

I wasn't going to leave because if I did, there would be no one to save Bobby, just like Kathryn had told him. I couldn't abandon my poor, innocent brother. Ever.

What I'd half decided the night before was now sealed in my mind.

After Kathryn had laid seven lashes across Bobby's back she told him that he could stand straight.

He turned around, smiling wide with crooked teeth, as proud as could be. And I smiled back, holding back a well of tears that wanted to cleanse my eyes of what they'd just seen.

I love you, Bobby. I will take care of you. I promise you, I will never leave you.

"It is finished," Kathryn said, spreading her arms wide.

Wyatt started to clap and was joined first by Bobby, and then by me.

"It is finished."

But really, it had all just begun.

Five years later

KATHRYN STOOD at the kitchen sink and watched through the window as Wyatt's truck pulled to a stop beside the house. He'd left long before sunrise and had been gone all day, hauling barrels and repairing a copper still for Zeke.

Now, dusky shadows reached deep into the surrounding bayou. Despite the approaching night, the summer air was still thick. She didn't mind at all, though, because it reminded her of the day her precious lamb had come to her. Their first night together as a family had been a night just like this one.

Had it been five years already?

Five years . . . Amazing how quickly time slipped away. Eden had been so beautifully naive then, clueless about the ways of redemption and purity and yet so innocent.

Five years . . . She was so much more now. Not always perfect, but as close as any human was likely to be. It hadn't been an easy path— righteousness never was. Her role as mother and teacher had required never-ending attention and wisdom. Eden's had required trust and obedience.

But there was no price for purity in the eyes of God. No cost too high for absolution. No task too great for the sake of love. And no mother or daughter could possibly love each other the way she and Eden did.

Wyatt's work boots clomped up the rickety porch stairs, and then the rusty screen door slammed shut behind him. His footsteps stopped a few feet behind her.

"Zeke wants to see you," Wyatt said.

She turned. He stood in the kitchen doorway, still dressed in grimy work clothes, hair matted to his sweaty forehead.

"Right now?" She set the last dinner plate in the wire drying rack and wiped her hands with the dishtowel.

"Yes, sugar. I was just at his place, he's waiting for you."

"Did he say why?"

"No."

"Well, how was he? Was he cross?"

"I don't think so."

"What do you mean, you don't think so?"

"I mean I couldn't tell if he was cross."

"I swear, Wyatt . . . If a hornet stung you between the eyes, you wouldn't notice it unless someone pointed it out to you. And how many times do I have to tell you to take your shoes off at the door?"

He carefully slipped his work boots off, peeled off his socks, and placed them on a mat next to the door.

She hooked the towel through the refrigerator's handle and hurried past Wyatt, fidgeting with her fraying hair bun on the way to the bathroom. "I have to change. The children are in their rooms having quiet time. They will stay there till I return. No one goes outside. Not them, not you."

"Of course, sugar."

She entered the bathroom, filled the sink with scalding hot water, applied a dollop of Noxzema to her right hand, and scrubbed her face and neck. The medicinal scent of the white cream pleased her and she breathed it in deeply. There wasn't time to be as thorough as she normally required, but this would have to do. God would cover her haste with grace.

Cleanliness is godliness, and godliness is purity. Only the pure can see God.
Kathryn dried her face and pulled on a fresh dress—the white one with Texas bluebells on it. Her crucifix necklace. Her polished black flats would do too. Hair pulled back without a stray hair to be seen.

Without another word to Wyatt, who stared out the kitchen window with his back to her, she left the house, climbed into the truck and pulled onto the long gravel road.

Why would Zeke have sent for her so late in the day? What had she done or left undone? Nothing. So then it had to be about Eden.

Eden: the spotless lamb who'd quickly come to accept her true place in the world. And her mother's love.

Mother.

She'd wept the night Eden had first used that word with full sincerity. She'd come so far. They all had, and for that Kathryn thanked both God and Zeke every day.

Kathryn turned left into Zeke's compound and rolled to a stop next to his spotless, black pickup—an F-350 he'd said. Next to it, hers looked like a piece of junk, but that was only proper.

She killed the engine and got out of the truck. Zeke's dogs ran back and forth in a nearby chain-link pen and barked as she climbed the flagstone steps to the house, wiping beaded sweat from her hairline with a handkerchief.

A lone rocking chair sat on the covered porch beneath an overhead fan that labored in the heavy air. She gathered herself and knocked on the door with a slight tremor in her hand, then took a step back.

A brief moment, then the door swung open. Zeke wore a black button-down shirt, tucked in, with his sleeves rolled neatly to his elbows. His dark, lingering eyes had always unnerved her—there was no hiding from them. He could see through a person's veneers, straight to the true wickedness of the heart.

"Kathryn." Zeke dipped his head. "Thank you for coming so quickly."

"Of course."

"Yes . . . Of course." He pulled the door wider and stepped to the side. "Come in."

The crisp chill of the air-conditioned home was refreshing and the pleasant musk of fine leather and wood nearly divine. To her way of thinking, every time she entered his house the air crackled with something that she could only call reverence. She imagined the children of Israel might've felt something similar upon entering Moses' tent.

The house had a modern kitchen to her right, filled with gleaming stainless-steel appliances and granite countertops. A mahogany dining table for twelve sat in front of a stone fireplace mounted with a huge elk. Hallways branched off on both ends to other rooms.

Zeke's kind of luxury was entirely out of place in the bayou, and yet that was the whole point because it was the way things should be—abundance in the midst of lack.

He led her toward a sitting area in the middle of the room. A pair of high-backed leather chairs sat on either side of a large couch and coffee table, which he'd once told her was hand carved from the trunk of a single redwood. On the corner of the table sat a silver tray with a half dozen highball glasses and a fancy crystal decanter half filled with amber colored liquor.

"Please." He motioned toward the couch and sat in the chair next to it.

She glanced around, wondering where Barbara was. Zeke normally took Kathryn to his office, beyond the earshot of his wife.

"It's okay, we're alone," he said, picking up the decanter.

Kathryn sat on the end of the couch with her hands on her knees. A thick silence passed between them as Zeke slowly poured the liquor. Even from where she sat, Kathryn could smell the whisky's sweet oak scent.

He eased back, crossed one leg over the other, and sipped from the glass. "Chivas Regal." He held the glass in front of him and turned it slowly. "Barreled the year I was born."

He took a drink.

"Good year. Only two hundred fifty-five bottles exist, and this is my last one so I drink it neat. Always neat. Watering down such a thing of beauty would be a sin because it would make it less true to itself."

He looked at Kathryn and winked. "And the truth sets us free."

She smiled and nodded. "Yes, it does."

"Tell me something, Kathryn. What's *your* truth?"

She felt the weight of his gaze. "You, Zeke. The life you gave me."

He took another sip of his whiskey. "It's been fifteen years since you came here. Isn't that right?"

"That sounds right."

"You were so lost when I found you. A vagrant on the streets. And now look at you. You're the pride of my heart, Kathryn."

She felt herself blushing. "Why, thank you, Zeke."

"Everyone else tossed you aside like the trash they thought you were." He paused. "But I, I saw a flower waiting to be opened. And flower you have."

"Because of you."

"I gave you beauty for ashes. The oil of joy for mourning."

Her mind spun back to those ashes. Her mother and father who'd both trampled on her and thrown her into the street. James, that monster, who'd taken Eden away and forced her into an institution.

The painful memories spread through her like a wildfire.

"Isn't that right, Kathryn?"

"I'm forever in your debt. All that I have is yours."

"Indeed. All. Because it was I who found you and gave you everything you have. I asked you to die to yourself—to give up what little life you had in return for a new one. Then I brought you back to life."

She absently rubbed the smooth nub where her pinky finger had once been. It had been Zeke's idea to fake her death in the Las Vegas hotel room so that no one would ever come looking for her.

"And then I found and gave you Eden, the daughter who would save your soul and make you whole."

"Yes, you did. Thank you, Zeke."

"Never forget that, Kathryn. And never forget that what is given can also be taken away." He offered her a gentle smile. "One word from me, and the authorities would swoop down on you and take Eden away forever."

She said nothing.

"Isn't that right, Kathryn?"

"Yes, Zeke. It is."

"I was very careful to make sure that my involvement couldn't be traced. I wanted you to bear the full responsibility for your daughter. After all, each of us must stand accountable before God and men."

He'd made the point only once before and hearing it again made her a little anxious.

"In this way you can also participate in the full blessing that Eden has been and will be for all of us."

"And I am so grateful. So very grateful."

"Then you will be even more grateful when you learn why I insisted we find Eden and just how great is that blessing."

Learn? She wasn't sure what he meant.

"Tomorrow, Eden turns eighteen," he said.

"Yes, she does." What did Eden turning eighteen have to do with any blessing?

"I've known for years that this day would come," Zeke said. "I thought it best to wait until now to tell you. So you could give your full attention to being a mother."

"Tell me what?"

"After you were institutionalized and Eden was turned over to child services, James Ringwald established a trust to provide for your daughter's future."

She sat speechless for a moment. "But he wanted nothing to do with her. Or me."

"Never underestimate the power of guilt, Kathryn. Or the mysteries of God. Remember, the wealth of the wicked is stored up for the righteous. This has been a long time coming."

"Wealth? James's wealth? How much?"

"The trust was funded with five hundred thousand dollars. The investments have since grown to three times that."

She blinked. "More than a million? And the money belongs to Eden?"

He smiled. "To all of us. But, yes, it's your birthright too. As one family, we will all share in this great abundance together. For what is yours belongs to all, just as what I have belongs to you and all my children."

"Yes, of course."

"The money becomes Eden's on her eighteenth birthday. All she has to do is claim it."

"How?"

"In two days, you and Eden will meet with a judge in town who is a very good friend of mine. He has arranged everything. The paperwork is drawn. Everything will be ready when you arrive."

"But what about the authorities? When Eden comes forward they'll know. They'll know we took her." A chill chased her spine. "They'll take her away from me."

"No. They won't. We'll have to be as wise as serpents, but I've handled everything. I hold all the strings, Kathryn. I always do. As long as you follow me, Eden's safe and so are you."

"But how?"

"The only answer to 'how' is 'yes.' All of God's promises are 'yes.' All you have to do is embrace them. Can you say yes, Kathryn?"

If there was anyone she could trust, it was Zeke. He'd practically gone to the ends of the earth to find her and give her a new start.

"Yes, of course. Yes."

"Yes."

"It just doesn't seem real. A million dollars? That's . . . that's a lot of money."

He chuckled softly. "Well, it won't all be yours, naturally. But, yes. It's a generous blessing indeed."

"I don't know what to say."

He set the glass down, reached across and laid his hand on top of hers. A rush of warmth filled her as he squeezed her hand gently. "Thank you is a start."

"Yes, of course. Thank you, Zeke. Thank you so much."

"When God's blessing comes, it's important to embrace it with a heart of gratitude, Kathryn. Always remember that. I want you to dream about it tonight. Imagine what it will be like to finally see your harvest come in after all these years."

"I don't know how I could ever repay you."

"When the time comes, you will."

She nodded. "Of course I will. Anything you ask."

"I've taken steps to make sure Eden's claim draws as little attention as possible. What you don't know is that the way I first found Eden was through her birth father's attorney, John McDermott. It was then that I also learned of the trust fund the senator had established in her name. I saw fit then to dig up some—let's call it leverage—that would ensure the attorney's cooperation. Some details of his life that would ruin him if ever exposed, if you catch my meaning."

He offered her a whimsical grin, the boyish kind that always made her heart flutter just a little. The ways of God were mysterious and sometimes beyond the law. Isn't that how they'd rescued Eden in the first place?

She nodded.

"It's a private matter and he'll do what we need him to do—there's virtually no chance the authorities will ever learn of her claim. But we also need Eden to do what's right."

"She will. Of course she will."

"Still, we can't take any chances. This will be the first time she's ever left the property. It'll be a controlled environment, but there's always the chance she'll talk to someone we don't have control over."

"I'll be with her."

"You can never be too careful. It's important that she really knows what happened to her the night Wyatt rescued her in case she happens to talk to anyone."

"She'll say anything to stay with me."

"I know she will. She's a wonderful girl, Kathryn. You're raising her right. Now you're being rewarded for your faithfulness."

"Thank you, Zeke."

"Believe me, the pleasure is all mine."

He picked up his glass and took another drink. The darkness that sometimes crossed his face filled his eyes.

"Don't fail me in this, Kathryn. We've come too far."

"I won't. I'll do exactly as you say. I owe you my life."

"Never forget that." He set the glass down. "There is one more thing."

"Of course. Anything."

"I know I've prohibited you from celebrating Eden's birthday, but I'd like to make an exception tomorrow for Paul. She seems to enjoy my boy's company and it would be fitting to let them spend some time together. Consider it a special gift on this day of redemption to soften Eden's heart. I need her to be in good spirits tomorrow."

"Whatever you think is best."

"Your redemption is at hand, but you must remain steadfast."

"I will."

"Good. Make sure Eden does as well. I know I would hate to see judgment fall on her unexpectedly."

I CAN'T say that I really kept track of how many years had passed since I'd been saved. But I was eighteen today, and that meant I'd been with my mother and father for about five years.

I had grown taller, but not by much, and I was still rail thin, maybe because of my special diet. I looked more like my mother each day, that's what my father kept saying, and that made me happy.

But the passage of time wasn't marked by years or birthdays. Mother thought celebrating the flesh in any way only drew attention to what was fallen. Bobby's birthday was always special because he was fallen and couldn't help it. I, on the other hand, was special, so we didn't celebrate my birthdays, although I think Wyatt secretly wanted to.

For me, time's passing was marked by how well I followed the rules every day and by the weekly baptisms. I wasn't as fond as I should be about being drowned every Sunday, but the baptismal ritual was a blessing because it meant I could start over each week and set things right for all of us since I never failed to defile myself during the week.

Mother was patient with me most of the time, and with so much making and changing of rules, I felt sorry for her. There were many times I felt sorry for myself too, because following her rules wasn't easy, I can't lie. But the real burden was on Mother; *she* was the one who had to make sure I stayed pure—she reminded me of that often in the early days when I used to cry.

At times I thought that my life was just one long purification ritual, but that was my privilege—I was set apart. Sometimes I even took some pride in my purity, even knowing that pride always came before a fall—maybe that's why I kept falling each week. I couldn't properly remember how it was to live without rules, or how my life had been before my father had rescued me from a situation that would have ended terribly for me. Even the memory that I'd decided to stay with Mother for Bobby's sake had faded. My old life, in my old wineskin, now seemed like a distant dream of another world.

The number of rules had increased over the years as I became better about following them. The only way to follow the rules properly was to love them, my mother taught me. Every time I hardened my heart and thought of the rules as restrictions, I felt a sickness in my heart because that's what sin does to you. It makes you feel upside down inside. That was the Holy Spirit's voice whispering to my conscience.

If Mother told me that, for the next month, I wasn't to go outside because it was the seventh month of the year and I had to stay extra pure, feeling sorry for myself only made me angry which was sin and then I only felt guilty and would have to endure more purification.

If Mother told me that I couldn't have any chicken for dinner because she'd decided to leave the tasty skin on for the rest of them, feeling sorry for myself as I watched them bite into their drumsticks wouldn't put the chicken in my mouth. I already knew that I couldn't eat any meat with skin on it because I had new wineskin—I should be thankful.

There were too many rules for me to keep track of so I kept an eye on Mother, who warned me if I was about to forget one.

The rules I'd been practicing for a long time were easy enough to remember. Like not allowing my bare feet to touch the ground outside, ever. Or my legs. Or my arms. Or any part of my skin except the palms of my hands, and then I was to cleanse them with moonshine or soap and water before coming inside.

Like never going outside without material covering my legs to my ankles and my arms to my wrists. The sun damaged my skin.

Like bathing every morning to rid my body of all the invisible bed mites and at night to wash off all the oils and dust that collected in my pores during the day. Complete with a hair wash, nail scrub, and ear cleaning each time.

Like reciting my long and very specific prayers as I knelt beside my bed at six o'clock each morning, at precisely noon, and at six o'clock each night after which I went straight to bed even when it was light outside and Bobby was still up, playing. Rest and my special diet made sure my organs stayed healthy.

Those kinds of rules were easy to remember. The rules that Mother announced out of nowhere—only for that day, or that week, or that month—were harder, because just when I was getting used to them, the rule would change, to keep me on my toes, she said.

Like not speaking any words that began with the letter *s* on certain days, a rule Mother had made a couple years ago to help me watch my tongue. There were many impure words that defiled me—like *dirt*, and *garbage*, and *bug*, and *pee*—and, so that my mind would stay constantly vigilant, she added all words starting with *s* on some days because *s* started the word *snake*, and a snake led to the deception of the first woman in the garden of Eden. To further help me remember on those days, every time I said a word that started with *s* I would be made to keep moonshine in my mouth for ten minutes without spitting it out or swallowing it. The moonshine made my mouth raw.

The rules went on and on. For example: "For the next two days you will not sit on any of the furniture, angel."

"Why, Mother?" I knew better than to ask, but she would allow me this curiosity with only a harsh glare before explaining.

"They aren't clean enough and I don't have time to clean them until Friday. So you won't sit on any furniture and you'll stand at the table when you eat."

"Yes, Mother."

"You will not so much as *touch* any of the furniture. That will help you remember."

"Yes, Mother."

All of the rules were there for my own good, and as soon as I began to understand that, I was able to practice loving them. Which I did. To the best of my ability. At least I think I did.

But there was one rule in particular that I struggled with more than any of the others. Mother had always made it perfectly clear that I was to have no impure relationships with any other person. By this, she meant no impure contact with any girl or boy or man or woman. And even more, no impure thoughts.

"What are impure thoughts?" I asked her.

"You must not think about their flesh, especially the flesh that's covered. Adam and Eve were covered by God for a reason. Only animals engage in fleshly activity, and even they don't think about it. A human only reverts to the animal in them when impurity sets in, only worse than an animal because humans think about it too, which is doubly worse. You're not an animal so you don't act like one."

"What about everyone else?" I wanted to know.

"The rest of us can't help acting like animals at times. But you're pure, sweetheart."

I didn't really understand her comparison, but I accepted the explanation at face value.

"If you ever have an impure thought, or if you ever let anyone touch you where your skin is covered, you will tell me," she said.

"Like who?" I asked.

"Like Paul, Zeke's boy. Or like any other boy you ever see."

I hadn't seen any other boy besides Paul, and I thought of Paul, who was my age, like a brother.

"And you'll tell me immediately if so much as a single impure thought crosses your mind," she said.

"I will, Mother."

"So we can cleanse your mind of it."

"Yes, Mother."

At first, the rule was easy to keep, but as Paul and I grew older, he began to look at me with tenderness in his eyes. It made me feel special and one day about a year ago, as he helped me clean a brown smudge off my dress before my Mother could see it, it occurred to me that he liked me. I mean *really* liked me. I wasn't sure what to think of that.

As time went on, I began to think about Paul more and more, and words from my prior life, like *boyfriend,* would pop into my mind without warning. Sometimes even crazier thoughts like being married and maybe even having a baby one day. With Paul, because I didn't know any other boys.

I only told my mother about the thoughts once when the thoughts first came to me, and then only in general terms without mentioning Paul. Her reaction was immediate: she gripped her head and paced back and forth, nearly frantic, informing me in no uncertain terms that I was on a very slippery slope to defilement that would forever bring ruin to not only myself, but to her, and to my father, and to Bobby. And to Zeke.

I spent the next twenty-four hours in my bedroom closet, where the darkness was meant to wipe away all of my imaginations. She baptized me twice that next Sunday, just to be sure.

But neither the darkness nor the extra baptism worked. I didn't tell my mother about the defiling thoughts that kept jumping into my head, because I didn't want to upset her. But the harder I tried to guard against them, the more frequently the thoughts seemed to come.

What would it be like to hold hands with Paul? Or to kiss him? Or to tell him that sometimes I got butterflies in my stomach when I thought of him?

I felt terribly guilty for both having these thoughts, and for not confessing them to Mother as I'd promised. I was living a lie, you see, and I knew that if I continued living it, I would put us all in hell.

In fact, I'd already put myself in a hell, here on earth, at least that's what it felt like, and the only way out was to tell Mother, at which point she would only put me in another hell of sorts, and that hell wouldn't stop the thoughts from coming so I would only go back into the first hell. And God wasn't helping me with my lustful thoughts, likely because he hated liars. No amount of pleading on my knees seemed to get his attention.

And why would he listen to me? I was in hell.

So you see, I had worked my way into a terrible spot by the time I turned eighteen, with no way out that I could see.

And still, the moment I heard that Paul was coming for a few hours on my birthday, my heart began to beat faster. Mother had seen fit to invite him over to play with Bobby and me.

I had dressed properly, in rain boots and a long, light-blue dress that covered my legs and arms. We spent an hour or so wandering around the property and in the stillhouse where Paul talked about making moonshine. I had never helped with "the business," as Paul put it, but I'd often heard Wyatt talk about it. Zeke made the finest 'shine and had customers from Arizona to Virginia who were willing to pay handsomely for his limited batches. Two nearby farmers supplied high-quality, organic corn exclusively for Zeke's mash, and a natural spring on the property provided a steady flow of pure water that gave the 'shine its uniquely sweet flavor. The whole operation, from source to distribution, was sophisticated and Zeke ran it like a skilled businessman who was as shrewd as he was ambitious. From the custom-made copper kettles used to cook the mash to the selection of each season's bottling, he oversaw every decision and was training his son to take over his empire someday.

Paul wasn't like Zeke, though. He was kind and short—Mother sometimes called him a runt under her breath—and he had curly blond hair and a smooth face and plump lips. I didn't really remember other boys too much, so in my mind, Paul was all there was, and to me he looked about as magnificent as any boy might look.

But it was the way he treated me that made my heart flutter. The way he would quickly open the door to the still house for me, as if I were a queen. The way he slowed to match my pace so he could stay close. The way he smiled at me, bright blue eyes flashing. How could I not return that smile?

I asked Bobby if he could get a blanket from the house, which he was only too willing to do. Fifteen minutes later we had it spread it out under a tree behind the house, and I was seated with my legs folded back to my right, facing Paul, who sat cross-legged watching me make one of my straw dolls.

"Eden likes making dolls," Bobby said, picking at his nose.

"That's right, Bobby," I said, mindful of where he might put his dirty fingers. "And this one's going to be very special."

"Why's that?" Paul asked.

When I glanced up I saw that he was watching me with that look of great interest and for a moment longer than I had planned, I returned his gaze.

He wasn't required to follow my rules of cleanliness, naturally— none of the other kids were, he told me. And he thought that made me very special. I think he was actually in awe of me.

And maybe I was in awe of him because he *didn't* have so many rules, and could wear whatever he wanted, and get his hands dirty, and go into the swamps—not that I wanted to, mind you. I was terrified of both the water and whatever lived under its surface. But his freedom was as wondrous to me, as my cleanliness was to him.

I looked back down to my hands, busy at work on the doll I was weaving from long stalks of half-dried swamp grass. But I wasn't thinking about the doll. I was thinking about the fact that I was sliding, this very moment, down that very slippery slope my mother had warned me about.

And I didn't seem to be able to stop myself.

"It's just special," I said. "Actually, they're all special." I had a collection in my room, eight of them, each one named and specifically appointed to match the personalities I'd given them. Mother wouldn't let me have any real dolls, but Wyatt had convinced her to let me keep the ones I made. Apart from Bobby and Paul, they were my best friends.

"How do you make it so smooth?" Paul asked.

"By tucking in every strand." My attention returned to my thin fingers working nimbly with the grass. "It just takes a little practice and some patience. See?"

"You do it so well," he said.

"Eden likes to make straw dolls," Bobby repeated. At fifteen he was nearly the same he'd been at ten—maybe a couple of inches taller.

"What's her name going to be?" Paul asked.

"How do you know it's a girl?"

He hesitated. "I don't know. I guess I just think of dolls as girls."

My dolls looked like miniature scarecrows, complete with arms and legs and different colored seeds for eyes, some dressed in pants for boys, some in dresses for girls.

"Then I'll name her Alice."

"Alice?"

"Eden dreams about Alice," Bobby said.

"Hush, Bobby. Paul doesn't want to hear about my dreams."

"Sure I do."

"Sure he does," Bobby said.

I felt shy—Paul might think that my recurring dreams were stupid.

I mean, who dreamed they were named Alice and lived in a psychiatric hospital? Nobody sane, right?

"Just dreams," I said, embarrassed.

"Silly dreams," Bobby said.

We were quiet for a little while, but I could feel Paul's eyes on me as I worked, which made it hard to concentrate.

"Bobby, do you want to go on a mission?" Paul finally asked.

Bobby perked up. "I'm good at missions."

"You think you could run to the house and bring back a drink?"

"I'll go to the house and bring back a drink," Bobby said, pushing himself to his feet. And then he was ambling off, consumed with his mission.

The thought that Paul had sent Bobby away so that we could be alone didn't occur to me until Bobby was already halfway across the back yard. One look at Paul's face and I knew that I was right.

"Can I ask you a question?"

"If you like," I said.

"Have you ever kissed a boy?"

My face flushed and I glanced at the house, afraid that Mother was close. But we were still alone.

"We shouldn't talk about that," I said.

"Randal has a girlfriend." One of the other boys who I hadn't met. "He likes Susan. He told me that they hold hands and kiss. His father doesn't mind. He says it's normal."

"And maybe normal's not so good."

"Maybe. Or maybe normal's okay."

I knew I was defiling myself by not running away right then, but I didn't want to run away. So I kept working on Alice.

"What would Zeke say about that?" I asked.

"My father kissed a girl when he was fifteen. He knows that I'm growing up."

"And what would he say if he knew you were talking this way to me?"

Paul didn't answer, but I suspected that Zeke would beat him silly if he knew he was trying to tempt me. We both knew that I was different from the other girls.

"I think you're very pretty," he said.

By now my face had to be beet-red. Paul wasn't as sheltered as me, but I had a feeling he wasn't as experienced as he would like to be. I should have reprimanded him right then.

But I didn't.

"Thank you," I said, embarrassed.

"I like you."

Liking was good, right? It was okay.

"I like you too, Paul."

Like a brother, of course. But that's not what my heart was telling me. And my mind was telling me that I was going to hell.

"Will you be my girlfriend?"

I stopped my fiddling on the doll and looked up at him. Then past him to see if anyone was coming. We were still alone.

"You know I can't do that!" I whispered.

"I know. So we don't have to tell anyone. Even our parents got married, you know. We aren't just kids anymore. And besides, I think you like me too."

"Of course I like you. But not . . ."

"I can tell by the way you look at me."

"Me? You're the one always looking! And you have to stop it."

"Why?"

"Because!" I whispered. "It makes me uncomfortable."

"Why? Because you like me too?"

I couldn't just lie to him, so I hesitated, suddenly at a very uncomfortable loss.

"Eden!"

I jerked my head up and saw that Mother was rounding the house, walking our way.

"Here, Mother," I called, waving a hand.

Paul spoke quickly, under his breath. "Come to the field at four o'clock on Wednesday. I'll be there."

I kept my eyes on Mother, heart pounding.

"I just want to talk to you. Wednesday at four o'clock, okay? In two days. I know four is your free hour before dinner. Just sneak out to talk to me."

"It's getting late, sweetheart," Mother called. It wasn't getting late—that was her way of ending whatever was going on. "I think it's time for Paul to go home."

"Don't forget," he whispered. "Four o'clock."

"Sweetheart?" Mother walked up from behind Paul, glancing between us. "Did you hear me? I said I think Paul needs to go home now."

With a parting gaze into my eyes, Paul pushed himself up and flicked a stick he was fiddling with into the grass.

"Why don't you walk, Paul. Be good for you."

He dipped his head. "Sure. Thank you for having me." He faced me. "See you around."

And with that he walked away.

"I don't trust that boy," Mother said, watching him vanish from sight around the house. She looked at me. "Why's your face red?"

"Only because it's hot, Mother."

She cast a disapproving glance down my dress, and I was afraid she might question me further, uncover my lie, and make me spend the rest of the day in penance.

I had lied to her; guilt racked my mind.

Instead, she sat down across from me and drew her legs back like mine.

"Did you enjoy that?" she asked. Something had shifted her mood.
"Yes, Mother."

"I know we don't celebrate your birthday, sweetheart, but you're eighteen today. I know you don't get to spend a lot of time with friends."

"Thank you."

She smiled. Reached forward and brushed my cheek with her thumb. "You're such a beautiful angel."

Relief cascaded over me. "Thank you, Mother."

"You don't think I'm too hard on you, do you?"

"No," I said.

"Tell me why I keep you away from dark waters."

"So that I don't fall in and drown."

"Good girl. The only drowning you'll do is in the clear waters of salvation."

She was referring to my baptisms. "Yes, Mother."

"What would have happened if we'd never rescued you?"

"I would have drowned."

"And did you come willingly?"

I knew this part all too well, and having narrowly escaped being caught in a lie, I was only too eager to rehearse my rescue.

"Not at first. But sometimes children don't see the danger they're in. They have to be disciplined so they don't get too close to the water. Or the fire."

"Fires of hell," she said, offering me a proud grin. "That's right. God delivered you and restored me. And today is a very, very special day. Do you know why?"

Besides my birthday, which wasn't a very special day at all, I had no idea. So I just looked at her.

"It's a very special day because today God is returning what the locusts have eaten sevenfold, darling. I have some very exciting news for you."

I had rarely seen Mother so excited.

She continued, beaming. "All of our hard work is paying off. You've been faithful and remained pure and now that you've turned eighteen, God has seen fit to bless us all beyond our wildest imagination."

"He has? How?"

"By giving us a large sum of money. For all of us to share. Isn't that wonderful, sweetheart?"

I hardly knew the value of money, but it clearly made her very happy.

"That's wonderful," I said.

"All we have to do is go and get it." She took a deep breath. "So tomorrow I'm going to take you into town and we're going to meet with some important people and they're going to give us our blessing."

I blinked. "Into town?" I'd never been off the property.

Mother placed a reassuring hand on my knee. "I know it will be a challenge for you, but Mommy will be right beside you the whole time."

"Why do I have to go?"

"Because you're the one through whom all blessings flow, sweetheart. That's how God works. He's blessing me and Wyatt and Bobby and Zeke and all of us through you. Isn't that wonderful?"

I was going into town?

"Yes. Yes, it's wonderful."

"Now . . . it's very important that you are especially pure tomorrow. If anyone asks you any questions it's very important that you give only the answers God would have you give to show how grateful you are for his provision all these years. He rescued you from the hell you were in and brought you into the loving embrace of your mother."

I nodded but my mind was spinning with thoughts of town. And with Paul. What would he say if I told him I was going to town? He would be proud of me and for some reason that made me happy.

"I'm going to help you prepare for our big day tomorrow," Mother said. "You have to be perfectly pure or God might withdraw his blessing at the last moment. You wouldn't want that would you?"

"No, Mother."

She shook her head slowly, smiling gently. "No, I didn't think you would. So I'm going to suggest we start preparing by having you spend the rest of the day in darkness, praying. Do you think that's a good idea?"

The closet? A chill washed down my back.

Then I thought about Paul, and how proud he would be that I was going into town and that brought me some comfort. If I was blessing Zeke, I was blessing Paul as well because Paul was his son.

"Yes, Mother," I said.

WYATT DROVE the truck down the gravel road as the morning sun crested the tall, moss-draped trees to Kathryn's right. It was a thirty-minute drive into town if they followed the main streets, forty-five if they took the back roads, which they would. Kathryn had chosen the route herself to make sure of that.

Zeke had arranged everything, he always did. Still, the uneasiness that haunted her whispered its worry, like a ghost trying to get in where it wasn't welcome. But it was always there, wasn't it? No matter how pure Eden was. No matter how many baptisms.

Always, always there.

Kathryn stared out the passenger window, chewing her fingernail, trying to quiet her mind. She should be happier, more at peace. It was a day of great blessing, wasn't it? But she was also all too aware that danger crowded in on all sides.

What if something went wrong? What if this was a test from God and she failed? She could live without money; she had for a long time. What if someone recognized her? What then? She couldn't live without Eden.

The moment they drove off the property, Eden would be in harm's way. That was the truth and no one, not her nor Zeke, could guarantee Eden's safety off the property.

"Right here. Stop the truck," she said.

Wyatt brought the truck to a stop. She could see Zeke's house just ahead to the left, surrounded by trees. His Dobermans were barking, probably because they'd stopped the truck.

Kathryn turned and looked at Eden, who sat behind Wyatt in the crew cab's back seat, face pressed close to the window. She passed a black hood over the seat.

"You need to wear this, sweetheart," she said. "Just for a little while."

Eden took it without a word.

"It's for your own protection."

Eden stared at her with round brown eyes, then shifted her gaze back out the window.

"Are you all right?" Kathryn said.

She hesitated. "It's just . . . the dogs."

"Don't you worry about them. We're safe. Isn't that right, Wyatt?"

"They're chained up during the day. Nothing to worry about."

Eden held the hood in her hands. Ran her fingers over the fabric.

"You're quiet this morning," Kathryn said. "This is a wonderful day for all of us, and especially you. You're not excited?"

"I didn't sleep well. That's all."

"I'm a little nervous too, but soon enough we'll be back home where it's safe. I promise." She smiled. "Now, go on. Put it on. It's a short drive to town so I want you to lie down in the back seat and rest your eyes until we get there."

"Yes, Mother." She carefully pulled the hood on, lay down, and rested her head on the seat.

They resumed their drive down the gravel road and past the other houses, which were scattered between Zeke's and the county road.

There were now eleven families in the community, all who lived on plots of land not unlike their own, and all who were as much a part of Zeke's family as his own children. They did what he said, and nothing less. He owned the land, didn't he? He guided them in the ways of truth. He was the one who kept the law off their backs and food on their tables.

No one really expected moonshine to flow from the swamps, which was why Zeke had bought the land and set up his operation in Louisiana, he said. It made sense if you were smart.

Everything Zeke did was smart.

It took them thirty minutes along the back roads to reach the highway and follow its short jaunt into Lafayette and to the address Zeke had given Kathryn. She hated the city, always had. Too many people without a head on their shoulders, walking the wide path straight to hell. More than that, civilization and all of its laws represented the world that had taken Eden from her in the first place. And would again if given half a chance.

Wyatt pulled into a large parking lot next to a shiny, ten-story office complex. He angled the truck into a free spot and killed the engine.

This was it, then. Just in to see the judge, sign the papers, and get out without any hitch.

Kathryn wiped her brow with a handkerchief, and turned around. "You can take it off now, sweetheart. We're here."

Eden sat upright and worked the hood off her head.

"Careful not to mess your hair. You want to look your best."

Kathryn got out of the truck while Wyatt opened Eden's door, which was locked from the inside with a child safety latch. Eden climbed out of the truck and blinked in the sunlight. She turned slowly, taking in a world that had long been hidden from her. And for good reason.

The less time Eden spent outside, the better.

"We should get inside. We don't want to keep the judge waiting."

She put her arm around Eden and led her toward the building, glancing around nervously as they walked. They entered the building, walked across the glass atrium to a bank of elevators, and took the slow ride to the tenth floor.

"You okay, sweetheart?"

Eden nodded as the elevator rose.

"I know this must be hard for you being away from home, but I'll keep you safe." She smoothed her daughter's hair. "Just don't leave my side. Okay?"

"Okay."

Kathryn glanced at the business card Zeke had given her—Suite 1003, the office of the Honorable Harlan Cobb, a long-time friend of Zeke's who would take care of everything. They found the office at the end of a vacant hall.

"Here we go. Wyatt, you stay behind me and keep your mouth shut."

When they entered they were met by a receptionist who took her name and showed them into the judge's office where he was already meeting with the attorney Zeke was blackmailing: John McDermott, James's old snake-skinned lawyer from Nevada. This was the very soulless bastard who'd probably made the arrangements for Eden to be stolen from her eighteen years ago. Served him right—she hoped the dirt Zeke had on him would end up putting the man in a grave.

He sat to the judge's right, looking the part of an expensive suit from the city. His sunbleached hair was practically white, as were his eyebrows.

An imposing figure, Kathryn thought, but underneath all that shine likely no better or smarter than Wyatt. It was in an office like this that Eden had been snatched away. And today that curse would become her blessing.

Fitting.

Judge Cobb sat at the end of the long table, examining a short stack of legal documents laid before him. He was a thick man, smartly dressed, with fleshy jowls and thinning hair.

After quick introductions, the judge invited them all to sit. Kathryn took the chair to the judge's left, with Eden and Wyatt by her side.

The judge cleared his throat, sat back in the leather chair and removed the bifocals perched on the end of his pudgy nose.

"Everything appears to be in order. I've got a full docket today so let's not waste anyone's time. Mr. McDermott, I presume you have no objections to expediting this matter."

"No, Your Honor," he said.

"Wonderful. It's nice when counsel is agreeable. I'm not one for . . . unexpected surprises."

"Nor am I."

The judge turned toward Eden. "First off, congratulations, young lady. Must feel good to be an adult now in the eyes of the law."

Eden glanced up at Kathryn. Poor girl was as frightened as a mouse.

"Go on. You can answer him."

"I guess," Eden said.

"You guess?" He chuckled. "When I turned eighteen, I thought I was the king of the world and could do anything or go anywhere. Looks to me like you've got a good head on you."

Kathryn reached over and squeezed Eden's hand. "She's a very special girl. A gift from God."

"I can see that. And you obviously have a loving mother who's raised you right," the judge said. "I'm not sure you need much more than that."

Eden nodded.

"There are several items to address today, but I'll cut to the quick. I'm sure you're ready to get on with this."

"She is," Kathryn said. "We all are."

"And you, Eden?" the judge said.

"I'll be speaking on Eden's behalf today, Your Honor."

His brow arched. "Is that so, Eden?"

"Yes."

"Very well," he said. "But if you have any questions, just ask."

"Of course."

"As you know, we're here to execute the final provisions of James Ringwald's trust. As his sole biological child, Eden is entitled to assets he established for her benefit. Before ownership of the trust can be transferred, there are a few legal requirements to fulfill. As representative of the Ringwald estate, Mr. McDermott's first responsibility is to confirm that Eden is, in fact, the congressman's daughter."

The judge slid the stack of legal documents in front of Kathryn.

So this was it. A few forms—simple bits of paper that would make the world right with a few strokes of a pen.

He tapped the top piece of paper with his finger. "These affidavits are sworn written statements that confirm Eden's identity as Alice Ringwald, also known as Eden Lowenstein."

Kathryn scanned each form and passed the affidavits to Eden to be signed. One by one, the judge talked about the significance of each document, but Kathryn hardly heard what he said. She was focused on doing what needed to be done as quickly as possible.

Eden didn't hesitate either and played her role just as she was expected to, signing where indicated. There were no questions and no problems.

Kathryn gathered the documents and gave them to the judge, who scrawled his signature on each one.

He glanced at the young lady in a gray suit at the opposite end of the table. "Miss Chatwick. We're ready for you."

The woman stood and approached Eden.

"Miss Chatwick will administer a simple paternity test. To satisfy the stipulations of the trust, a sample of Eden's DNA must be compared to the late Congressman Ringwald's to verify that he's her father."

The tall brunette stopped beside Eden, placed a small black kit on the table, then pulled on blue surgical gloves.

"You need her blood?" Kathryn asked.

"No, ma'am. Just some saliva," she said and carefully pulled a capped plastic tube from the kit.

The woman uncapped it, then slid out a long cotton swab. "This won't hurt at all, Eden. I just need you to open your mouth so I can run it along the inside of your cheek. A few cells are all I need for my analysis. Okay?"

"Okay." Eden opened her mouth.

Watching her daughter, a chill prickled Kathryn's forearms. Eden had her father's lips. They were full like his, an unmistakable detail she remembered because it was the first thing she had noticed about James long ago.

Miss Chatwick leaned close and carefully scraped the inside of Eden's mouth with the swab, then returned the swab to the tube and sealed the sample with an orange sticker.

"All done," she said, and stood. "I'll have my findings to you by end of day today, Your Honor. And to you as well, Mr. McDermott."

"Thank you, Miss Chatwick."

"There's one final order of business," the judge said. "I understand that a bank account in Eden's name has been established, is that right, Kathryn?"

"That's right."

"Also that Eden is electing to sign a durable financial power of attorney to you."

"She is," Kathryn said. "I'll be handling everything."

The judge nodded and turned to Eden. "Since you're legally entitled to the assets, I need to be sure you understand what this means. By designating your mother as financial power of attorney, you're stating that you're either incapable or unwilling to manage your affairs. You're surrendering the legal right to access the funds to your mother and she may use them for your benefit as she deems fit. Do you understand that?"

"Yes."

"Is that your intention?"

It occurred to Kathryn that with a few simple words here, before the judge, Eden could destroy everything. She wouldn't, of course— she'd learned the true blessing of obedience, both to God and to those God had placed in authority over her. But for a moment, Kathryn felt a pang of empathy for her. In a way, she was no more than a slave doing the bidding of her master for her master's gain.

Then again, that's the way it was with God. They were all his children, for his sake. And when his children were obedient, even unto death if so required, they were blessed. So this was really Eden's blessing.

She let the empathy pass and smiled at her daughter, who glanced up at her with questioning eyes.

Eden turned back to the judge. "Yes."

"Very well then." He gave the power of attorney document to Eden. "Powers of attorney aren't forever. As long as you are mentally capable, you may revoke it at any time and regain full control of the accounts."

"I can't think of a reason she'd change her mind," Kathryn said. "Can you, Eden?"

Eden hesitated, for just a moment, then answered as Kathryn knew she would. "No."

"Regardless, it's a protection for both of you. Do you understand that?"

"I do."

"Good. Go ahead and sign the form."

Fact was, Kathryn was sure that as soon as she had legal access to Eden's trust, Zeke would want her to transfer all the money out. Eden would no longer have access to any of it, ever.

Eden signed the form and then passed it to the judge.

He shuffled the forms together into a neat stack and smiled. "Well, that's that. Congratulations, Eden. It's quite an accomplishment to become an adult and a millionaire all in the same day. The good Lord smiles on you."

"He most certainly does," Kathryn said.

"Your Honor, may I say something before we adjourn?" McDermott said. "Off the record, of course. I think it's appropriate considering the absence of my client, Eden's father."

The judge nodded.

A knot tightened in Kathryn's gut. The man had sat silently the entire time. What could he possibly have to say now? Not that it mattered—everything was finished and there was nothing he could do to ever hurt Eden or her again. Not without ruining his own life.

McDermott cocked his head and studied Eden for a moment. "You resemble your father. I didn't see it at first, but I do now."

Eden said nothing.

"I realize you never knew him, but he was a good man. Maybe the finest I've ever known."

Kathryn harrumphed. "Good? James Ringwald was as evil as they get."

"He made plenty of mistakes, but he tried to do what was right. If that wasn't true, I wouldn't be here today and neither would you. The trust was his idea, to make sure his daughter would never go without."

"How dare you? James was a liar and a betrayer! I don't appreciate you trying to poison my daughter with your filthy lies. If not for him, my daughter wouldn't have been stolen from me in the first place."

"Mrs. Lowenstein," the judge said and gave her a stern look.

"It's okay, Mother," Eden said.

Kathryn sat back in her chair, eyes fixed on the wolf across the table.

McDermott smiled at Eden. "You're strong like him too. I can see it in your eyes. I worked with your father from the early days and saw him climb his way to the top. Tough business, politics. It takes an iron backbone to stand on your own. It's a lot easier to be a puppet on a string. To let others think for you. That's what I admired most about him. He thought for himself."

His gaze shifted to Kathryn and lingered there. "He was his own man, not what others wanted him to be. No one ever had him under their thumb. Ever. He was too strong for that."

"What are you trying to say?" Kathryn said.

"Mrs. Lowenstein," the judge said.

"It's okay, Your Honor." McDermott said. "I appreciate Mrs. Lowenstein's vigilance for her daughter. Being the parent of a girl who's coming of age is a very frightening thing. I understand, but eventually we all have to let go."

Kathryn glared at him.

He stood, took the documents from the judge and slid them into his steel briefcase. "I'll have my assistant execute the paperwork first thing tomorrow morning. Per the trust, the assets will be released after a thirty-day cure period that begins tomorrow."

"Cure?" Kathryn demanded. "What do you mean thirty days?"

"I mean the trust specifically stipulates that thirty days must pass following proof of paternity before any funds can be accessed. A waiting period that ensures proper vigilance. After that, you will have access to the money."

First she'd heard of it. But Zeke likely knew. Of course he did.

McDermott shook hands with the judge, then nodded toward Wyatt and Kathryn. "It was a pleasure meeting you both. Eden, good luck to you. I wish you only the best."

"Thank you."

Kathryn's pulse hammered in her ears as the man closed the door behind him. It really was over, just as Zeke had said it would be. James was gone and now his dog too. No one would ever come after Eden again.

Wherever James was, she hoped he was burning for his sins, weeping because she had won. All the years that had been stolen from her, God was returning to her sevenfold.

Everything would be different now. She had Eden and there was nothing James could ever do to take her away again. No one could. She and Eden would always be together and no one would ever change that.

No one.

BOBBY WAS often with me when I went outside, particularly when I ventured to the woods that butted up against the swamp about seventy-five yards behind the house. Or to the lake, which was less than a minute's walk, hidden from the house by a bunch of trees that grew on dry ground.

We'd been like glue for years, spending much of our free time together, protecting each other. He kept me safe from the swamp and the dark waters and whatever alligators might take a bite out of me, and I kept him safe from Mother.

I didn't actually believe that Mother would hurt him, at least not while I was pure. But she reminded us both quite often that Bobby would be lost without me and by that she meant thrown out. In her way of thinking, God had restored all of us through me. If I failed, God would punish all of us.

At least that's what she said, and I had no reason to doubt her. So I kept close to Bobby, like a guardian angel, if only to assure him at all times that I was there for him. Mother loved Bobby, I think, but her attention to me overshadowed every other concern in her life—I knew that no sacrifice, including Bobby, was too great to keep me pure.

Still, as Bobby and I grew older, we spent more time doing our own thing during my free hour. He might be off catching frogs while I worked on my dolls or helped Wyatt at the still. Now and then, I would find my way to the lake, even knowing that Mother didn't favor it.

The afternoon after my big day in town, Bobby was messing around in the still with Wyatt, and Mother had gone off the property. Unable to turn my mind off, I hadn't gotten much sleep the night before and I was dead tired, but I decided to head down to the lake by myself.

Evidently turning eighteen was a very special thing. Suddenly I was valued for more than my purity. Important lawyers wanted to talk to me. I was worth a lot of money, which was a big deal to all of the adults.

For that matter, *I* was an adult now.

All of it was a bit mind-bending, but that's not the only reason I wanted to be alone. It was Paul, you see? More to the point, his request that I meet him alone in the field the next afternoon.

The "field," as we called it, was halfway down the road to his house—a large portion of higher dry ground spotted with trees where Bobby, Paul, and I sometimes hung out when I was allowed. It was the farthest I had ever ventured from the house.

At four o'clock, having dressed properly in rain boots and black slacks with a long-sleeved T-shirt, I grabbed a small blanket, sneaked out of the house, and made my way to the lake. I wasn't breaking any rules, but just knowing that Mother didn't like the lake made me nervous. Either way, I felt I could take this liberty after giving such blessing to so many through the trust money now that I was eighteen.

Spreading the blanket on the grassy bank, I settled down and stared out over the crystal-smooth water. I'd always been afraid of water, but the one thing I liked about the lake was the view. I could see all the way across to the far side, so far yet so close. Everywhere else on the property, all you could see were trees. Here, the world looked almost never ending and it gave me some calm.

Mother had ruled out fishing because of the hooks and slimy fish and grime that might harm or defile me. Anyway, I was just as happy to hear Bobby wax eloquent about his skills as he hurled his line out and sometimes reeled in a small catfish with all manner of hoopla.

The water lapped gently on the bank and a hot, late-afternoon still-ness hung over the water. It was peaceful, without a soul in sight. All was well.

I ran through the events of the day for a while, thinking about how grateful I should be. I was eighteen now. I was loved and valued. But the more I thought about the last two days, the more unsettled I became.

All should be well, but I didn't feel well. My stomach was tightening into a knot and my brow was sweaty and I wondered why.

I picked up a stick and toyed with it between my pale, nimble fingers.

Maybe I'd become so used to the task of maintaining my purity through endless daily ritual that even the thought of being more than I always had been made me anxious. That's what was happening, right?

No . . . no, it wasn't that. It was this business with Paul. The fact that I wanted to know what it was like to be a girlfriend. To hold a boy's hand. To be special to someone for more than just my ability to stay pure and take away their sin.

To kiss someone.

To kiss Paul.

My mind went blank for a moment. I flicked the stick into the grass as shame washed over me. Why couldn't I just let the temptation go? I was wicked to the bone, that's what it was. Here I was, eighteen years old, and I was growing more sinful with each passing day.

No, Eden . . . It's natural to want to kiss a boy. What do you think all the rest of the people in the world do? Kathryn's put you in a prison and you secretly hate her for it.

The thought came out of nowhere and stopped me cold. How could I think such a thing? I suddenly felt panicky, dreadful, sick to my stomach. If Mother knew I'd had such a thought she would confine me to my closet for a week. I couldn't allow myself to think that way!

I was a blessing, not a prisoner in my own home.

It's not even your real home.

"Stop it!" I muttered.

I had to get back to the house.

I jumped to my feet, grabbed my blanket, and ran back to the house where I went straight to my room and lay down in the comfort of my own bed. This was where I belonged, right? Whatever pathetic complaints might tempt me, this room was my home. I belonged here.

It may seem strange, but the thought of being confined brought me peace, and I embraced it, as I often did. Soon the world around me faded and, tired to the bone, I fell asleep.

I don't know how long I'd been asleep before the vivid dream visited me. In it, I was back at the lake that same afternoon, as if I hadn't left. The breeze blew in my face, the water stretched out to a distant horizon, I was in peace and I closed my eyes, grateful.

That's when I heard the gurgling of water to my right. I snapped my eyes wide and spun around.

There, less than a stone's throw away, just rounding the bend in the shore, came a small rowboat. And in that boat, a man pulling at two oars, guiding the boat toward me.

I froze. A part of me knew that I was in a dream, but only a very small part because the dream was as vivid as any I'd ever had. And right there in front of me was a boat. It was actually there. But in a dream.

I'd seen a few boats on the lake but never so close, and never angling for the shore. My heart pounded and I thought I should turn and run, but my feet didn't want to move.

The man had dark, wavy hair that fell to his shoulders, and he eyed me with interest, wearing a smile. But it was his eyes that drew me as the boat came closer, faster than I would have guessed, effortlessly gliding through the water.

I had to run! I had to get back to the house! Mother would never approve of this.

Why, Eden?

It didn't matter why. She just wouldn't. I was hers and hers alone. No one was supposed to even know I was here!

"Hello, my dear."

The man's voice was low and gentle. He lifted the oars from the water and let the boat slide forward. A wooden boat maybe four feet wide with a single board across the center on which the man sat. He was dressed in blue jeans and a denim jacket, wearing black boots.

"Beautiful day, isn't it?" the man said.

I wasn't sure if I should run, or talk to the man. My mind said run, my heart told me I was eighteen now. It was okay to speak to a stranger even if he was a man.

The boat slid to a stop on the bank and the man looked at me, smiling, eyes as blue as the sky. He wasn't as large as Wyatt, but he looked strong enough to throw me over his shoulder with one hand and hardly notice I was there.

"You're an awfully pretty girl," he said, voice as gentle as a dove. "What's your name?"

I hesitated for a moment.

"Eden," I said.

"Eden." He said my name as if it held great significance. "Like the garden of life. You're very lucky to have such a beautiful name."

Run, my mind screamed.

Wait. Hadn't I just run, only to end up right back here?

Stay, my heart demanded.

"Thank you," I said.

He dipped his head. "I don't mean to intrude. I saw you sitting alone." He scanned the shore. "Are you okay?"

No, I thought.

"Yes," I said. "I'm fine."

He looked at me for a long moment, as if trying to decide if he could believe me. And why should he? He'd caught me in a discombobulated state of mind.

"Well, Eden, do you mind if I get out and stretch for a spell on your beach? It took me a bit to row this boat across the lake."

I forgot that I was in a dream. It all felt absolutely real. The breeze, the smell of the water, the sight of the stranger, the sound of his voice. Which meant that I was at a crossroads, because this was the first unfamiliar person I'd ever met alone. Sure, I'd briefly met some of the other men and women who'd come to our property over the years—all members of Zeke's community—but always in the company of Kathryn, and then only to say hi as instructed by my mother.

"No need to be afraid, my child," he said with a whimsical smile. "The alligators lurking beneath the waters in your mind pose far more of a threat than me. And I've been known to take care of even those. Besides, you look like you could use a friend."

I was at a crossroads, but suddenly I was past it, because I then thought, *why not?* There's no sin in making a new friend. And I'm eighteen now.

"I guess," I said.

"Thank you. That's very kind of you." He promptly set the oars down, slung a leg over the boat, dropped into foot-deep water, and walked up onto the shore, not bothered that his boots were soaked.

He stretched his arms over his head, then leaned this way and that, working the kinks out of his bones. "Ah, that's better. Sitting so long can give you the cramps."

Without further invitation, he strolled up to me and sat cross-legged on the grass beside the blanket, which he promptly patted.

"Have a seat here, Eden."

Again I hesitated. The sudden appearance of the stranger had taken me completely off guard and now here he was, sitting by my blanket, speaking as if we'd been friends our whole life.

But that was just it. In a way, as strange as he was, I actually felt as though we had. So I sat on the blanket beside him, cross-legged.

"You can call me Stephen," he said, reaching his hand across to me. "Some call me Outlaw."

Thoughts of touching unclean flesh spinning through my head, I took his hand. "Hi, Stephen," I said. His hand was warm and strong but it held mine gently and only for a moment.

We sat in the still afternoon, staring out at the lake together and at first I thought how strange and awkward it was, sitting there doing nothing together. But as the silence stretched I thought how nice it was, sitting there staring out at the water, doing nothing with someone new.

For no reason that I could understand, emotion suddenly rose through my throat. Good emotion. Warmth and contentment. Here I was, just being with someone new. What a strange and wonderful thing.

"So . . ." he finally said. "How long have you lived here, Eden?"

"Five years." Then I added, for no good reason, "I'm eighteen now."

"Eighteen. That's wonderful. How do you like it?"

"I just turned eighteen yesterday."

"I meant living here. How do you like it?"

I shrugged. "It's all I know."

"Well, it's not a bad thing to know." He took a long draw through his nose. "Reminds me of where I grew up."

"Where was that?"

He chuckled. "A long way from here in a jungle across the world. On a mountain near swamps not so different than these. We had crocodiles instead of alligators, and more kinds of birds than you could count in a day. It was a wild place. Every day brought enough adventure to last a lifetime."

"You were there with your family?"

He eyed me kindly. "I grew up with my . . . father."

"Just your father?"

"Just my father until I was twenty."

That was a little bit like me, I thought. And with that thin connection I began to feel like I really did know this stranger named Stephen.

"It's a long story," he said, looking out at the still water. "Brimming with freedom." He took another draw of the air. "There's nothing like the clean smell of freedom, wouldn't you say?"

I didn't really know what freedom was.

"I guess so," I said.

Stephen nodded. "One day you will know so." He lifted his arm and motioned out to the middle of the lake. "When you climb in a boat and row out into the middle of the lake, all you see around you is water and all you hear is stillness, and you think, *I am safe. I am at peace. There are no troubles that can touch me.* Tell me that isn't so."

"I wouldn't know. I'm afraid of the water."

He faced me. "You're afraid of the water? But you're in a boat, yes? You're protected from the water."

"I've never been in a boat."

"You live on the lake but you've never been out on a boat?"

"No."

"Why not?"

"Because we don't have a boat. Besides, like I said, I'm afraid of the water."

"Well then . . . today is your lucky day!" He stood and held out his hand. "Step into the boat, my dear, and see how wonderful it feels to float, carefree on the water beneath your feet!"

"Oh no! I could never get in the boat."

"Why not?"

My mind swirled with images of Kathryn and dirty water and baptisms. "I would get dirty. It's not safe!"

He lowered his hand and eyed me gently for a moment, then sat back down. "Well now, dear. There's nothing in life that's safe if you think about it. No matter what you do, there's always a threat lurking, isn't that what they say?"

He was right, in a way. That's why I had to stay pure.

"Think of the water like the trouble that comes your way in life. And think of the boat like the kinds of things you have to do to save yourself from those troubles. As long as you stay in the boat, you're safe, right?"

"I suppose."

"You keep yourself free from the trouble that wants to drown you and you do so by doing all the right things and following all the rules, because you don't want to drown. God knows that wouldn't be a good end."

I'd never thought of it that way, but it made perfect sense. That's why I followed all of Mother's rules. That's why she put me under the water every week, so that the rest of them wouldn't have to drown in their own sin.

"Yes," I said. "And that's why the water is dangerous."

"Yes, but we have a boat. For now, think of the boat as your freedom. You do want to be free don't you?"

Yes. Yes I did. But the thought of being free seemed scandalous to me. Wrong even.

"As long as you live in fear, you aren't free, I can assure you. Wouldn't you like to step into the boat just once to see how it feels to be free of even that one small fear?"

"Why are you trying to talk me into doing something I don't want to do?"

"Because you seem like you could use some help."

"You only just met me. You don't know anything about me."

"Oh, but I do, my dear. I know you're afraid of water. And I know that you are afraid of so much more."

I stared at him, suddenly wondering if he really did know me. And all I saw in his eyes was kindness and love. They pulled me in a way I had never felt.

"You must know, Eden . . . If I could rush you away from all of your troubles, I would. But only you can free yourself from your fears. Only you can take the path to freedom. In fact, you must. It's your destiny."

"My destiny? How do you know?"

He lifted his hand and swept his hair behind his ear, staring out over the water. "Because it's my destiny too. It's everyone's destiny."

His words were unlike any others I'd heard. Who was this man that he seemed to know so much?

"You are in a prison of your own making, my dear Eden," he said softly. "As are the vast majority of those who walk this earth. The troubled waters always come, threatening to drown us all."

Stephen faced me and a glint came to his eyes.

"But before you can deal with those troubled waters, you have to find the courage to step into a boat. What do you say? Just to prove to yourself that you can. Is it forbidden?"

I thought about that.

"No," I said.

"No. Do you think you will drown?"

I looked at the small boat. At the dark water slapping up against its hull. At the dirty slope disappearing into that water.

"I can't get dirty. Mother wouldn't like it."

"No? Well then . . . I will carry you!" He bounded to his feet and held out his hand as if expecting me to jump to my feet and agree. "What do you say?"

"Carry me?"

"To the boat. I'll just pluck you up and set you safe and sound in the boat."

I don't know why I didn't just get up and run away then, but I didn't. Maybe because his words about freedom were working their way into my mind in a way that was both terrifying and thrilling at once. I was eighteen, right?

"How do I know you're a safe person?" I asked. But I knew he was safe. At least as safe as Mother.

"Because I am. I think you already know that. But it's your decision. I can put you in the boat and you can float for just a minute. Then you can get out and I'll be on my way."

"Just like that."

"Just like that."

"And nothing bad will happen to me."

"On the contrary, my dear. You will have found a slice of freedom."

So I thought, why not? Why not? It's just a boat.

I stood to my feet, eyes on the boat. "Are you sure?"

"I'm sure," he said, and he stepped toward me, put one arm under my knees and the other around my back and swung me from the ground before I could protest.

"Careful!"

But he was already down the bank and in the water, which was a foot or so deep and sloshed as he strode forward. I was too stunned to speak.

And then he hoisted me over the edge of the boat as if I weighed no more than one of my straw dolls, and set me on my feet.

The boat wobbled a little and I flung my arms wide, terrified.

"Oh no! Oh no!"

"Jika jika jawa. You're floating on water! Look at you, Eden. You did it!"

The boat settled and I tentatively stared down at my feet. They were on solid wood. Not a speck of water was leaking through.

He splashed at the water with his right hand, beaming.

"Ha! You see? You see? You're on the water. What did I tell you? You just stepped beyond one of your fears only to learn that it was an illusion. That, my dear, is quite an accomplishment."

His excitement was infectious, and I couldn't help but return his grin. I was standing in the boat! Like a statue, tall and proud, albeit with arms spread wide just in case.

"Jika, jika, jawa," I said.

He winked. "Now you're talking."

I stood there for a few moments, feeling more courageous than I had for a long time. It was nothing, I knew, but for me, it was something. And no one was watching, so I didn't feel stupid.

I shifted my weight and felt the boat shift a little. Actually, it was nothing, even to me.

"Now all you have to do is get out and walk back to shore," he said.

"Walk to shore? No, I can't do that."

"Sure you can. Is it forbidden?"

I wanted to say yes—it would give me an excuse. But technically, it wasn't.

"And even if it was, not all forbidden things are wrong. If your mother told you to cut off your hand, would you?"

I blinked at him. Did he know about Mother?

"No, I didn't think so," he said. "The fact is, boats really offer you only an illusion of safety. There's still the water, you see? What if the boat sprang a leak or broke? Or what if a storm rose up? The only way to really be safe is to have no fear of the water under any circumstances, but that's a bit advanced for today, I would say. Now . . ."

He pointed to the water at his feet . . .

"I can guarantee you this water, which is only a foot deep and won't even come above your rain boots, can't hurt you. All you have to do is get out of the boat and step in it. You'll see. Do that, and you will be more free than you have been in a very long time."

"But . . ."

But suddenly the thought sounded quite appealing. Not stepping out of the boat. But being free.

And the water was only a foot deep.

I'm not sure what came over me in that moment, but I was flooded with a surge of courage and I found myself grabbing the edge of the boat, flinging one leg over, then the other, and dropping into the water.

My boots landed in mud and I came to a jarring halt.

"Jika jika jawa!" Stephen said, stepping back. "Look at you!"

I looked down at the brackish water around my boots, a foot up. And a balloon of giddiness rose through me so that I felt like I was on a cloud.

I gripped my hands together and squealed, knowing that I sounded like a little girl and not caring.

"Walk!" Stephen urged, backing out of the water. "Walk out of the water."

So I did. And it was simple. I just put one foot in front of the other and I walked.

What would Mother say to this? In that moment, I didn't care. I was eighteen and I was bold and I was free.

And then I was also out of the water, standing on the bank. Staring up at Stephen, who wore a grin as wide as my own.

He stepped forward and placed a hand on my shoulder. "That's my girl. I'm so proud of you, Eden."

I didn't know what to say.

"Know that you are loved, my dear," he said in soft voice. "Know that you can and will rise above all of your fears. I now call you water walker."

"Water walker?"

"You walked through the waters of fear, didn't you?"

Yes. I had, hadn't I? And that immediately brought to mind my other fears. Like being afraid to see Paul. What was wrong with seeing Paul?

"Do you think it's wrong of me to have a boyfriend?" I asked.

He stared at me, and at first I thought he would think the idea absurd. Who did I think I was, asking a stranger what he thought about such things?

But he didn't feel like a stranger, and when he answered, his voice was sincere.

"You're eighteen. In this country that gives you the right to make that decision for yourself."

"It does."

"Only you will know if that helps you or hurts you. Always remember one thing: God isn't a boat, or the water, or any boy for that matter. He's in your heart. Let go of your fears of this world and find him there."

His eyes seemed to be melting me. I suddenly felt like I was going to cry.

He continued to hold my shoulder in his gentle grasp. "I wish I could save you from all of your troubles, my child. But you must walk the path before you and walk your own waters to the place where only love resides."

He kissed my forehead, stepped passed me, and bounded into the boat, which glided deeper into the lake.

"You're leaving?" I asked.

"So pleased to meet you, Eden. You give me courage. I have to go . . . Not to worry, I'm sure we'll see each other again." He grinned wide. "Go find yourself a boyfriend, you look like you could use some fun."

And then he was rowing.

I watched him until he was around the corner, still glowing with courage at my accomplishment. It struck me that in just two days I had turned eighteen, I had been asked to be Paul's girlfriend, I made my first visit into the city, I had become very wealthy, I had met a new friend, and I had walked on water. Kind of.

What would Mother say?

The question jarred me and my eyes snapped wide. The ceiling, not the lake, hung in my vision. It had been a dream. Yes, of course, a dream.

But that was just it: it hadn't felt like a dream—not at all. And thinking about that, something else struck me: I was going to honor Paul's request and meet him at the field the next day during my free hour, wasn't I?

My heart was racing and my skin was wet with sweat. Yes, I was. I was eighteen, I could do that. I wanted to do that. In fact, I *had* to do that.

Mother will drown you if she finds out.

No . . . No, she couldn't. I was a water walker.

How little I knew.

EPISODE THREE

HAVING MADE the decision to accept Paul's invitation to meet him in the field, I could think of nothing else. Actually, as I thought about it, I hadn't so much made a decision as given myself permission, because I could now. I was no longer a young child under the thumb of my mother's every wish. I had become an adult, and with that came a new kind of freedom.

Mother would say that I was in a state of denial, that place she often accused me of being when I wasn't readily aware of my sinful thoughts. That I wasn't feeling guilty about my plan to see Paul because my desire had blinded me.

But I wasn't blinded. In fact, I was seeing more clearly now than ever. I had faced my fears and I had walked on water so to speak, even if it was only in a dream. Well, I was going to walk some more, right down to the field at four o'clock during my free hour. I would see Paul because seeing Paul was what I wanted.

I must have looked at the clock a hundred times that morning and through the afternoon as I counted down the hours. Never before had my daily rituals or household chores seemed so tedious.

Mother was in an exceptionally good mood, which made perfect sense—she had just come into a small fortune, so when I asked if I could take Bobby to the field during my free hour she gave permission with only a small warning to be careful. I found Bobby playing in his room, and we were out the door before Mother could change her mind.

Bobby kicked rocks as we walked the gravel road toward the field. The day was still hot and the air thick, but I couldn't have cared less. My heart felt light and for the first time in a while the world seemed new. Hopeful.

He ambled ahead of me and sang so loudly that he startled a flock of birds in a nearby tree. With a loud rush of wings they took flight and disappeared into the dense cover of the swamp.

I laughed, which only made him want to sing louder.

"Bobby Joe, he played three! He played knick-knack in a tree. Knick-knack patty smack, dig the dog a bone! He wants his treats so he's swimmin' home!"

He turned around, smiled, and swept his arms through the air with a flourish. "He wants his treat so he's swim . . . ming . . . home!" He held the last note as long as he could, then beamed, toothy grin spread wide. "Wanna hear it again?"

I laughed. "On the way home, okay? After we're done at the field."

"Okay!" he said and pointed to the path just ahead on the left. I could see the field from where I stood and, there sitting in the middle of it, was Paul. "Race you!"

Bobby broke into a hobble-sprint, arms pumping, his clumsy feet kicking up dust as he went. I followed close behind and ran through the short patch of wild grass separating the field from the road.

"I won!" he said and lifted his arms high into the air as I pulled to a stop beside him.

"You're fast," I said, but my attention was on Paul who was waiting for me no more than fifty feet away. He was sitting on a checkered blanket he'd spread in the grass.

He stood and waved.

"Hi, Paul!" Bobby yelled and waved back.

"Bobby," I said, "I'm going to talk to Paul, okay?"

I didn't want to be rude to Bobby. Having him along was the only reason Mother gave me permission to come to the field. I couldn't simply abandon him to play alone while I talked with Paul. Yet, I wanted nothing more than to sit on that blanket by Paul's side. Alone.

"I'd really like to talk with him privately for a few minutes. Is that all right with you? Then we can all talk together. Okay?"

"Okay. Can I climb the tree?" He stared at a large maple to his right.

Mother wouldn't have approved, Bobby was better at falling out of trees than he was at staying in them. "I don't know . . ." Then again, it would occupy him. But then I spotted a turtle making its way through the thick grass ten feet away and I pointed it out.

"Look!"

His eyes went wide and he ran for the creature. "A red-eared slider. Wow. Can I play with him?"

"I tell you what, you wait here and watch the turtle while I talk to Paul. After I'm done we'll take him down to the lake. Deal?"

He chewed his lower lip and nodded his head, eyes fixed on the turtle. "Deal."

He sat cross-legged in the grass and began to trace his finger over its shell.

Others thought Bobby was simple, but that's what I loved about him. He saw the world like a child. Nothing was complicated; everything was fascinating, even a turtle, even though he'd seen a thousand or more.

"I won't be long," I said and looked toward Paul. "I promise."

"Okay," he said, but he was already transfixed with his new friend.

I took a deep breath, smoothed my dress, and started walking toward Paul. With each step my heart thumped louder and harder, just like it had when I stepped out of the boat the first time. No, it was more than that. This was joy and fear and something else I only felt when I was with Paul—something I couldn't explain.

I couldn't help but smile as I came closer. Paul was wearing a blue button-down shirt with khaki pants and black work boots. When I saw his eyes, a tingle spread through me. He wasn't simply looking at me. He was staring like I was the only other person in the world.

My heart was flirting with temptation, I knew that much was true.

I stopped at the edge of the blanket and looked into Paul's eyes. He took a step toward me and smiled. The summer breeze brushed his hair across his face. A wave of nervousness washed over me and I could hardly breathe.

"Hey," he said.

"Hey."

"I hoped you'd come," he said.

"Here I am."

"Yeah," he said. "Here we are."

"Here we are," I said softly.

Neither of us said anything for a moment.

"Oh, hey . . . want to sit down? I brought a blanket."

"I can see that."

"Yeah, I guess you can." He scratched the back of his neck, his only nervous tic. "Kinda stupid pointing out the obvious, huh?"

"No, it's nice. Thoughtful." I settled onto the blanket and nervously arranged my dress over my legs as he sat across from me.

We were both quiet and just looked at each other for a while. It was strange how Paul and Bobby were the only people I felt like I could simply *be with* and not feel like I had to fill the silence with small talk.

Paul smiled and fidgeted with his hands.

"What?" I said. "What are you thinking?"

"Nothing."

"No, what?"

"You look nice. I like your dress."

"You're just trying to flatter me."

"Maybe a little," he said. "Is it working?"

"A little." My face got hot and I knew I was blushing.

The wind blew gently, bending the taller grass near the far edge of the field. Paul and I had spent time together before, but this seemed different. We weren't kids anymore, simply passing the time with games and stupid things while the adults did the important things of life.

"I brought you something," I said and reached into the deep pocket Mother had sewn into my skirt.

Paul's attention went to the small package of brown paper and twine that I'd handed to him. "What's this?"

"Just something I made for you. It's not much, but . . ."

"Really?" He peeled the paper away and unwrapped the straw doll that I'd made for him the other day. His eyes went wide.

"Do you like it?" I asked.

He cradled it in his hands. "I love it."

"You do?"

"You made it, so I love it. Thank you. I'll keep this forever and think about you every time I see it."

"I hope so," I said. And I meant it.

We talked for a half hour as the sun sank lower in the sky. We talked about what we liked and didn't like about living in the swamps, how I loved math and how he hated it. How his father wanted to bring him into the moonshining business even though Paul didn't want to.

"Well, what are you going to do then?" I asked.

"I'm going to be in a rock band."

"Rock band?" I asked. "Does your father even allow you listen to that kind of music? Mother never lets us listen to anything other than that old gospel music."

"He lets me when my mom's not around. My dad says the music he grew up with was the last time rock and roll was good. He lets me listen to all of his old records—Led Zeppelin, Queen, the Eagles. I'm even learning to play the guitar."

There was a long pause in the conversation and he scooted closer. "I thought about you all day, Eden."

I hesitated. "I thought about you too."

"Really?" He blinked.

"You seem surprised."

"Well, a little bit. What'd you think about? I mean, when I crossed your mind."

I shrugged. "I don't know. Little things, I guess. It's stupid. Forget it."

"No, tell me. Just one thing."

"One thing?" I said.

He held up one finger. "Just one. I won't ask anymore. Promise."

I fidgeted with the blanket. "All right then. This morning I thought about how you kind of snort when you laugh really hard."

"I don't snort."

"You do. A little, but it's cute."

"I must get it from my mom."

I laughed. "I think you're right. I've always liked it, though."

"If you like it then I'm happy. What else?"

"You said one thing."

"C'mon, just one more. Please," he said. "Then I'll tell you something I like about you."

I looked at him and smiled. "Well, there's the way you make me smile. You always know what to say to me. No one else treats me like you do. It's . . . nice. Besides Bobby, you're my only real friend. You accept me for who I really am."

"Liking you is easy. You're perfect, Eden."

"No," I said. "Don't say that. I'm not."

"Maybe not in your mind." He gently placed his hand on top of mine. "But you are."

The warmth of his skin against mine sent a shock up my arm and through my whole body. I drew a short breath. For a moment I felt like that one touch would send me soaring on the wind and high into the sky.

"Would your father approve of you holding my hand?" I asked.

Paul's eyes shifted to the tree line. "What he doesn't know won't hurt him." He had a far-off look when he said it. So he was here without his father's knowledge. He had taken his own risks to be here with me.

His fingers lingered across the back of my hand. I knew he was as nervous as I was because I could feel the slight tremor in his hands. "Do you see me as more than a friend?"

I hesitated. I felt like I was standing on the edge of a dam that was held together by a single pebble, and I was about to kick it loose. I wanted nothing more than to do just that no matter what might happen because of it.

"I don't know. I think so."

His eyes searched mine. His mind was churning, I could practically hear it. But what was he thinking? What if he didn't really like me too?

"Yes," I said. "I like you."

Paul smiled and squeezed my hand. "You know I like you too. I kinda think of you as my girlfriend."

Girlfriend. I liked the sound of that.

I turned my hand over until my palm pressed against his, and I held his hand. Wrong or not, I felt something special for Paul and I wanted him to know it. But only him.

"Girlfriend," I said. "What does that mean? I've never been anyone's girlfriend before. And what does it mean that you're my boyfriend?"

Paul caressed my hand with his thumb. "It means we'll be here for each other. Always. I'll protect you and think about you. Just you, no one else."

I smiled. "I like that idea."

"We're growing up, Eden. No one can stop that, not your mother or my father. Even they know that part of growing up is loving someone."

I stopped. Looked him in the eye. "Love?"

"I've never felt this way about anyone before. Have you?"

I shook my head slowly.

"How else do you describe it?" he said.

"I don't know. But love, it seems—"

"It seems right, doesn't it?"

I nodded. "I think so."

In that instant I'd kicked the pebble away and now joy crashed through the dam like I'd never felt before. Joy that I don't think could have any other name but love, and not in the way Mother or Father loved me. But it wasn't just happiness that spilled out. It was fear too. Mother would eventually find out. She would know how Paul felt and how I felt about him. What would happen then?

"Eden!" Bobby yelled from the tree line. He held his turtle high over his head. "Can we take the turtle to the lake now?"

How long had we been there? "I'll be there in just a minute, okay? Then we'll go to the lake."

"When can I see you again?" Paul asked.

I turned to Paul and held his hand tighter. "I don't know."

"Tomorrow. You always have the free hour at four, right?"

"But my mother—"

"Won't have to know why you came. Did she know today?"

"No," I said.

"See. As long as we're careful no one will know. If no one knows then why can't we see each other?"

I released his hand and stood to my feet. "All right. Tomorrow, a little after four. I'll probably have to bring Bobby."

"Eden!" Bobby yelled.

"I've got to go. Mother will come looking for us if we're not back soon."

Paul stood and took my hand again. "I'll be thinking about you tonight."

"I'll think about you too."

"Do you promise?"

"Promise."

He took a step closer until his body brushed against mine, then leaned close and kissed me lightly on the cheek. "Tomorrow can't come soon enough."

I closed my eyes as his warm lips lingered on my skin. I was sure my heart would explode just then. Nothing else mattered and the world fell away. There was only Paul and me. And his kiss.

He stepped back and gently wiped his thumb on my cheek where he'd kissed me. "Tomorrow."

"Tomorrow," I said softly. But inside I was singing at the top of my lungs.

MOTHER HAD always told me that the reason we ended and started each week with a ritual baptism was to, once again, get rid of the old and make all things new. That's why every Sunday morning Mother, Wyatt, Bobby, and I would gather in the holiness shed, as Mother called it, and drown me. That's why Mother would lay seven straps against Bobby's bared back. That's why she would recite scripture, and rejoice after our sin was properly dismissed through the lamb and goat.

I was the lamb and Bobby was the goat, because I was born beautiful and Bobby was born ugly, she said.

I always felt much cleaner after baptisms each Sunday, glad to be rid of all of our sin. However much I hated the thought of being held under water until I was sure I was going to drown, I loved the feeling of being saved even more. The first few hours following my cleansing were always the happiest hours of my week, if only for the peace that purification brought me. We all felt it. Manna from heaven, Mother called it. Euphoria from God.

But none of that had prepared me for the exhilaration that had swept me away in the field with Paul the previous afternoon. I spent the rest of the evening and the following morning walking as if I were on a cloud, heart throbbing with feelings I hardly knew existed.

Though I tried, I couldn't hide my excitement from Mother. But she was in quite a good mood herself and thankfully didn't press beyond a question or two as to why I went about with a smile on my face, humming.

I felt a little guilty for keeping my love for Paul to myself—after all, I had vowed to tell Mother if I was ever even tempted to be romantic with anyone.

But I was eighteen now, you see? That gave me certain rights. I was old enough to handle my guilt directly with God and not through my mother. And I didn't think he minded that I was in love with Paul.

That's what it was, right? Love. The thought made me dizzy. And if just a small kiss on my cheek felt like heaven, I wondered what being married to Paul would feel like. Didn't all girls my age think about marriage? They must, surely, and God had created marriage so he must not mind.

I couldn't remember a time when the whole family had been so happy. Bobby was happy because I was happy. Wyatt was happy because Kathryn was happy. Kathryn was happy because Zeke was happy. Zeke was happy because God had blessed us all with a lot of money, or so I figured.

Mother was in such a good mood, in fact, that when I told her I was going to go for a walk alone during my free time, she only gave me a word of caution to stay clear of any trouble and seemed satisfied with my assurance that I would.

That was how I ended up on the gravel road for the second day in a row, this time without Bobby, who was occupied with building a miniature fort out of small wood blocks in his room. It was about ten minutes after four and I was a bundle of nerves, mostly good ones.

Taking that quarter of a mile walk all alone was unnerving, sure— the swamps were on either side and there was no one to warn me of any danger, like an alligator. But again, it was only like stepping out of the boat. I was a water walker now, wasn't I? That meant facing my fears to reach the shore.

But this time that shore was Paul and my stomach was full of butterflies. Good butterflies. Wonderful ones that made me lightheaded with exhilaration. It was strange how only a few days ago I had tortured myself for the very thoughts that now excited me so much. It was like a dam had burst and suddenly my life was flooded with newness.

I imagined the man from my dream would approve, even if he was just a figment of my imagination. Or maybe my true self, speaking some truth into myself.

The edge of the field came into view and I picked up my pace.

If the Outlaw could see me now, he would say, "Jika jika jawa, Eden! Look at you go!"

And what would Mother say? But I already knew the answer to that, didn't I? She didn't like . . .

I saw the big black truck then, sitting out in the middle of the field, and I stopped cold. Zeke's truck.

My heart began to pound like a fist. I quickly glanced along the tree line, but didn't see Paul. Only Zeke, sitting behind the steering wheel, watching me.

My first thought was to run, because Zeke could only mean trouble. He'd come to punish me.

But that thought left as soon as it came, because I'd never been the kind to run from anything. I'd learned to face whatever was in front of me—it was better to pay the price than invite even more trouble.

Besides, who was to say that Zeke being here was trouble? Sure, the man made me cringe because I knew that he was the closest thing to God on earth and God always made me cringe. But maybe Zeke had come to thank me for my blessing.

That's what I told myself as I started toward the truck, too afraid to dare think anything else.

The driver's door swung open when I was twenty yards from the truck, and I stopped again, feeling totally exposed.

You shouldn't have come, Eden. You see what happens when you cross the line?

There was still no sign of Paul—only Zeke, who slowly climbed out of the truck, dressed in black slacks and a black button-down shirt. He didn't look at me. He just walked around the crew cab to the back passenger door, and opened it. Then reached in and gave a hard yank.

Paul stumbled out of the truck, held up by Zeke who gripped his collar. I recognized him by his body and his hair but not by his face because it was swollen and bruised.

The blood drained from my face and I suddenly felt as though I was going to throw up. Paul's right eye was swollen, and there was a gash on his cheek, dried shut with blood.

He'd been beaten. Badly. His father had discovered our secret and had punished him. In the space of one breath, my whole world came crashing down around me because I knew that I had done this to Paul.

Zeke hauled Paul toward me, still holding him up by his collar as if he was nothing more than one of my straw dolls. He stopped by the front of the truck, eyes now burning a hole through me.

Paul was staring at the ground with his one good eye.

"Take a good look, Eden." Zeke's voice was calm and cut straight to my heart. "I can't say that I'm surprised by Paul; he always was a rebellious little turd. But I'm deeply disappointed that you so fall so easily."

I felt myself shrinking away to nothing under his glare. Guilt, the kind that made me feel like a worm, wiped away all of the courageous thoughts that had filled me with such happiness just a few minutes earlier. In that moment, I hated myself. It was all my fault. I should have known better.

Zeke jerked Paul backwards, nearly off his feet.

"Get back in the truck."

Paul stumbled toward the cab, limped around the open door, and disappeared inside. He'd been too afraid to even look at me. I lifted my eyes to take in Zeke's hard stare as he strode toward me.

He's going to do the same to you, Eden. He's going to punish you and he should.
Zeke stopped within arm's reach, towering above me.
He's going slap you hard and hurt you bad.
But as I stared up into his eyes, ready for what I deserved, his face softened. His mouth formed a thin line—a half-smile.
He lifted his hand and gently brushed my hair back from my face. "You're a very pretty girl. I wouldn't think of hurting you." He paused. "No. No, that wouldn't do."
Zeke lowered his hand.
"Do you know why I punished Paul?"
I didn't think I could talk; my throat was in a knot.
"Please don't be rude, Eden. Answer me when I speak to you."
I tried to tell him, but had to clear my throat. When I did speak, my voice sounded distant and frail.
"Because he disobeyed you."
"And why is that a problem?"
"It's disobeying God."
"That's a good girl. You see? You do know better." He paced to his right, hands held loosely behind his back. Mine were trembling by my sides. I was already shutting down my mind—I had long ago learned that it was the easiest way to endure what couldn't be avoided.
"I give you an inch and you take a mile. Is that how a child of God returns their gratefulness for his blessing?"
He paced back to his left, eyes back on me.
"No, I don't think so. Clearly, you need to be reminded of a few things. The first is that I know everything that happens. Everything. There's nothing wrong with an innocent kiss, now is there? But breaking a rule isn't innocent. One rule becomes two and before you know it, you're burning with the rest of them. But you already know that, don't you, Eden?"
"Yes."

"Yes?"

"Yes, sir."

"Yes, sir." He flashed a grin. "You see, already you're breaking more rules. So let me put this in very simple terms for you. Without me, you would be nothing. I gave you your life back and provided a way for you to bless us all in a very significant way. But with great blessing comes great responsibility. You, of all people, know that."

"Yes, sir."

"I trusted you, Eden. I entrusted you with my son, thinking it would be a nice gift on a day of such blessing, knowing that you would never break the rules. And yet here we stand."

Tears sprang to my eyes. I felt like dropping to my knees and begging his forgiveness.

"I . . . I won't do it again. I promise . . ."

"No, of course you won't. You won't see him again until I've determined that you know your place."

"Yes, sir."

The thought of not seeing Paul again struck a new fear in my heart.

"I've decided not to tell your mother of your indiscretion. God knows she wouldn't take it well. So we'll keep this between us. Consider it my small gift to you, however undeserved."

A measure of relief washed through me.

"Thank you, sir."

"But if you so much as take one misstep in the next thirty days, that changes. Do you understand?"

"Yes, sir."

"Don't be so selfish, Eden. Think about the rest of us for a change. You saw what happened to Paul. Think of your mother. Think of me. Think of God." He eyed me, steadfast. "Think of Bobby."

I could not mistake his veiled threat. If I disobeyed, he would hurt Bobby.

I think something deep in me snapped then, thinking of Zeke laying his hands on Bobby. It was just a subtle shift, but I felt a small part of my guilt turn to anger.

"Yes, sir."

"We're surrounded on all sides by swamp and alligators—the only way out is by my good grace. Earn it and maybe one day I'll give it to you. In the meantime, you will be a good little girl and follow your mother to the letter as God has instructed you to do. Is that clear?"

"Yes, sir."

Zeke looked at me as if trying to decide whether or not he could trust me. Not just a moment or two, but a silent spell that stretched out until I thought he might change his mind and punish me anyway.

When he spoke, his tone was soft.

"Have you ever seen one of those pictures of a shepherd carrying a lamb around his neck? A soft white lamb over the shoulders of a strong caretaker in a brightly colored robe."

I'd seen one of Jesus like that.

"Yes."

"What most don't realize is that the shepherd has an errant lamb on his back. One that tried to break out of the flock and in so doing lead others astray. So, if the shepherd is good, he does them all a favor. He breaks the lamb's leg so that it can't go astray. That's why he's carrying the lamb around his neck."

Zeke's right brow arched.

"When you get tempted to feel sorry for yourself, think of that lamb, Eden. All that I do, I do in yours and the flock's best interest. Can you accept that?"

"Yes."

"Yes?"

"Yes, sir."

"Consider this your final warning."

"Thank you, sir."

He reached into his jacket pocket, withdrew the straw doll that I'd given to Paul, and calmly twisted the head off as I watched. Then he dropped it on the ground, broken and torn.

"Paul won't be needing this anymore," he said.

And he left me like that, staring after him with my doll at my feet.

IT TOOK all of my courage to present myself at peace when I got home after seeing Paul beaten at the field that afternoon. I didn't dare show the slightest concern, because Mother had a hawkeye for my disposition and would immediately begin digging. So I smiled as best I could, ate supper with the family, and thankfully retired to my room for my evening prayers.

But inside I was falling apart. Kathryn had never beaten either me or Bobby. She was stern to the bone, don't get me wrong, but she used words, disciplines and rituals, not her hand, except around my throat to push me under the water each week. Seeing Paul beat up terrified me.

Alone in my dark room, I wept for him. For me. For us. It felt like God had immediately and forcefully yanked back his blessing, which had been Paul. And why? Because I'd disobeyed. So I lay in bed sobbing silently into my pillow, begging him for forgiveness.

But there was more than just guilt and sorrow in my heart. I was angry at Zeke.

He could have put Paul in a closet for a day or something instead of beating his face with his fist. God might do that and more, sure—he sent people to hell, didn't he? And Zeke was his prophet on earth, sure, so he could be God's voice. But no matter how much I prayed for forgiveness that first night, I couldn't get the anger out of my heart.

Which scared me because it was the first time I had really struggled with anger.

And the next day was even worse. I still went about my chores and rituals with a calm face, but inside my anger began to boil.

So I prayed even harder. I repeated my prayers with more intensity. I took an extra shower that night, with the water extra hot. When Mother asked why, I told her that I wanted to be extra pure because things were different now that I was eighteen. She smiled and told me how proud she was of me.

The third day after Paul's beating, my anger finally began to calm down and I knew that God had finally heard my prayers. But as my anger settled, my sorrow for Paul only grew worse, so it was just as hard to put on a brave face around Kathryn.

The fourth day was Sunday, and I'd never been so eager to be drowned. I asked Mother to make sure she got all the sin out. I was eighteen now.

"Are you sure, sweetheart?" she asked.

"Yes. I have to be sure."

She smiled. "That's my brave little girl."

As she held me under the surface in that dark place of death, I felt the same panic that always came after a couple minutes. But I was surprised by a sudden temptation to just suck in a lungful of water and end it all.

It's too much, Eden. You can't do it. You can't spend one more day living in this hell!

The thought roared through me like a ball of the blackest darkness, and with it a terrible rage at the injustice of my situation.

Mother pulled me up. I gasped and for a split second I was disappointed to be alive. And then Kathryn's hallelujah wiped the darkness away and I felt gratefulness sweep in.

After Mother laid her lash against Bobby's bared back, she celebrated with more glory than I was accustomed to seeing. She was very happy.

My happiness, on the other hand, was fleeting. I was relieved to be cleansed, of course—I always was. But within half an hour of my baptism, the sickening sadness that had swallowed me the day before returned. And to make matters worse, my anger was back.

By nightfall, I could hardly contain my emotions. I wasn't used to having such a terrible struggle and that fact alone confused me, which added fear to a mix of terrible feelings that refused to be calmed.

Still, I managed to keep it all inside.

Until Monday afternoon, that is. On Monday afternoon it all fell apart.

It started early Monday morning, while I was sleeping. I often had dreams of being Alice, trapped in a hospital with mentally disturbed patients, and in those dreams I'm quite lucid, aware of how insane everyone but me is. It's a safe place for me, because I can play along as a patient without fearing the consequence because I know that I'm only in a dream. I even help other patients to see things differently.

But the dream I'd had of the Outlaw named Stephen was different, if only because I'd completely lost any sense that I was in a dream. Every detail had been fully fleshed out without any break in sequence. And when I awoke, I could remember every detail, as if it had really happened.

Just before waking early Monday morning I had another dream, just as real.

This time I was in a boat out on the lake and there was a storm brewing. The wind was blowing and foamy waves beat against the boat and I was terrified.

I'm going to die, I thought. *I'm going to drown!*

Then I heard the distant call and I turned to see a man on the shore. It was Stephen. He was smiling and beckoning me with an outstretched hand. My first thought was, *He's back!*

Then I remembered where I was.

"Come to me, Eden!" he called, voice distant. "Step out of the boat and walk to me."

I looked at the wood hull under my feet and then at the water, surging and slapping against the boat. Then at him, dressed in a black coat, long hair whipped by the wind.

"Step out of the boat, Eden. Walk to me. Be a water walker. It's okay, I promise. Step out of the boat and walk to me."

I was scared, but I knew that if I didn't do what he said, the boat would capsize and I would drown. So I slung my feet over the edge of the rocking boat, held my breath to fight back my fear, and, closing my eyes, stepped out onto the water.

But I didn't walk.

I plunged under the surface.

Flailing hopelessly, I dropped straight down, deep into murky black water that filled my nostrils and ears, cold as ice. It was like a baptism, only this time the water was a bottomless pit and this time I was going to drown, really drown.

I started to scream and jerked up in bed, soaked in sweat, panting.

I was alive. It had only been another dream. Thank God. I was safe. But the moment I thought that, a new awareness struck me, as cold as the water I'd dreamed about.

I was still in the lake, wasn't I? I was still drowning in the water.

Not real water in the lake, but here, in the house. My whole life was that troubled sea and I was drowning in it. I didn't understand why or how, really, but I was. That's what the dream meant.

And with that awareness, a simple question dropped into my mind, as if it had come from heaven itself. *What if I'm being used?* Just that, but for me, asking such a question bordered on blasphemy. I hadn't dared even think it before.

While I had dealt with raging emotions all week and embarked on a never-ending struggle to seek forgiveness for my anger, for the first time my mind dared ask that simple, logical question.

What if I'm being used? Or even worse, abused.

I mean, what if all of this had been an elaborate plan to get to the money all along? Not Mother's plan, no—I couldn't see that. But isn't that essentially what Zeke had said? His words reached to me from the field.

Without me, you would be nothing, he'd said. *I gave you your life back and provided a way for you to bless us all in a very significant way.*

As if he'd orchestrated my coming here so that I could give them all a significant blessing. Meaning the money.

It hit me square between the eyes, and once in my mind, I couldn't get it out. I didn't want to get it out. It was as if someone had turned a light bulb on in my head.

What if all of this—the baptisms, the teaching, the rituals, the prayers, the confinement, the rules—all of it was only to get me to be his obedient little girl so that when I turned eighteen, I would readily just hand over all the money to my mother who would just hand it over to Zeke?

What if it was all a sham? Not my belief in God, or that Kathryn was my real mother, but all this other business. And on the heels of that question, a whole slew that battered my mind and pushed my anger even deeper until my body began to display signs of it regardless of any attempt on my part to keep it calm.

I got out of bed and went through my normal morning cleaning rituals. I did my chores and said all the right things. But I couldn't stop sweating. Noticing, Kathryn asked me to wash my face three different times to keep it clean. Even worse, I couldn't keep my fingers from trembling when the thoughts overtook me, and twice I didn't hear questions put to me by Mother.

It all came to a head during lunch, when I inadvertently knocked over my water glass.

"Eden!"

I began to dab up the water with my napkin. "Sorry."

"What has gotten into you?"

"It's just water, sugar," Wyatt said, rising to help me clean up the spill.

"Sit down, Wyatt. It's her spill, not yours. She's been acting strange all day."

Wyatt hesitated, then retreated to his seat, knowing better than to defend me in front of the whole family, though I think he did so in private on occasion.

"It's just water, Mama," Bobby said.

"Shut up, Bobby."

We ate the rest of the meal in silence and Wyatt headed for the door as soon as Kathryn excused him.

"Bobby, go with your father."

"We're going to the still?" he asked.

Wyatt flashed Bobby a smile. "Wanna help me change a tire, boy?"

Bobby hopped off his chair and marched for the door as if to defend the fort against invading marauders.

"I can change the tire!"

"Of course you can."

Wyatt gave me a glance of understanding and followed Bobby, who was already outside, raring to go.

Mother turned to me the moment the door closed, hands on her hips.

"What's wrong with you today? It's like you're not even here!"

"Sorry, Mother. I just . . ."

You see, already I was feeling guilty. And then angry that I was feeling guilty.

"You just what? Stand up. Have you lost your mind?"

I stood and stared at her, feeling my face flush red.

"That's right. You *should* feel ashamed."

But it was anger, not shame, that heated my face.

"Well? Are you just going to stand there?" she demanded, expecting me to apologize.

I almost didn't. But my habits had grown too deep, like roots that had worked their way into every cell in my body.

"I'm sorry."

She eyed me suspiciously for a spell.

"You've been weak all day, haven't you? In fact, you've been off since last night. I could see it when you went to bed. We accepted our blessing in baptism yesterday and you went to bed ungrateful and in a foul mood, didn't you?"

I've been in a foul mood all week, I wanted to say. But I didn't.

"You answer your mother when she asks you a question, Eden Lowenstein."

So I did.

"Yes."

"And you didn't bother to confess?" Her face grew red. "What has gotten into you?"

"I don't know." It was a lie, but I was past feeling guilty for such small sins. My true demons were far more frightening and were tearing me apart.

"Well you had better *start* knowing!" Mother glared at me and for a second I thought she was going to blow up, something she rarely did.

"I've given you too many liberties, haven't I?" she said. "All this business of you turning eighteen and I've let my guard down."

"No."

"No? I think *yes.* I think your head's getting the better of you."

I could see the wheels spinning behind her eyes. She was suddenly worried that I was going to ruin things for all of them, wasn't she? For her and Zeke. All they wanted was my money.

"You're hiding something from me, I can see it in your eyes."

"I . . ." But I couldn't form a response. Anything I said would be a lie, and I suddenly couldn't bring myself to keep up the charade.

"You what? Speak up!" Mother snapped.

"I don't know."

"Well that's a problem, isn't it?"

"I guess."

"You guess? You *guess?* You can't do this to us, Eden! Not now. Not after all we've been through." She began to pace in front of me, and concern replaced her anger. Genuine worry, I thought. She was as much a victim as me, but realizing this didn't calm me.

"What do you think Zeke would say to this?" she demanded, turning on me.

It was the way she pulled him in to the conversation that pushed me over the edge of the cliff I'd been desperately balancing on.

"Zeke?" I asked.

Your voice is too loud, Eden.

"Zeke?"

You're falling.

"Since when is Zeke more important to you than your own daughter?"

You're shouting, Eden.

My face was hot and my breathing was coming quick, but I was past making any attempt to stuff my emotions. It was suddenly all boiling over and I didn't have the strength to stop it.

"Eden!"

"I'm not a straw doll, you know?" I snapped. "You can't just use me to get what you want!"

Mother's jaw fell open and she gasped. I had never raised my voice to her, and now that I had taken the plunge, I just kept going.

"Do you know what he did to Paul? Zeke beat him up. Smashed

his face with his fist and cut him up! He brought Paul to the field and showed me, then threatened to hurt Bobby if I ever crossed him."

You would think I had slapped Mother and sent her staggering back. Her face went from red to white, gripped by fear and shock.

"You went to the field without me knowing? How dare you!?"

"Of course I went to the field, no one said I couldn't. And now I'm confessing that I let Paul kiss me on the cheek. There. Now you know, Mother. I went to the field and let Paul give me a kiss. Is that so bad? Of course it is! Do you know why? Because I have to do exactly what Zeke wants me to, regardless of how absurd the rules you two come up with are."

"How *dare* you!"

"You have to keep me perfectly obedient, don't you? It's the only way Zeke can get his hands on the money! All he's ever wanted is my money, can't you see that?"

Kathryn was trembling.

"Blasphemy!"

"Of course it is. Anything I do that doesn't make your life better is blasphemy. You don't *love* me. You're only using me to take care of your own guilt and get your hands on my money."

Kathryn gawked, speechless.

"Well, that's too bad," I said. "Because you're not going to get my money and neither is Zeke. I'm going to undo what I did. I have thirty days to do that, and I'm going to tell them I've changed my mind." I took a breath. "I'm not going to let Zeke use me like this. It's not right! I don't like that man!"

"Eden Lowenstein!" Mother shoved her hands against her ears, as if to protect them from my words. "You stop this right now! Stop it! The devil has gotten inside of you!" She shoved her finger at the hallway. "You go to your room right now and cleanse your mind of all this garbage!"

I hadn't planned on saying any of what I'd said. Or undoing the power of attorney I'd signed. The words had all just come out. But having said them, I felt a surge of courage and I realized that it was exactly what I was going to do. I didn't know how or when, but I could do it and I would.

That monster who'd beaten his son up wasn't going to get his hands on that money. Neither was my mother, for that matter.

For the first time, I wondered if my mother wasn't a monster too.

But I had the sense to know that saying any more wouldn't help my cause. I wasn't even sure what the full extent of my cause *was*.

So I took a deep breath, set my jaw, and forced myself to calm down.

"Fine," I said. "I'll do that."

And I turned on my heel and walked to my bedroom.

KATHRYN STOOD silent in the kitchen, holding her head with trembling hands, unable to hold back the anger that washed through her like an ocean that threatened to drown her where she stood.

No, it wasn't just anger. There was fear too, raw fear that was pitch black and ran bone deep.

How could Eden be so foolish? Not only had she rebelled, but Zeke knew. He'd smashed Paul's face to show her the wages of her sin—a warning. And yet her response was sin heaped upon more sin, rather than humility and repentance.

The little fool had no idea what she'd set in motion, or what Zeke was capable of. Her pride was inviting disaster upon all of them, not just herself.

Stupid girl. Too blind to see that . . .

Kathryn stopped. Another thought came, fully formed, and she shuddered. If Zeke knew of Eden's rebellion, he also knew of her failure as a mother.

You have to set this right, Kathryn. You have to set this right before Zeke does.

Mind spinning, she walked to the front door and pushed through it. The screen door banged shut as she descended the porch steps and angled across the yard. She had to think, had to find a way to fix this. Fix Eden and return her to the path of righteousness so that everything could go back to the way it was.

Eden was deceived. She'd been deceived by her own sinful nature and that nature was bent on devouring the good Kathryn had cultivated in Eden all these years and replacing it with poison thistles and stones.

And poison they were. With each passing moment Eden's venomous words bit deeper.

I'm not a straw doll, you know.

That's where Eden was wrong. She *was* a straw doll. And she was a fool if she believed anyone was controlling her. No, Eden's corrupted flesh wore her like a glove, manipulating her every thought and desire. Her rebellion was blinding her to that fact, wasn't it?

"Wyatt!" Kathryn yelled. She glanced at the truck parked beside the house. Its front tire still sagged, unchanged. Where was that man?

His distant reply called from her right. "Here! Down near the lake with Bobby."

Jaw clenched, she hurried toward the lake where the two of them stood with fishing poles in hand.

Wyatt watched Kathryn as she approached and reeled in his line, smile fading as she stopped next to them.

"Go to the house, Bobby," she said.

Bobby's eyes flicked between them. "Am I in trouble?"

"Now," she said. "I won't ask twice."

After a moment's pause, Wyatt quietly took hold of Bobby's fishing pole. "Do as your mother says. I'll take care of that rod, all right?"

"All right," he said quietly. He took a few steps then turned around. "Is Eden in trouble for spilling her drink?"

"Now, Bobby!" She jabbed a finger toward the house. "Go! And don't talk to your sister, you understand me?"

"I won't talk to her." Bobby shook his head and then hobbled up the path in a hurry.

Kathryn paced by the water's edge, her thoughts clawing one over the other like a desperate mob. Wyatt stood there and watched her with nervous eyes.

He finally spoke. "If this is about the tire . . ."

"Shut up, Wyatt! I don't give a damn about your truck right now."

"I'm sorry, sugar."

"Well you'd better be. We've got a problem."

She told him what had happened with Eden, how she'd betrayed her by going to the field, how she'd given in to her lust for Paul and how Eden had betrayed not only her, but Zeke too. He listened without comment and a dark look of worry crept over his face.

"What's gotten into that child?" Kathryn said. "She's rushing down the road to hell, all the while dragging us close behind her. I've done everything for her. Everything! She has no idea what grief I've suffered for her sake. I've asked for nothing. Nothing! What do I get in return? Rebellion and contempt."

After a thick silence, Wyatt spoke. "Maybe we're being too hard on her."

Kathryn's eyes narrowed. "Excuse me? Too hard?"

"I just—"

"What's wrong with you, Wyatt? If anything I've lightened up too much! Despite rearing her to stay on the narrow way, she's chosen the lusts of the flesh. That's why she went behind my back. She knew better than to sneak around, and she still disobeyed me. Who knows how long this has been stewing in her."

Kathryn continued her tirade, steaming. "She's been deceived into believing a lie about herself. She's forgotten who she is. I'm losing her! I have to stop her before she does something even more foolish."

She cast him an angry glare, knowing it wasn't his fault but at the moment she wasn't in the mood to quibble about details. It was both of their fault. All of their fault. The whole world seemed to be coming down around her.

"What if she actually tries to do it, Wyatt?"

"She won't, su—"

"What if she tries to get into town? Says the wrong thing? There's no telling what Zeke will do. You know as well as I do that if the wrong people find out how we got her, Zeke could go to prison. He won't allow that to happen. You know what he's capable of doing."

His silence confirmed the truth of her words.

"I have to deal with this," Kathryn said, pacing again. "I let her go down this path, and now I have to bring her back."

The proper course of action hit her then, like a whisper from heaven, and she stopped, staring out at the lake. A calm edged into her mind, like the still waters before her. That was it, wasn't it? You put new wine into a rotten vessel and it only rots the new wine.

Eden's vessel had been corrupted.

"A rebellious spirit is spoiling Eden." She spoke with biting certainty now. "It's like a poisonous weed working its way into her heart and there's only one way to deal with a weed. You have to rip it out by the roots and burn it. And that's exactly what I'm going to do. I'm going to save my little girl before it's too late."

Kathryn turned on her heel and headed toward the house. Wyatt made no attempt to follow her, and neither should he. She was the one who'd birthed her. She was the one who would now offer her rebirth.

She climbed the porch stairs, entered the house, and marched into the kitchen. She found the scissors in the drawer by the sink, crossed the living room, and turned down the narrow hall that ended at Eden's room.

Without pausing to knock, she twisted the knob and pushed the door open.

Eden sat motionless in a chair across the room. She stared straight ahead, her face as expressionless as stone. Still, Kathryn could feel that poisonous spirit lurking behind those eyes, quietly mocking her.

Kathryn walked into the room and stopped at the foot of the bed. Eden slowly turned and looked at her, face still stone. She held her daughter's stare and straightened, chin up.

"You've violated my trust, Eden," she said. "Not only have you sinned against me and Zeke, you've rebelled against God. And like a Jezebel, you lured Paul into sin. And I've come to realize why."

Eden showed no emotion.

"I remember what it was like to be eighteen, to be tempted by the ways of the world and all it has to offer. I know how it feels to get swept off your feet by the promise of love. But it's an empty promise. You cannot serve the flesh and the spirit at the same time. They're at war with one another and you will be lost if you choose the flesh. I won't let that happen."

She took a step toward Eden. "Stand up, sweetheart."

Eden looked at the scissors in Kathryn's hand.

"I said stand up. You will listen to your mother. I won't have any more of your foolishness."

For a moment Eden did nothing, then she slowly rose to her feet.

Kathryn smiled and ran her thumb across Eden's cheek. "The light is shining in you. We simply have to get everything else out of the way so it can burn bright."

She took Eden's hand and led her to the bedside. "If your left hand causes you to stray, you must cut it off. If your right eye makes you sin, you must gouge it out. It's better to enter life maimed than to be thrown into hellfire with both hands or eyes."

She released Eden. "Kneel."

Eden eased to her knees and planted both elbows on the mattress.

Kathryn kneeled behind her and removed the rubber band holding Eden's ponytail in place. Her hair cascaded over her shoulders, beautiful and smooth, and Kathryn gently combed the tangles out with her fingers.

"To destroy the works of the flesh, we must separate you from them." She brought the scissors to Eden's hair just behind her right ear.

"You must come out from among the world of sin and death."

With a metallic snip, the razor-sharp blades sliced through her hair. It fell onto the back of Eden's legs.

"Until you repent and change your behavior, no food will touch your lips. You will have only water and the bread of God's discipline."

A second cut. The hair drifted to the floor.

"You will not be allowed to bathe or wash as a reminder that the stench of sin clings to you as long as you are rebellious."

Snip.

"You will not have the comfort of your mother, neither my tender words, nor my gentle guidance."

Snip.

"You will be outcast. No one will speak to you and neither will you speak to anyone."

Snip.

"You are confined to your closet for the next seven days, from the time the sun rises until it sets. You will not leave your room for the next twenty-one days."

Snip.

"You will not lay eyes on or speak to any boy for a year."

The scissors made the final cut and the last, thick strands of hair fell loose to the ground and scattered.

"So be it."

Kathryn leaned close until her lips were next to Eden's ear. "Your beauty is taken from you, Eden. You have whored yourself out to sin and you will be a vile thing in my sight until you repent. You will not be my angel because you cannot be. You will be my demon, a twisted thorn in my flesh sent to torment me until the day you turn from your sin."

Kathryn set the scissors on the bed and rose to her feet. "Rise," she said.

Eden pushed to her feet.

"Turn around so I can see you."

Eden turned slowly and met Kathryn's gaze. Tears pooled in Eden's eyes. Seeing her daughter like this, stripped of her innocence and beauty, Kathryn's own heart cracked. However hard this was, it was the only way.

"This is what a fall from grace feels like," Kathryn said. "This is the price of your sin. Ask yourself if it was worth it. Do not be deceived, God cannot be mocked and neither can I. You're only reaping what you've sown, Eden. You brought this on yourself. You did this, no one else."

Kathryn took a step back. "From this moment forward, you will be cut off from life until you repent. When you're ready, you let me know. And so you know, the phone is no longer functional. There will be no contact to or from the house by anyone until you've come to your repentance."

Eden wasn't permitted to use the phone, even when it was working, but Zeke had been very clear: any sign that Eden could not be trusted and the phone had to be cut.

Kathryn walked toward the dresser that sat against the wall and gathered Eden's collection of straw dolls.

"My dolls?" Eden said.

"Not anymore. It's time to set aside childish ways. You want to be an adult and so I'm helping you become one. We have to sever all of your old ties to this world so you can be free."

"What are you going to do with them?"

"The same thing we're going to do with your hair. Burn them," Kathryn said. "Now gather up those clippings and place them by the door. I'll be back to get them in an hour."

I CAN'T rightly describe the darkness that swallowed me in the day
and a half following Kathryn's punishment.

A small voice somewhere in the back of my mind kept telling me
to repent. Kathryn had endlessly drilled the idea into me over the years.
I needed to change my behavior and be more pure.

Repent, Eden. Repent.

*Change your behavior. Breathe and let it go. Just do what's expected of you and
all would be fine. After all, weren't you reasonably content when you didn't rock the
boat?*

Wasn't life bearable before you decided to step out of the boat?

But the voices of offense screaming through my head made that
tiny whisper nothing more than an absurdity. And hadn't my dreams of
Outlaw shown me that I was my own person who didn't need to suffer
my fears?

A shift had occurred in my psyche. I know what had happened—I'd
run through it a hundred times as I lay in bed, staring at the ceiling with
a fixed jaw. I was finally seeing the light. The dam that had held back a
lake of dark waters had finally collapsed and truth was pouring out like
a torrential waterfall. Why walk on the waters of that lake? Better to
drain it. Why?

Because I was being abused, that's why.

Because I was the victim of a monster, that's why.

Because I was a prisoner in my own room, but Kathryn might as well have put me in a dungeon deep under the house, hidden away from the rest of the world. I was nothing more than her slave, her precious lamb, her sacrificial offering to be used for her gain.

Five years of being abused had secretly filled me with an ocean of bitterness and anger and it was all gushing out, fueled by the realization that I was right.

She'd walked in shortly after I'd stood up to her on Monday and she'd announced her rules as only Mother could, with complete sincerity and conviction, fully embracing her own delusion. Odd, how it was all so plain to me after so many years of living in deception. Someone had turned on the light and I could see everything clearly for the first time. I'd been blind, but now I could see.

Kathryn was insane, if not naturally, then in Zeke's manipulative grasp. I knew it as she hacked off my hair. As she laid down her list of rules: No eating, no speaking, no washing, no hair, no leaving my room. No boys, ever. A year, she'd said, and to me that was forever.

True to her word, Kathryn had delivered only water to my room, three times in a large pitcher since issuing my new sentence. I hadn't seen Wyatt or Bobby, and I hadn't bothered to face my mother when she'd come in with the water, which she left on the floor by the door next to a pot in which I relieved myself.

I was in prison forever. My room was my eternal hell and I hated it as much as I hated my mother. I hated her for hacking off my hair and making me ugly. I hated her for kidnapping me five years earlier. I hated her for being so weak. I hated her for burning my dolls.

You don't hate her, Eden.

But I did. And that hatred only seemed to grow with each passing hour. I even gave up praying. Had God ever heard me before? I had said the sinner's prayer and begged his forgiveness and sworn my allegiance over and over, thousands of times over the years. I had made myself pure and followed his servant's every rule and committed myself fully to being pure, and where had it put me?

In hell. God, my Father in heaven, was either angry with me or didn't care, or he was deaf. This after I'd done everything asked of me.

Everything!

If she thought I would cave in and play her insane game, she had another thing coming. Her punishment had backfired.

By Tuesday evening, my grievance toward her was so great, I thought I might die of anger, lying right there on my bed. She wanted to starve me, right? Well I would do one better. I would just die of rage. Her perfect, sacrificial lamb would pay the ultimate price to save them all from their miserable hells.

That's when I decided I would run away. Yes, I know that I'd decided the same thing five years earlier and then rejected it for Bobby's sake, but I decided it again, and this time I knew how I would do it.

By the time Kathryn came in with my pitcher of night water Tuesday night, it was all I could think about.

"Good night, sweetheart," she said.

They were her first words to me in a day and a half, spoken with empathy, as if trying to seduce me into feeling guilty. She wasn't going to succeed. But I wanted to give her some hope so she would sleep while I escaped.

"Good night," I said, not bothering to turn to her.

A moment later I heard the door close.

I was an adult now and I was going to be free. And I was going to be free that very night. Nothing else mattered to me anymore. I was going, I was going, I was going, and that was that.

But I had to be smart or I was going nowhere. And I had to take Bobby with me.

The next six hours crawled by like a snail inching across my wall. Only after the house had been completely quiet for two hours did I slowly crawl out of bed and stand up.

Even then I waited for several long minutes, listening for any sound. The house remained silent.

Desperately hoping that I was the only one awake, I crept to the door, still dressed in my bed clothes. I didn't want to risk any more movement than I needed, and proper dress wasn't important. Only getting away was. Once I reached the police, I could worry about clothes.

I cracked the door open, listened for another second. If Kathryn woke up and caught me now, I would tell her that I was going to get her to beg her forgiveness—that's what I'd worked out. Once outside that excuse wouldn't work.

Heart thumping in my ears, I sneaked into the hall on my tiptoes, then crossed to Bobby's room.

His door creaked when I opened it, but only one squeak, and no one called out. I eased the door shut and listened again.

Okay . . . Okay, you can do this, Eden. You have to do this.

Bobby snored softly in his bed, mouth ajar, neck stretched at an odd angle. I bent over and gently tapped his shoulder.

He snored on, lost in his dreams. So I shook him and this time his eyes snapped wide.

"Sh . . ." I held a finger to my mouth.

"Eden?"

He'd said it aloud, albeit in a soft voice. I clamped my hand over his mouth, twisting toward the closed door. No sign he'd been heard.

I spun back to Bobby. "Sh, sh, sh . . . Don't say anything."

His round eyes stared up at me, but he remained silent.

"Come with me outside," I whispered. "But don't make any sound, okay?"

"Outside?"

"Yes."

"We're going outside?"

"Yes. But we have to sneak out or the alligators will hear us coming."

"We're going to hunt alligators?" His eyes brightened.

"Sh . . . You have to whisper. It's a special mission. Just come with me. Walk on your tiptoes, okay?"

He jerked up enthusiastically—this was Bobby's way, throwing himself into any adventure with all of his heart.

"Sh . . . Slowly, Bobby. We can't make a sound."

He looked at the door, the floor, then up into my eyes. "I can walk like a ghost," he said.

"Good. Like a ghost. Come on."

I crossed to the door, eased it ever so slowly open, poked my head out into the hall, and, seeing no one, waved Bobby forward.

He crept past me, walking on his tiptoes, bent over and intent. Glanced back at me once out in the hall. I nodded and motioned him on. Then followed him out into the living room, to the front door, where I stopped him.

We were making it! There was no sound, no sign at all that Kathryn had woken up.

But it was there that the first hitch presented itself. Next to the door, the nail from which Wyatt's truck keys typically hung was bare. My heart lurched.

I spun toward the kitchen counter. Nothing. The table, the coffee table—there was no sign of the keys that I could see by the dim moonlight. And I didn't dare turn on any lights.

My pulse was racing and I couldn't think straight. I'd been sure that Kathryn wouldn't feel the need to hide the keys—I didn't know how to drive. Maybe Wyatt had inadvertently left them somewhere else. Or maybe Kathryn had thought ahead of me.

"Do you need a gun?" Bobby whispered, leaning close.

"No. I need the keys to Wyatt's truck."

He looked around. "Wyatt's going with—"

I put a finger on his lips and hushed him, hopes dashed. "We have to find the keys!"

The thought of remaining in that house even one more minute was too much for me to bear. I had to get out.

I pulled Bobby forward, carefully unlocked and opened the front door, and quietly stepped out onto the front porch. Bobby followed me, down the steps and out onto the driveway. We were out.

But we didn't have the keys.

"Is Wyatt hunting alligators too?" Bobby said.

"Sh! No one can hear us."

"Sorry, Eden."

"No . . . No, Wyatt's not coming. We have to go into town."

"Into town?" His eyes were as round as the moon. "How are we going into town?"

"With the truck."

"You know how to drive the truck?"

"No. But you do, Bobby."

Bobby had bragged on numerous occasions that Wyatt was giving him lessons on how to drive. I knew that these lessons consisted of nothing more than talking as they drove around, but that was far more instruction than I had. Our trip to sign the papers at the lawyer's office had been my first drive in any vehicle since coming.

"I do?" Bobby said.

"I've never watched Wyatt, but you have. You're going to tell me how."

"I am?"

"Yes. But we need the keys."

"I don't have the keys."

My mind raced. Where could he have put the keys? In the bedroom? If so, I would be hard pressed to get to them. Maybe he had an extra one somewhere.

"Does he keep a key in the truck?"

Bobby looked in the direction of the old truck, fifty yards from us, near the shack. "I don't know. I don't think so."

"How about in the shed? Or in the still house?"

He shrugged, doing that flicking thing he did with his thumb and forefinger. "We can ask Wyatt," he said.

"No. Wyatt can't know."

"Why not?"

"Because this is a surprise."

My mind was racing. Trying to drive the truck was going to be hard enough, but walking out would be nearly impossible. The dogs would give us away or attack us. If Kathryn discovered me now things would get even worse.

"We have to find the keys!" I snapped, now near a panic.

A plop at my feet startled and I spun, immediately thinking: frog or snake. But it wasn't a reptile. It was Wyatt's truck keys. Right there, on the ground a yard from me. How . . .

I spun back to the porch and saw how. Wyatt stood on the porch, watching us. A chill washed over me. We were caught! At any moment Kathryn would fill the open doorway behind him, wearing a scowl.

Only then did I realize that Wyatt didn't appear to be upset. He stared at me, wearing a sad face, arms loose at his sides. For several long seconds, neither of us moved.

He wasn't trying to stop me. And he'd just thrown us the keys.

With a single nod, he suddenly turned, stepped back into the house, and closed the door behind him.

I stared up at the porch, stunned by what I'd just seen. He was helping me. In his own way, he was telling me to leave. He didn't have the courage to actually drive me away and he had to get back to bed before Kathryn woke up, but he was doing his best to help me, even if it meant that everything might go badly for him. At least this way, he could say I must have found the keys and gone on my own. That would be harder if he got caught helping us.

Either way he was helping me and that froze me up. How could I do this to Wyatt? If I went to the police, they might send him to prison—that's what Mother had said.

Run, Eden. Run now!

I bent down, scooped up the keys, and ran. "Hurry!" I whispered.

Bobby tore after me, stumbling with an uneasy gait.

I reached the truck, threw the door open and jumped into the front seat, with Bobby panting by my left side, staring in through the open door. Now what?

"Get in, Bobby! The other side."

I glanced back at the house as he hurried around the front of the truck. The porch was empty. But if Kathryn had woken, she would be out any moment.

Bobby slid into the front seat next to me.

I searched eagerly for the key hole in the darkness. "Where does it go?"

"There!" Bobby pointed a stubby finger at the column under the steering wheel.

Now . . . I wasn't totally clueless as to how vehicles worked, naturally. I had six months of memory before being taken by Wyatt—but I was too young and too busy learning other things to have paid much attention to the precise mechanics of driving. And trucks weren't the same as cars.

But I had some general ideas. Like inserting a key and twisting it to start the engine.

So that's what I did.

The motor cranked and the truck lurched forward and I let out a little yelp.

"You have to push the clutch in," Bobby said excitedly, pointing to the floor.

I stared at the three pedals at my feet, all within fairly easy reach.

"The clutch? Which one?"

"That one," he fairly yelled.

"Not so loud, Bobby!" I whispered.

"Sorry. That one."

I put my left foot on "that one" and pressed it to the floor.

"Now start it?"

"Yes."

This time the engine cranked over a couple times and rumbled to life. Beside me, Bobby beamed, as if he himself had brought the truck to life. Ahead of me, the gravel driveway stretched into the night like a long gray snake.

"Now what?"

"Now you press the gas and go."

"Which one?"

He hopped off the seat and reached down by my feet as if to do it by hand for himself. "This one!"

"Okay, get up, Bobby. You can't help me down there!"

"That one!" he said, pointing and climbing up.

"Just press it? What about my left foot?"

"You have to let the clutch out. If you let it out too quick, it will stop."

"That's how you stop?"

"Yes. But you have to use the other brake to stop."

I stared at him, deciphering his speech. Then at my feet. The third pedal was clearly the brake. I thought I had the general gist of it.

"Okay. Hold on."

The truck did exactly what Bobby said it would on my first try. It jerked to a stop.

"You did it too quick," Bobby said, smiling wide. To him, our night ride was only another grand adventure.

I tried again, and this time we started rolling forward and gained speed. Too much speed, I thought, and we were pointed at an angle that would take us into the swamp fifty yards ahead.

"What now! What now!"

"Now steer!" he said, pointing ahead. "You have to stay on the road. You have to steer."

He grabbed the steering wheel to show me how.

"You have to—"

"Let go, Bobby!" He released his grip.

I turned the wheel back and forth and was rewarded with a redirecting of the truck. It came to me quickly and I managed to put it down the center of the road. But the engine was roaring loudly, far louder than I knew it should sound.

Only then did it occur to me that I had the gas pedal pushed all the way down, so I eased my foot off the pedal and we slowed.

"You have to turn on the lights," Bobby said.

"Where?"

"Here." He reached forward and pulled a switch. Light flooded the road in front of us.

For a few seconds, neither of spoke. We were driving. With the doors still wide open, and slowly, but down the road.

"We're doing it," I said.

"Eden's driving!" he hooted.

"Is anyone behind us?"

Bobby turned and peered through the back window.

"No."

We were getting away! There was still Zeke's house up on the left and his dogs, but they couldn't hurt us in the truck.

"Close your door, Bobby."

We both did. And then we were driving down the middle of the road, away from Kathryn, toward civilization. Just like that. It had all seemed too easy. And yet . . . here we were. So maybe God had answered my prayers after all.

My plan was simple. I would drive out onto the main road, stop the first person we saw, and tell them to take me to the police. That's all. And that was enough.

"You have to change gears to go faster," Bobby said.

"I don't want to go faster."

"You're in first gear."

"First gear is fast enough."

We drove like that, silent for a while, right up the road, right past Zeke's house, right past the barking dogs who chased the truck for a little while before being left in our dust.

"You're a good driver, Eden."

"You're a good teacher, Bobby." I smiled.

"I don't like the dogs," he said.

"I don't like them either. But they can't hurt us now."

We were going to make it. We were actually going to get away from the compound. A hundred thoughts crowded my mind. What about Wyatt? What would Kathryn do when she found out I'd escaped? How would I explain myself to the police? What if they didn't believe my story? How much should I tell them? Where would Bobby and I live? How would I get the money? What would I do with the money?

Was what I was doing wrong?

I bit my fingernail and chased that last thought away as we rolled on, seemingly forever. Even if going was wrong, I would find a way to live with it, because I could no longer live as Mother's precious lamb.

The road was long, as straight as an arrow, and, at this time of the night, empty except for us, which is exactly what I'd hoped.

And then suddenly it wasn't straight; it came to an intersection directly ahead of us. And it wasn't empty; there was another truck parked across the road, blocking that intersection. A dirty white truck with big, thick tires, covered in rust.

My heart jumped into my throat.

"That's Claude's truck," Bobby said. He looked over at me. "Is he coming with us?"

"Who's Claude?"

"He's Zeke's friend."

I shifted my foot and slammed down the brake pedal. Our truck slid to a jerking stop and the engine died, less than twenty yards from Claude's truck. Zeke's friend, which meant he was here to stop us. I couldn't breathe.

"You have to press the clutch," Bobby said, pointing at the floorboard again.

I searched the road on either side of the truck, thinking through a full-fledged panic. There was room to get by on the right, maybe. I might scrape the other truck, but I might get by. I might still be able to find a way.

But before I could piece together the mechanics of restarting the truck and forcing it past Claude's, a bright light filled the cab. It came through the back window and I knew before I twisted around that Zeke was behind us.

"Is Zeke going to help us?" Bobby asked, staring back.

No, I thought. No, Zeke's going to hurt us.

I SAT frozen to stone in the truck next to Bobby, who stared wide-eyed at Zeke's truck, then at the white truck in front of us. My veins were ice. My head throbbed. I couldn't move.

But my mind was moving, filling me with images of Paul's beaten face and Zeke's dark glare. It didn't stop to consider how they'd found out I was trying to escape, only that they had and now I was going to suffer the same fate as Paul, or worse. Surely worse.

And then my mind wasn't so much thinking as commanding without thought, reacting out of pure survival instinct.

I grabbed at the key and twisted it hard. The truck jerked and I shoved down the clutch and twisted the key again. The engine tried to start and then fired and the moment that roar filled my ears, I slammed my foot down on the gas and released the clutch, twisting the wheel as far as I could to my right, because I had to get past that white truck, see?

I had to escape now or I was going die.

We surged forward, jerking, and I turned the wheel harder. The lights illuminated a deep ditch to the right of the white truck and it struck me that we might go straight into that ditch, so I yanked the wheel to the left a little, but by that time we had covered the distance to Claude's truck—we were going to hit it!

Again without thinking through it, I pulled my foot off the gas and somehow managed to cram down the brake.

And then we smashed into the front of Claude's truck and came to an abrupt halt.

The engine ticked and hissed.

"You hit Claude's truck," Bobby said.

The engine ground to a stop.

There were two men in Claude's truck, both just looking back at me, uncaring it seemed, that I'd just hit them. I twisted back and looked at Zeke's black truck, expecting to see his tall form stalking toward us. But no one got out—the truck just sat there like a demon panther, lights glaring.

For a few seconds nothing happened, but even that silence seemed to be screaming at me, telling me that I was nothing that could possibly threaten or escape from these men. I was only a slightly annoying gnat that could be easily crushed.

One of the men in the white truck lifted a cell phone to his ear, spoke for a few seconds, then put it away. He pushed open his door, climbed out and walked toward me.

Opened my door, grinning.

"It was a mistake, Claude," Bobby said in a thin voice. "Are you going to hurt us?"

The man was skinny, with messy red hair and a long tangled beard. His fingernails were dirty as were his plaid shirt and his blue pants.

"No, Bobby. I'm not." He looked at me and his grin flattened. "You hit my truck."

"It was a mistake," Bobby said.

"Shut up!" Eyes back on me, glaring now. "Scoot over. I'm taking you back to where you belong."

I wanted to scoot. I should have scooted. But the thought of going back to Kathryn had turned my muscles to paste.

"Move!"

I moved. Quickly, then, panicked.

Claude climbed in, started the truck, shoved the gear shifter all the way back, and backed away from the white truck, which was turning around, driven by the other man, who slid over to take the wheel.

It was Zeke that I was more concerned with, but he was turning his black truck around, then heading back in the direction we'd come from. By the time Claude got our truck turned, I could only see the taillights of Zeke's black truck. He'd left us in Claude's care, as if totally unconcerned.

But that couldn't be true. Of all the possible scenarios I'd imagined during my planning, being found out by Zeke himself was the worst. I sat in the seat next to Claude, hands folded in my lap, hardly daring to breathe. My palms were sweaty and my face was cold. I felt like what a corpse must feel like, ten feet under the ground.

The white truck was following us.

Beside me, Claude chuckled.

"My, my, my, you have gone and done it now, haven't you?" He shook his head. "Not too smart."

"My dad helped us," Bobby said. "He gave Eden the keys."

Claude cast a side-glance at us. "He did, now did he? Even dumber."

I wanted to defend Wyatt, I really did. But my voice wasn't working and I didn't know what to say.

How much Claude knew was beyond me. I wasn't even sure he was aware of who I was, other than Kathryn's daughter. But I couldn't help feeling like he was part of a bigger plan that I'd been kept in the dark about all these years. Like maybe getting my money.

"You really did piss him off. I wouldn't want to be in your shoes, I can tell you that much."

The same road that had taken us much longer to travel stuck in first gear, now flew by. The dogs barked as we sped past Zeke's house. And before I could fully process what had just happened, we skidded to a stop in front of our house.

"Are you going to hit us?" Bobby asked, face drooping.

"Get out," Claude snapped.

We both climbed out.

"Get in the house."

Without waiting for us, he marched up to the porch, rapped his knuckles on the front door, and yanked it open. "Kathryn! Get your sorry butt out here!"

He'd told us to get in the house but he was blocking the front door and all I could think was, *Kathryn's going to see me standing outside. She's going to catch me. I'm in terrible trouble.*

I could see Kathryn stumbling out of the hallway in her night dress, eyes wide.

"What's going on? What on earth are you doing here?"

"Zeke wants to see you," Claude said. "That's what's happening."

"Now?"

"Yes, now. Why else would I be here in the middle of the night?"

Wyatt appeared behind Kathryn, buttoning up his pants. I didn't think Kathryn had seen me or Bobby yet.

"Why?" she demanded.

"Why? Because your rat made a run for it, that's why. Now get your butts down there, both of you. He's waiting and he ain't happy. Don't bother dressing."

With that, Claude stepped aside, brushed past me, and headed toward the white truck which had pulled in behind us.

Kathryn could see me now, that much I knew. But I couldn't bring myself to look at her face. I couldn't bear to see her accusing eyes boring though me.

It took a few seconds, but she finally spoke, and the low, biting tone of her voice did the job plenty well, anyway.

"What have you done to us?"

"I showed Eden how to drive the truck," Bobby said, stepping up beside me.

Mother shoved her arm back into the house. "Get back in your room this instant, you little runt!"

Bobby scurried up the steps, ducked into the house, and vanished into the hall. I started to follow, eager to get away from her.

"Not you," she snapped.

I finally found the courage to look her in the eyes and they were as fired as I could remember seeing. She glanced at Wyatt's truck, then found me again.

"Where did you think you were going?"

What was I supposed to say?

"Answer me!" she screamed.

"Away from you," I said.

She blinked. I could see her jaw flex. I knew that hitting her in the face would be kinder than the words I'd just spoken, but I was done with not telling the truth. So I said some more.

"I don't want to be your slave anymore."

My mother stepped forward, trembling. She lifted her arm and pointed a finger back into the house. "You get back in that closet this very instant and you get down on your knees and you start begging God for mercy and you don't stop until you have accepted the full weight of your repentance. Go! Now, before God strikes you down where you stand, you hear me?"

I looked at Wyatt who was dressed—maybe he knew this was going to happen the moment he heard Claude's voice. He certainly knew that I was in trouble and his eyes showed me great empathy.

But that look gave me the courage I needed to set my jaw, step up onto the porch, and walk past Kathryn into the house.

I knew that I was done. That I was going to face a new kind of hell. But I also knew that I wasn't going to get down on my knees and repent for trying to run away from a monster.

Not this time. Not ever again.

THE NIGHT was hot and the air heavy, but something far more threatening suffocated Kathryn as Wyatt guided the truck down the gravel road.

Dread.

"How dare she?" Kathryn breathed through gritted teeth. "How *dare* she do this to me!"

Wyatt stared out the windshield, silent.

"Why? How dare she?"

Tears gathered in her eyes. Every stitch and seam that held her life together seemed to be unraveling.

Zeke was waiting. Dear God . . .

"There'll be hell to pay for this," she said. "Hell to pay for all of us."

Kathryn's mind spun. "How'd she get the truck? It doesn't make sense. I told you to keep your keys in the nightstand. How could she have gotten her hands on those keys?"

Wyatt kept his eyes straight ahead.

"Answer me! Don't just sit there like a wart. Say something."

He glanced at her nervously.

"Don't you dare tell me you knew about this."

"No. No, of course not."

"We're all in a world of trouble here. How'd Bobby show her how to drive? He can't drive."

Wyatt shrugged. "I showed him a few things."

"If you know anything, it's gonna come out. Zeke will know. You realize that, don't you?"

He began to speak, then stopped.

"What? Spit it out."

"I can't remember what I did with the keys. Maybe I left them on the kitchen counter by mistake."

"Maybe?"

"I'm sorry, sugar. If I'd known . . ."

"Shut up, Wyatt! Just shut up!"

He offered no response.

"All that matters now is that I failed. Zeke told me there would be consequences if she ever got out of line."

"We'll talk to Zeke and he'll understand—"

"You think Zeke called us to his house to have a conversation? Eden tried to leave us, for heaven's sake! She meant to find that judge and tear up the power of attorney. She betrayed him!"

The turn into Zeke's was just ahead. She stared at the moonless night beyond the window.

"There's gonna be hell to pay, I swear."

Wyatt pulled into Zeke's compound and brought the truck to a stop. Claude leaned against a pillar on the porch, watching them as they climbed out of the truck and made their way to the front door.

Claude pushed the door open. "He's waiting in the study."

The study. Judgment was in the air and there was no running from it.

She cinched her night robe tight, entered the house, and angled toward Zeke's office to the left of the living room. Through the door she could see him sitting at his desk.

They entered the study without a word, followed by Claude, who stopped at the doorway, arms crossed.

Zeke's piercing stare was as dark as midnight and for several seconds he simply studied them. She felt naked, stripped to the bone, nothing more than a desperate failure. The bitter disappointment on his face said everything.

"Sit." He nodded to the two leather chairs opposite him, watching them from his black, high-back chair, whisky glass cradled in his hand.

Kathryn eased into a chair and Wyatt began to take the seat beside her.

"Not you," Zeke said.

Wyatt stood upright, confused for a moment. "Sure, Zeke."

Zeke tilted his glass and took a drink. "Why'd you give her the keys, Wyatt?"

Wyatt stood stock-still, like an animal trapped in a cage.

"Do you take me for a fool?"

"No, Zeke. Of course not."

"No. Of course not. Stupid, Wyatt. Very stupid."

"I . . ."

"Like that boy of yours. But at least he's honest. He must get his backbone from his mother."

Kathryn's pulse drummed in her ears.

"You gave Eden the truck keys and walked away. Unless Bobby's lying, in which case I would have to punish him. You know how I hate liars."

Wyatt's hand began to quiver at his side. "Bobby's an innocent boy."

"You're right, Bobby wouldn't know duplicity if it smacked him in the mouth. Tell me Wyatt, are you duplicitous?"

Wyatt shifted on his feet.

"It means two-faced, double-dealing," Zeke said. "Deceitful. Or is that not a clear concept in that thick skull of yours?"

"No," Wyatt said quietly.

"No what?"

"No . . ." A tremor had taken to his voice. "I mean . . . Yes."

"Yes what?"

"Yes. I understand."

"Understand what, Wyatt?"

He hesitated. "That I was deceitful."

His eyes, guilty as sin, flitted to Kathryn, then darted back to Zeke. She felt the room begin to close around her. Wyatt had betrayed her too. The whole world had turned against her.

"Why did you defy me, Wyatt?"

"I'm sorry . . . I wasn't thinking."

"No, you weren't. And unfortunately I can't allow people who don't know how to think to remain with me in an hour like this." He drilled Wyatt with an uncompromising stare. "I'm sending you away."

Wyatt blinked, dumb, face white. Blinked again.

"You understand I have no choice, don't you?"

"Yes."

"Whether or not I ever allow you to return to Bobby will depend on how you conduct yourself these next thirty days. Do you understand?"

"Yes, Zeke." He cleared his throat. "Thirty days."

Kathryn could see the beads of sweat on his forehead, but her mind was on her own head. If this was Wyatt's sentence, what would be hers? Dear God, it was all falling apart. All of it!

"Well, now, I can't have a traitor around while we reap our blessing, now can I?"

Their blessing, Kathryn thought. Eden's money. It was Zeke's fixation as much as their obedience.

She kept her eyes on Zeke, now unnerved by any impulse to look at Wyatt—it would constitute some kind of betrayal of Zeke. She couldn't allow herself sympathy. Not now. But she didn't have to look at him to know that he was shrinking and for that she couldn't help but to feel strangely conflicted.

Zeke glanced at the door. "Show him out."

Claude stepped forward, took Wyatt by the arm, and pulled him way.

Hot tears blurred Kathryn's eyes as the front door thumped shut. She was alone now. Alone with Zeke.

Zeke took a long breath and let it out slowly. A heavy blanket of silence settled over them. He gently tapped the desk with his fingertips, eyes cutting so deep she felt her very soul being severed in two.

But this was his way, wasn't it? A good and righteous and pure way, deeply dividing the truth like a sword. Bone and marrow.

"You disappoint me, Kathryn."

"Forgive me, Zeke." The words came out in a half sob. "Please. I didn't know . . . I did what you asked. She didn't know she could—"

"Shut up, Kathryn."

"Yes, Zeke."

"The issue has nothing to do with what you did or didn't know. The issue is Eden. And here I was so sure that you'd brought her up in the ways of truth. Now I see you have a slut for a daughter."

He was right. She couldn't possibly offer any defense. There was nothing to be said. He let the statement stand and continued to tap the desk with the tips of his fingers.

Only when she didn't think she could bear his dark gaze a moment longer did he shift it to the wall behind her.

"Like a shepherd I watch over the sheep that God has entrusted to me. Tell me that I haven't cared for you, Kathryn."

"Yes, Zeke, you've cared for me."

"That I haven't been merciful to you in every conceivable way."

"Your mercy knows no bounds."

"That you don't owe your own life to me."

"I do. All of it."

He looked into her eyes again.

"That Eden and everything she is belongs to me."

"She's yours. Your lamb. Your gift to me and I am so grateful."

"And yet this is how you treat me? What have I ever asked in return for what I've given you?"

"Nothing."

"Wrong. Not nothing. What is the one thing I ask of you?"

She hesitated only a moment. "Love."

"That's right, love. And how will I know whether or not my flock loves me?"

"By their obedience."

"Good girl. And as obedience brings the blessing, rebellion brings the curse, and, with it, judgment."

"Yes, Zeke."

"You are the people of my pasture, the sheep of my flock, and I am your good shepherd. Who knows what's best for you?"

"You do, Zeke."

"And who knows what's best for Eden?"

She swallowed hard. "You do."

"You've allowed her to forget who she is. She's proven herself a stray sheep prone to wandering. One of these days she just might wander too close to the cliff and bring us all down with her."

"I'll do anything."

"Yes. You will."

"Just tell me what to do. Anything, I promise. This won't happen again."

"No it won't, Kathryn. It won't because you're going to teach that stray lamb not to wander from the fold."

"I will. I swear I will!"

"Just like a good shepherd teaches any precious lamb."

"Yes, just like that. Just like a good shepherd. Tell me, Zeke. Just tell me what I have to do."

He picked up his tumbler and drained the last of his whisky. Then set it down and slowly turned it with his thumb and forefinger, as if it was a delicate crystal.

"I want you to break one of Eden's legs."

EPISODE FOUR

Charleston, SC

CLOUDS THE color of cast iron hung low over the restless ocean and drifted inland. Gentle waves stretched up the beach, splashing over Special Agent Olivia Strauss's bare feet as she jogged along the water's edge.

C'mon, Liv. Pick up the pace.

The approaching storm had kept the usual crowd of early morning runners off the sugar-white beach. Besides a solitary figure standing fifty yards ahead, Olivia was alone with her thoughts and the rhythmic slap of her feet on wet sand.

Since moving here to supervise the Charleston field office, running was her daily therapy, the one place that put life's madness into perspective. It would take more than a summer storm to keep her from it.

Olivia's eyes were drawn to the man standing motionless on the shore. Something was curious about him, she thought. She slowed her stride.

She'd jogged this stretch of beach every morning for the past six months and knew the regulars well—the joggers, the fishermen, the retired couple that rose before dawn to search the sands with metal detectors in hand.

He didn't carry himself like a tourist, which she could easily spot. Yet, he seemed strangely familiar.

The man looked out to sea with his arms by his sides, the sea breeze lifting his dark hair. Even in the dull, gray light of morning she could see he was barefoot. He wore dark jeans and a stark white T-shirt that stretched taut over his muscular frame. Behind him, a pair of black biker boots lay in the sand just beyond the tide's reach.

She settled to a walk ten feet to his right. Did she know this man?

"Hello, Olivia."

She stopped. He knew her?

The man turned. Staring back was a face she'd thought about countless times over the years. She blinked twice, half expecting him to vanish. But he didn't.

"Stephen? Is that you?"

He walked toward her, eyes as gentle and strong as she remembered them. How long had it been? Four years? No, five. Five years since Stephen had shown up and spoken life into her shriveled soul.

Five years since she'd lost Alice Ringwald and unexpectedly found herself along the way.

Stephen stopped in front of her, smiling. "You look well."

"How'd you find me?"

"You run every morning, don't you?"

He studied her for a silent stretch. "I see you've found some peace. Light in your eyes."

"I never got a chance to thank you. What you said that day . . ." She drew a breath. "It changed my life."

"We all play our roles. One person plants the seed, another waters it, but it grows only when the season is right."

His words soaked into her like the radiant warmth of the sun. But there was something else—a distant look of deep concern in his eyes.

"What are you doing here?" she said.

"Keeping a promise I made to you. But you already knew that, didn't you?"

"Alice Ringwald?" she said.

He nodded once. "I said I would tell you if I ever learned anything new."

The image of the young girl still haunted Olivia. Even years after the case had gone cold, she believed Alice was out there somewhere, terrified and waiting for someone to come.

"She's alive, Olivia."

The world seemed to still around her.

"You're sure? She's alive?"

"For now at least."

"How do you know?"

"Because I spoke to her."

Her pulse quickened. "You found her? When?"

He dipped his head. "A couple of times. This last week."

"Where is she?"

"I don't know."

"What do you mean you don't know? You said you found her."

"I did. In a dream."

A dream? Olivia held his gaze and let the words settle. Coming from anyone else it would have sounded ludicrous, but this was the man who'd told her things about herself that no one else knew. His eyes were unflinching, and there was certainty in them.

"And this . . . dream . . . You're sure it means she's alive?"

"She's alive," he said.

"How do you know it wasn't *just* a dream? What if it was just wishful thinking, a trick of the mind? We both want to find her; we have for a long time. You know as well as I do that the mind sometimes sees what it wants to see. That doesn't make it real."

"The wind blows wherever it wills. How and why is a mystery. It's enough to simply know that it *is*. In the same way, I know that my awareness and hers are somehow connected."

"*How* do you know?"

He shifted his gaze and looked at the horizon again. "A dream called to my mother's heart once. Drew her across the ocean. What she thought she would find and what she actually did were worlds apart. Her story came with great blessing, but also much death. You see? Both life and death were birthed from a dream." He looked back at her. "I *know* because I know.*"

She nodded slowly. "Okay. Then tell me where she is in your dream."

"I'm not sure."

"Yes, but assuming the dream is real, there must be clues to where she is."

"My dreams are of that place where heart calls to heart. Even what I do see may not be a direct reflection of what's outside that heart."

"Is she in danger? That's a matter of the heart, right?"

"Terrible danger."

"And?"

"I believe that she's with her birth mother."

The prevailing theory at the time. So she was right.

"And that's just another dead end. There must be something else. Anything that could at least narrow our search."

"She was standing alone on a lakeshore, in fear of her mother. I came to her in a rowboat—from where I have no clue. There were thick trees covered in stringy moss and the air was tinged with the scent of salt."

Olivia paced as he spoke, mind spinning through the possibilities. "She must be near the coast. Swamp lands near the ocean . . . that describes half of the Gulf coast."

"Or perhaps not. It may only represent something more. What I can tell you for certain is that she's alive, and, wherever she is, she's trapped in a state of great fear and suffering. Truthfully, I may be the only one who can help her find emancipation."

Drizzle began to fall as Olivia worked the problem in her mind. "What about sounds? Traffic? Maybe an airport? Anything that would put her near a landmark that we could use to narrow a search."

He shook his head. "Nothing."

She stopped and faced him. "That's it, then? Nothing but a dream with no helpful details."

"Not nothing. Alice is alive and she's opened up to me. That's something."

"What good is that if we can't get to her?"

His right brow cocked. "But I can. I thought I'd mentioned that."

"Through a dream."

"Exactly."

"Then can't you tell her how to escape in that dream? Tell her to call a number or make a mark on the shore . . . Anything that might help—"

"I can only speak to her heart. What she chooses to do is entirely up to her . . ." He paused. "You must understand . . . there's no guarantee she *will* get out. And even if she does, her freedom may only come at a great price to her or to others."

"What kind of price?"

"I don't know."

She stared at him. "We're helpless then."

"Not helpless, no. We can hope that Alice will find that narrow way to her freedom. You must remember that she's not just any child, Olivia. Not at all."

He was referring to her upbringing in the monastery, a history totally lost to Alice.

"What was it about that monastery?" she asked.

Stephen stared out at the ocean, thinking.

"She was protected from this world. Taught the virtues of love, beauty, and peace in ways very few are. Although she doesn't remember, there's a deep place in Alice that still knows . . . Mountains can be moved, the blind can see, the lame can walk if only one can let go."

"In my experience, the best way to move a mountain is with a bulldozer."

He offered a slight smile. "That would be in your experience. In either case, I doubt Alice has access to a bulldozer at the moment."

Touché.

"And if she can't let go?"

He didn't respond.

The rain fell harder and a peal of thunder shook the sky. "We'll find her," Olivia said, watching the waves.

"I hope you do. But I don't think she's ready yet. She'll only be found when she is. It's why I only met her in my dreams recently."

"Because she wasn't ready."

"I can assure you, it wasn't for a lack of trying on my part."

All this talk of life and death and readiness was such an inverted way of thinking. Offensive even. Wasn't any abducted girl always ready to be rescued?

Yes, yes, of course . . . but Alice wasn't just any girl. And this was all coming from Stephen. She couldn't bring herself to object.

"And it won't be for any lack of trying on my part either," she said. "I'm going to do everything in my power to find her."

"As will I." He dipped his head, gave her a parting smile, and walked to his boots. "As will I."

BREAK HER leg. That's what Zeke had said.

Break her leg. And with those three words Zeke had broken Kathryn's heart.

She'd driven home in Wyatt's truck, mind numb, head ringing. It all made sense, she knew it did, but she wasn't in the place to piece all the scriptures and bits of reasoning together yet. She could only trust in what she knew to be the truth.

And the truth was, Zeke had saved her. He'd led her down the path of righteousness and, when she wasn't righteous enough herself, provided a way for her to be reconciled with God. Eden, the lamb of God, come to take away all of her sin.

And now she had to break Eden's leg so that she couldn't stray and fall off a cliff and bring them all down with her.

So why did it break her heart? Why did the thought of breaking Eden's leg feel like an order had been given to break her own leg? Or worse.

Because you love Eden, Kathryn. Didn't God love his child?

She walked straight to her bedroom without checking on either Bobby or Eden, knowing they wouldn't dare make another attempt. Not tonight anyway. And not tomorrow because Eden wouldn't be able to walk tomorrow.

She lay in bed and stared at the dark ceiling, only dimly aware. An hour passed. Two. Three, and sleep didn't even bother tempting her.

Slowly her mind began to settle into that place of deep understanding that was far beyond the world's way of knowing.

There were times when you had to shut your mind down and trust in what you knew at a deeper level. She'd invested her whole life in Zeke, and, in some ways, he'd invested his in her. All she knew now was that she had to follow him, regardless of where he took her. Regardless of how terrifying the path or sickening the thought.

And that meant she had no real alternative but to do exactly what he said.

Break her leg. She's the lamb who would stray into guilt. By breaking her leg, you will save her.

Spare the rod, spoil the child. Give them an inch and they'll take a mile. Put them on the slippery slope and they'll slide all the way to the bottom. That's just how it was. Hadn't God put Jacob's hip out of joint to help him understand?

Didn't the good shepherd lovingly break the leg of the wayward lamb to teach it not to stray, just like Zeke had said?

And hadn't God asked Abraham to sacrifice his only son, Isaac? It didn't matter that God had sent a ram from the thicket to spare Abraham; what did matter was that Abraham had been obedient. Sometimes the righteous were called upon to do what seemed humanly impossible in order to bring blessing to the world.

Truth was, the first time she'd drowned Eden in baptism, she'd been terrified. And yet she'd been obedient, and held her daughter down, covering up her own fear with exclamations of praise and long quotes of scripture.

And, having died to the flesh, hadn't Eden come out of the water with tears of gratefulness? Hadn't they all been abundantly blessed for her obedience?

That was the path of being dead to the flesh.

So Kathryn shut down her reasoning mind and embraced the word of life that had saved her for this day of great blessing.

"Praise be to God," she whispered, and doing so she felt even more calm. "Praise be to God."

By the time first light was graying the sky outside her window, Kathryn had found a measure of resolution. It wasn't her place to think or reason; only to obey. And the only way to obey was to shut out the tempting voice of the serpent that would seduce her into eating from the tree of death.

Kathryn lay in bed for another hour, trying her best not to think, remaining as best she could in that place of obedience, until it occurred to her that she might only be procrastinating the good will of God, which was only another clever temptation of the serpent.

She swung her legs off the bed and placed her feet on the floor.

Break her leg. So she would.

She stood, took up the small package Zeke had given her, and walked to the door, aware that she was moving slowly, as if through water. Drowned. Numb. Dead to the flesh.

She opened the door and listened in the silence for a long moment that might have stretched into a full minute. Not a sound in the house. They would be fast asleep.

Walking slowly so as not to disturb the children, she headed to the kitchen to retrieve the ball of twine. She'd never tied Eden up before.

Dead to the flesh, Kathryn. This is the path, walk ye in it.

She opened the drawer next to the refrigerator, removed a pad of paper and a small tray filled with incidentals, found the string in the back, and withdrew it. How many times had she pressed forward toward the goal through seemingly impossible situations, keeping all tempting thoughts in the grave where they belonged? This was no different.

So why did it feel different?

No Kathryn. Stay dead. Keep the flesh in the ground. Lean not on your own understanding. Take up your cross. Follow. Just follow Zeke.

Back across the living room, into the hall, to the bathroom. She reached for a white towel, then stopped, thinking that there might be blood. Red would stain the towel.

She closed her trembling hand, turned to her right and reached for a dark blue towel instead.

Back out of the bathroom and down the hall, one step at a time, just one step at a time, that was all. Walk, walk, walk. Placing one hand on Eden's doorknob, she took a deep, shuddering breath, let it out through her nostrils, and twisted the handle. Slowly pushed it open.

Eden lay on her side, still dressed in the same pajamas she'd worn to bed, watching her with empty eyes. Defeated.

Terror sliced through Kathryn's mind. She was awake.

For a few seconds, she looked at her daughter and knew she couldn't follow Zeke in this. How could she? He was asking too much!

But only for a few seconds, because she was mature enough to realize that this objection was only the flesh, trying to climb out of its grave. If the serpent tricked her into turning away from obedience, there would be hell to pay. In this life and the next. Zeke might even kill Eden. She had to do this for Eden's sake, not just Zeke's. That would be the most loving thing. And she loved Eden more than she loved her own life.

The seconds ticked by and the terror eased, but Kathryn found that she still couldn't move. It was Eden's eyes. They watched her without so much as blinking. A hardness seemed to have set into them. She felt no ill will toward her daughter for this—she might feel the same way if their places were exchanged.

A knot filled her throat. The room blurred as tears seeped into her eyes. The only way was to obey quickly, without further thought, before she lost her nerve.

Taking one last deep inhale, she ignored the voices of protest in her head, walked up to the bed, lay the towel and the string on the nightstand, and reached for Eden's shoulder.

"Roll onto your back, sweetheart," she said.

Eden hesitated a moment, then did so, turning her head away to face the window.

It was almost as if Eden knew what was coming and had accepted it. An obedient lamb who knew not to resist anything her loving mother would do to her. She'd never been physically harmed, had she? She had no reason to suspect what was coming.

I'm sorry, Eden. I'm so sorry.

Kathryn opened the package, withdrew the syringe, slipped off the protective sleeve, and jabbed the needle into her daughter's shoulder.

Eden jerked her head around, startled by the pain.

"I'm sorry," Kathryn whispered, shoving the plunger to its hilt.

She didn't know what was in the syringe, only that Zeke had promised it would put Eden to sleep immediately and keep her that way for a long time.

Kathryn jerked the needle out and stepped back.

Eyes wide with fear, Eden tried to push herself up, got halfway, and faltered.

"What's . . ." She tried to sit up again but failed. "Mommy? Mom . . ." Her voice trailed off and her eyelids drooped and her head settled on her pillow. She was out and limp within five seconds.

Kathryn swallowed hard, blinking away tears. *Now, Kathryn. Finish what you've started now, without thinking.*

She stepped up to the bed, gently took Eden's right wrist and tied it to the metal bedframe above her head, unable to stem the flow of terrible emotions battering her. Then walked around the bed and tied her left wrist in the same fashion, then her left leg to the bottom of the bed, leaving only her right leg free.

Without daring to hesitate even a moment, Kathryn lay the towel over Eden's leg, climbed onto the bed so that she was standing over her daughter's feet, and lifted her right leg by the heel.

With one last look at Eden's peaceful face, she threw one leg over her towel-draped shin, took a deep breath, and pulled hard, teeth clenched and eyes squeezed shut.

The leg didn't break, so she pulled harder.

"Use a sledgehammer," Zeke had said. "Bones are hard to break."

Lying on her bed in the early morning hours Kathryn had decided that she wouldn't be so cowardly. This was *her* correction as much as Eden's—she would do it with her hands, flesh on flesh, feeling the pain of inflicting pain as much as her daughter.

But the bone wasn't breaking.

She groaned and tugged, tears now streaming down her face. Her mouth parted and she moaned as if it was her own leg under such pressure.

Still, the leg didn't break.

And then Kathryn was wailing, because it was in that moment, while her head was tilted toward the ceiling and her veins bulging on her neck, that she came into the sudden realization that she couldn't bring herself to use the force needed to break Eden's leg.

Which meant that they would both end up dead. And surely in hell.

But she just couldn't do it. She couldn't. She couldn't!

Kathryn slowly sank to her knees, straddling Eden's leg, lifted her hands to her face and wept into them, feeling utterly worthless in her failure.

"Forgive me . . . Forgive me, Father. Please . . ." Her mind swam in a dark sea of fear and desperation from which she could see no escape. At another time she might have suggested that Eden be baptized or at the very least ritualistically cleansed to appease her mother's failure, but Eden was unconscious now, put to sleep by her wicked mother who was failing Eden, Zeke, and God through one profound act of disobedience.

She could only hold her face in both hands, and sob, begging God for mercy in this dark hour of weakness.

"Give me the strength," she whispered. "Please give me the strength you once gave Abraham. Let me rise in righteousness and wield your sword of judgment as commanded by your servant."

"Mommy?"

Kathryn spun her head to the door to see Bobby standing there, staring dumbly.

"Shut the door and get back to your room," she cried, shoving her finger at him. "Now!"

He spun away, pulling the door shut.

The interruption snapped her out of her mindless slobbering. Eden rested with her eyes closed, pale face tilted to the right, oblivious to any harm. Or so it seemed at first glance.

Kathryn blinked to clear her vision and looked at the corner of her daughter's eye. There, a single tear slid slowly toward her temple. She was unconscious, but crying? In her sleep?

Or was Eden somehow aware of her surroundings?

The sickening voices of objection that Kathryn had silenced earlier were back and this time she made no attempt to stop them. She had to listen now because she knew that she had a new problem.

She could not break her daughter's leg. She was too weak. God wasn't going to give her the strength he'd given Abraham and he wasn't going to send a ram from the thicket to take Eden's place because Eden *was* the ram as much as she was the lamb.

Kathryn slumped back to her haunches and turned toward the window, swallowing against the ache that tightened her throat. She simply couldn't follow through.

But Eden still had to learn her lesson in a way that she hadn't. She'd been too easy on her daughter—nothing else explained Eden's seditious rebellion and betrayal. Just as importantly, Zeke had to be appeased. He had to be assured that they wouldn't fail him again.

Even so, Kathryn could no longer bring herself to break her daughter's leg, not while Eden lay crying in her sleep. In fact, not ever. It was too much to ask of this mother.

Which left her with only one option, a small idea that had been whispered by the darkness during the night. One that now reasserted itself as a solution, never mind if it might also be a clever temptation.

How was a horse broken? Couldn't "breaking" mean bringing under full submission? If she was unwilling to actually snap Eden's leg, couldn't she "break" it by disabling it?

The point was to keep Eden from walking and escaping. That and teaching her just how evil her sin really was while offering correction. But both could be accomplished as easily with a bad sprain as with a break. Eden's mobility and her rebellious spirit would both be broken.

It was the only option Kathryn could think of other than going to the toolshed for a sledgehammer. She would sprain Eden's ankle badly enough to keep her from walking, then wrap it up to look like a break.

Kathryn turned back and studied her daughter. Saw another tear follow the trail of the first.

She had to do it now, before her nerve for even that was gone.

So she did. She quickly scooted to the end of the bed, ripped off the towel to expose Eden's leg, grabbed her foot, and twisted hard, grunting as much with anger at God's cruel nature as with exertion.

There. Surely that was enough.

Eden lay in peace, save those tears.

Her ankle began to swell within the first minute.

THE FIRST sensation I felt was a sharp pain in my knee and I think it was the acuteness of that discomfort that jerked me out of a dark, peaceful oblivion.

Immediately memories flooded me. My escape attempt with Bobby had failed miserably. Back in my room, I'd lost all hope and fallen into a deep despair, recalling all of the torment I'd suffered since I'd been kidnapped by my own mother five years earlier.

Every hour of forced prayer. All of the guilt heaped on me for not being perfect. Every day in the closet, every meal withheld from me, every turn of my mother's psychological screws, all of the abuse.

I was a slave. I had no rights. I was being used like an animal, a lamb, an offering . . . By whatever name, it was all the same to me.

And for that I realized that I really did hate Kathryn.

The moment this realization came to me, my hatred grew into something more. I loathed her. She disgusted me. Rage boiled in my veins as I lay staring at the wall, unable to sleep.

Then Kathryn had come in and injected something into my arm and my world had quickly vanished. Only to be jerked back into my awareness when the sharp pain hit my knee.

It was strange. I was unconscious, I knew that much. But I could hear and feel my mother standing over me, breathing hard and applying terrible pressure to my leg, as if she was trying to hurt me.

At first I dismissed the thought—Kathryn had said and done many cruel things to me, but she'd never struck me or injured me. But as her straining persisted, I realized that she was.

And then it hit me: she was trying to break my leg. My own mother was carrying out the very threat that monster, Zeke, had alluded to in the field. She was trying to break the leg of her wayward lamb so that I couldn't run away!

I was in a deep sleep, so I couldn't react at all, much less try to stop her. I could only lie there and let her do whatever she liked as great waves of anguish and revulsion rolled through me.

What exactly happened after that is a little dim. Outrage blinded me. All I knew was that the pain shifted from my knee to my ankle, then shot up my leg before she finally let go and left me alone in my room.

She might have broken my ankle, I wasn't sure. But it hardly mattered any more. In fact, a part of me was glad that she'd finally shown her truest offensive nature—it only validated and further justified my hatred of her.

Whereas before I might have had a sliver of doubt about my rights, and a tinge of guilt over my rebellion, I was now unequivocally certain that I would run and I wouldn't stop running until I got away from Kathryn and Zeke forever. I would go straight to the police and send them right to prison where they both belonged.

This was what I was thinking as I drifted in a sea of darkness for what felt like many hours, because a part of me was aware the whole time. I distantly wondered if it was the drugs that made it all so strange. Or maybe my own fear was keeping me half aware—she might come back.

But she didn't. I lay on my back for a very long time without dreaming or forming coherent thoughts. Swimming in bitterness.

No . . . not swimming. Floating. Yes, I was floating on a black sea.

Gradually, much later, I thought to myself: *This isn't a black sea. It's the lake. And I'm not on my bed, I'm lying at the bottom of a small boat.*

I jerked up, heart lodged in my throat. Spun my head. The calm, dark lake water stretched out to the distant shore in all directions. I was dreaming that dream again. The water walker dream.

But it felt so real, you see?

The lake was still and deathly silent, and waves of panic washed over me, as threatening as any storm. I was stranded in a boat without oars. There was no one to help me! The water was pitch black. A storm could come up and drown me!

The moment I had the thought, the wind began to blow and immediately the boat started to roll with the rising waves.

I scrambled to my knees and grabbed onto the side of the boat to steady myself. I still knew that I was in a dream, but the wood under my palm and the wind on my face felt so real that I was tempted to think I really was stranded in a storm. And as soon as I had that thought, I was.

It was actually happening! I really was going to drown.

Oh no! No, no, no!

"Eden . . ."

The familiar voice reached me from far away over the pitching waves and I twisted toward the distant shore. I could just see him when the boat rose up on a wave, then lost sight when it dropped back down.

It was him. It was the Outlaw!

"Walk to me, Eden . . ."

Then he vanished behind a wave as the boat dropped. The wooden hull smacked the water and shuddered.

It was getting worse!

"Eden . . ." Outlaw's distant call was whipped by the wind. "Step out of the boat and walk to me . . ."

"I can't!" I screamed.

"Walk to me, Eden . . ."

"I can't!"

The boat was bucking in waves so high now that I knew one was going to crash into the boat and crush me under its weight. And I now was certain that I was no longer dreaming. It was real! I really was going to die.

"Eden . . ."

Panic overrode my thoughts as a massive wave lifted the boat high into the air.

"Step out of the boat and . . ."

But his "walk to me" was lost as the boat crashed back down into the water with enough force to rip my grip free and send me sprawling.

I began to scream. Then was pitched forward and smashed my head on the boat's side.

"Help me!" I was out of breath and sucked at the night air, but spray slapped my face and stopped my breathing short.

"Help!"

The wind suddenly stilled and the lake calmed. I was breathing hard, steadying myself with both hands outstretched, sure that another wave would come.

Instead, the boat's rolling slowed to a gentle rocking.

I got my knees under me and pushed myself up so that I could see the water. The lake was flat again, and I immediately saw why.

Outlaw was walking toward me. On top of the water. Moving with even strides in boots that kept him afloat.

But no . . . No, he wasn't wearing boots. His feet were bare, splashing with each step.

Slap . . . Slap . . . Slap . . .

I was too astonished to move. All the while, he kept his gentle eyes on me.

Slap . . . Slap . . . Slap . . .

He'd stilled the water. Only then did I think, *Oh yeah . . . this is a dream. You can do things like that in dreams.* So I stood up and watched him all the way, amazed by just how real my dream looked. Only the fact that he was walking on water reminded me that it wasn't real.

Or was it?

He stopped ten feet from the boat and stared at me. Flashed a smile.

"Hello, Eden."

I wasn't sure what to say.

"I see you're stuck again."

I looked at his feet and saw that the water only came up half way to the top of them.

"Is this real?"

"Of course it's real. It's happening, isn't it?"

"Yes, but in a dream. I'm dreaming."

"Are you?"

"I think so. Yes, of course I am. How else could you walk on water? I'm just seeing this in my mind."

He walked a little closer, eyeing the boat now. "You're right, it's in your mind. But aren't all thoughts? Just in your mind, that is. And your memories, aren't they just in your mind? And your fears? And your hopes? Aren't they all just thoughts in your mind?"

"I guess so."

"And you guess right. Change your mind, and change what's real for that moment." He lifted an eyebrow, as if slightly amused. "How did you get out here?"

"I . . . My mother drugged me. She tried to break my leg."

He cocked his right brow. "And you found that quite disturbing, I'm sure."

"Of course."

"Just like the waves and the water in this dream. Quite a threat, wouldn't you say?"

I immediately knew where he was going, but it didn't stop me from saying how I felt.

"I suppose. Yes."

"You're threatened. Offended."

"Wouldn't you be if someone tried to break your leg?"

"No. But this is about you right now. It's up to you whether or not you want to be offended or threatened. And yet you feel threatened by your mother. By the water and the waves."

I didn't know what to say to this. He might be right, but it sounded crazy to me.

He ran one hand along the hull's wooden bow. "You're afraid of the thought that the water will drown you, so you stay in this boat which you are certain will keep you safe. But when the storm comes, you still tremble with fear, don't you? Because you're afraid of the water."

My last dream flashed through my mind.

"I sank last time."

"Of course you did. Because you were afraid and took offense at its threat. But what if there was a way to change that? What if you could see that there was no threat?"

"Change it? How?"

"*Metanoia*," he said.

"*Metanoia?*"

"It's a secret word. Greek. It means repent."

His use of that word struck a chord of fear in me. How many times had I begged God to forgive me from my sins and tried to correct my behavior as demanded by Mother? And look where it had gotten me.

He slowly shook his head, as if anticipating my objection.

"It doesn't mean to change what you *do*. It means to go beyond your thinking. To change your *mind*. To let go of what you think is true for a greater knowing. For instance, to let go of the belief that if you step out of that boat which keeps you safe, you'll only drown in all the troubled seas of your life. See? *Metanoia*. It'll be our secret word."

"But that's not true. I *will* drown!"

"So you believe. That's why *metanoia* requires faith, a tiny bit at least, like maybe the size of a speck of dust. Everyone believes what they believe, right? Only those who go beyond what their mind tells them can walk on the troubled waters of life." He winked. "Like me."

Metanoia. It had a ring to it. I suddenly liked the word.

"As long as you keep your eyes on the troubled sea, and believe that the wooden hull under your feet keeps you safe from that sea, you'll never be a proper water walker. And you are, Eden."

"I am what?"

"A water walker. Just like me."

"I am?"

"Sure. You walked on water before, didn't you?"

He was talking about the first dream I had with him. "Not really. I was walking in shallow water."

"Well then it's time you learned to walk on deeper water. To do that you have to let go of the knowledge that the boat keeps you safe and the water is a danger."

Hearing him explain it that way, it almost felt like I'd heard it before, a long time ago. Not from Kathryn, that was certain. Maybe before. Or maybe it only felt that way because I was in a dream.

"Let go of your fears of what can't hurt you, Eden. Find no offense in the water. Turn the other cheek, surely you've heard that before. Forgive the offense. Do that and it won't swallow you."

"Forgive?"

"It means let go."

The idea drew me. What if I could? What if I could just up and walk out of all the troubles in my life? But it was also absurd, wasn't it? I mean . . . How could I just let go of everything I knew to be true?

But then . . . that was my mind telling me it was absurd.

Then again . . . he was saying that *metanoia* was going beyond the mind. Using faith.

Outlaw held out a hand. "Wanna try?"

"Now?"

"Why not? It's the only way you're getting to shore. What do you say?"

His smile was infectious. And we were just in a dream. I could change my thoughts here. Anything was possible, right? I just had to change my mind.

"Okay."

A grin split his face and he slapped the edge of the hull. "Jika, jika, jawa! Now you're talking; dead man walking!" He thrust his hand out again. "Take my hand, and step on sand."

I couldn't help but grin with him. But looking at the water, I couldn't see that it was sand. We were in the middle of the lake—the water had to be a hundred feet deep out here. I was afraid.

"No need to be afraid, Eden," he said. "See no trouble. Have faith."

Now he could read my thoughts?

"No, I can't read your thoughts. But I read faces pretty good. Now step on out here before that hull goes up in smoke."

"Why would the hull go up in smoke?"

"Well . . . the boat's only an idea, right? A thought. All thoughts vanish. So waste no time. Walk with me."

I looked at the water, then back into his bright eyes, then at his hand. I reached for it and he held my fingers firmly but gently.

"Now you're talking."

Using my left hand on the hull and supported by his strength, I cautiously drew first my left leg, then my right over the side, so that I was seated on the edge. I kept my eyes on the water, struck by the fact that, even knowing that my mind was only making this all up, that wet, glossy surface rolling gently a few inches under my feet looked so real. So much like water.

And I knew that if I stepped on water I would sink. I just knew it.

My breathing came shallow and I frantically looked up at his smiling eyes.

"I'll tell you what," he said. "Why don't you close your eyes. Trust me, if you can't trust what I've told you."

I nodded, thinking that his hand was strong and if I did sink, he would hold me up.

So I closed my eyes, held my breath, and scooted-stepped-fell into the water, feet first.

But I didn't fall. The surface under my feet was firm. I was standing! I really was on solid ground and I was so stunned by this that I opened my eyes to see what had changed.

Nothing had. The moment I saw the glistening water, fear washed through me, and the moment I felt that fear, I became convinced that I was going to sink, and the moment I was sure I'd sink, I did.

Right up to my knees, gasping, squeezing my eyes shut.

He chuckled. "Keep your eyes closed."

I stopped sinking and he gently pulled me up. I was standing again. Once again relief flooded me.

"Walk," he said, guiding me.

I took a step, keeping my eyes closed.

"That's my girl. Look at you."

"No . . ."

"No, you're right, don't look."

I took another step. The water squished under my feet but I didn't sink.

"You see, Eden, it's not the water that changes. It's what you make of the water that changes. It's finding no offense in the water that keeps you safe, because there's nothing to be kept safe from when you're already safe. One step at a time. Walk."

I took another step, and then another, and another, and suddenly I could not stop grinning.

"Wow," I said.

"Yeah, wow. Now we're talking; dead man walking."

"You keep saying that: 'Dead man walking.' I'm not a man and I'm not dead."

"Just an old saying I learned in the jungle where I grew up. But actually, you *are* dead. At least the old you is. A good thing, because it's the only way you can walk on water."

"To die?"

"To let the old self die. To let go of the known patterns of this world and be transformed by a renewed mind beyond those patterns."

"Hmm . . ."

But my mind was on the thrill of walking. So I just kept walking with my eyes closed, trusting that he was leading me to the shore.

Slap . . . Slap . . . Slap . . . I was walking on water, filled with courage and feeling so elated that I thought I should scream with joy.

Instead, I breathed out another thought that had entered my mind.

"I'm so glad this is a dream," I said.

"But in some ways, it's not," Stephen said. "Open your eyes, Eden."

I pulled short. "Now?"

No answer came. I suddenly realized that no one was holding my hand. Without thinking about it, I snapped my eyes wide and stared into the darkness.

It took me a couple seconds to recover my orientation and see that I was lying on my back, in my bed, staring up at the ceiling, covered in sweat.

The reality of my situation crashed in around me and I jerked my head up.

It was night again. White bandages bound my right leg, from my knee all the way down around my ankle. The bandages were wet.

I'd been on the lake. No . . . I had sweated through the bandages.

Kathryn had tried to break my leg. She'd actually injected me with a drug, climbed on the bed, and done her very best to break her own daughter's leg.

A terrible rage washed over me and I swung my legs off the bed, not caring if or how much it would hurt. I placed my feet on the ground and put some pressure on them.

Pain cut into my right ankle, but not enough to keep me from standing.

I hobbled around the bed, favoring my right leg. It was too sore to walk much, but that would change in a couple days.

I sat back down on my bed, clenched my jaw, and let a quiver work its way through my bones. I had courage now. If there was one thing my dream had shown me it was that I could face all my fears. I could march right out of this hellhole, even if it meant walking right over Kathryn.

She was the troubled black water, but I was a water walker.

That's what I was going to do. As soon as my ankle could support a good walk, I was going to go, and this time, I was going to go all the way.

LIFE CAME in cycles. Some days were hard, others a blessing; some brought death, others life. For every sin, a lash was dealt, and for every moment of holy courage, a jewel stored up. Spare the rod, spoil the child. And they were all God's children.

Kathryn had lived her life by many principles, but none rang so true as the ageless law of compensation: you reap what you sow.

Although she hadn't found Abraham's courage to break Eden's leg, she'd faced terrible fears and done the next best thing by spraining it. Even doing that had been horrifying, followed by hours filled with terrible pain and heartache. How Abraham had found the courage to put his own son on the altar she could hardly fathom, but then he was the father of nations.

Perhaps in her failure to fully obey Zeke she would miss out on a blessing as great as Abraham's, but even for her small act of obedience, Kathryn was reaping the fruit of her faithful sowing.

Three days had passed since that dreadful morning—the first of which had been dreadful, the second, peaceful, and the third, today, quite beautiful.

She'd tenderly wrapped Eden's swollen ankle and leg with a splint to make it look like a break. Every hour thereafter, she'd gone to check on her daughter, making no attempt to hold back her tears of empathy while Eden slept in peace.

Looking upon the wounding she'd administered to her daughter was hard, but since when had being righteous not been? Didn't punishment hurt God even more than it hurt his beloved children? Was it God's fault that he had to level vengeance upon those who'd strayed from his love? She was only following his example, both in vengeance and in love. Her precious lamb was in a time of correction—hurting for her was appropriate even if it was best done in secret, just like God hurt in secret.

Zeke came by that first afternoon, took one look at Eden's heavily bandaged leg, and, clearly satisfied, walked to the front door where he'd turned and offered his gratefulness.

"Your obedience doesn't go unnoticed, Kathryn. When the time comes you will see that."

"Thank you, Zeke."

He nodded once. "I've cut the phone line."

"Of course."

He withdrew a small, black cell phone from his pocket and gave it to her. "It's programmed to call only my cell. Just press send. Keep it in your dresser and use it only if you find yourself out of your depth."

"Yes, of course. Thank you, Zeke."

"I want you to hide the truck keys in the shed. Somewhere neither Bobby nor Eden would think to look."

"Why? Eden can't drive."

He drilled her with a dark stare that had filled her with shame. For a moment she wondered if he already knew she hadn't broken Eden's leg and was only toying with her.

"Forgive me, Zeke. I didn't mean—"

"She won't be able to walk without a cast, but that doesn't mean she won't try driving out again. I would appreciate a little trust from you."

"Yes, of course."

"Hide the keys."

"Yes. Yes, I will. Thank you, Zeke. You're very . . ."

He'd turned before she could finish and was gone without another word. It was just as well, because really she was just stumbling all over herself and that wasn't a pretty sight, even for someone as understanding as Zeke.

Eden hadn't awakened that first day, which was a small blessing. Kathryn wasn't up to facing her daughter yet. When she'd gone in to check on her the next morning, she'd been filled with trepidation, afraid to see hatred and anger in those soft brown eyes.

She'd found Eden lying on her back, staring up at the ceiling, fully awake and seemingly at peace. When Eden had turned to face Kathryn, her eyes showed none of the bitterness she'd feared. Her daughter hadn't smiled or said anything that might show her repentance, but neither had she voiced any frustration at waking to find her leg in bandages. It was a very good sign.

Kathryn had approached her bed and studied her daughter lovingly.

"Are you okay, darling?"

Eden had slowly nodded.

"Yes."

"Yes?"

"Yes, Mother."

She smiled at Eden and, although Eden didn't return her smile, there seemed to be a light in her eyes.

"I think that you'll be glad to know that I've decided to lift my restriction on food. Your body needs to mend. Would you like some chicken soup?"

"That would be nice, Mother. Thank you."

"You're most welcome."

Kathryn left the room flooded with peace, quickly heated up some soup, and took it to her daughter on a wooden tray so she could eat it in bed.

Eden had spent the rest of the day in bed except to use the toilet, which Kathryn had also allowed. Watching her hobble to the bathroom had filled her with sorrow. It would have been easy to question her act of punishment, but Kathryn did her best to ignore the tempting whispers of the accuser.

Weren't they both already seeing the fruit of repentance? Eden seemed to have finally found some inner peace. The resurrection always followed the crucifixion.

By the third day, Eden was getting around better, though still limping noticeably. More importantly, she'd found her pure self, taking time to kneel beside her bed in prayer unbidden by Kathryn. A gentleness and kindness had come to her eyes—a look that had always melted Kathryn's heart.

"I love you, sweetheart."

"I love you too, Mother."

"I'm so proud of you."

"Thank you."

Kathryn had gone about the rest of the day humming with gratitude. The blessing that came after obedience and suffering never ceased to amaze her.

Bobby seemed quite distraught to learn that Wyatt would be gone for a while and, without a playmate, he was far too fidgety. So Kathryn had allowed him to spend some time in Eden's bedroom that afternoon. She'd listened at the door while Eden answered Bobby's questions about why she had a bandage on her leg.

"I hurt it," Eden said. "But don't worry, it was actually a good thing."

"Why is it a good thing? Does it hurt?"

"Yes, it hurts, but sometimes you need to feel pain so that you don't get hurt again. Like putting your hand in the fire—you feel the pain so you don't get burned again. Isn't that right?"

"Fire will burn you."

Eden had hesitated for a few moments before speaking.

"That's right, Bobby. Fire will burn. That's why we stay away from it."

It was all Kathryn needed to hear. Why it had taken a measure so severe to finally show her daughter the full nature of righteousness after so many years of faithful service in purity, she didn't know. God knew how it pained her more than it pained Eden. The important thing was that her correction had taken hold.

Zeke would be proud of them all.

On that third night, Kathryn had knelt at the side of her bed before retiring and offered a long prayer of thanksgiving for the great blessing, once stolen by the locusts, now being returned a hundredfold as they all humbled themselves and walked in obedience. Then she'd climbed under the sheets, folded her hands on her belly, and drifted into a peaceful sleep for the first time in many days.

She dreamed of Wyatt because she missed him. He was walking with her as she approached a towering cliff and at first she thought the cliff was an obstacle she had to climb to reach the top where heaven awaited.

"Where are you going?" Wyatt asked, in the echoing way people speak while dreaming.

"To the tomb," she said, and she thought, that's right. I don't have to climb the cliff. I'm just going to the tomb at the base of the cliff.

"What's in the tomb?" he asked.

Jesus, she thought. But no, it wasn't Jesus. It was someone else. And suddenly she was very curious about who exactly was in that tomb.

The dream was interrupted by another, this one about a dog and Bobby, and she was thinking that Bobby should have a dog as a friend. But then she was somehow back with Wyatt, at the base of the cliff, looking at the tomb with its stone rolled away.

"Are you going inside?"

"No." Her answer surprised her.

"Why not?"

"Because I'm already inside."

Why she said this, she didn't know. Dreams were just that way. But then she stepped up to the tomb and looked inside anyway.

Inside lay the body of a woman, arms and legs bound in strips of cloth. She blinked and saw that she was right—it was her, lying on her back with her hands folded over her belly.

"That's you," Wyatt said over her shoulder. "Are you dead?"

Was she?

She was no longer looking down at herself: she *was* herself, lying on her back, arms and legs bound. She tried to open her eyes, but couldn't. Tried to free her hands, but the strips of cloth held them together.

"Where are the keys to hell?" a voice asked.

I'm in hell?

Everything started to get muddled up in her head.

"Wake up!" The voice wasn't Wyatt's. It sounded more like an angel.

"Wake up!" Something pushed against her arm and she opened her eyes.

"Tell me where the truck keys are."

Kathryn twisted and stared up into the face of her angel. Only it wasn't an angel. It was Eden!

"Tell me!"

She was dressed up in a dark-brown wig Kathryn hadn't worn in years. Wearing one of her dresses—a white one with yellow flowers that Kathryn had recently outgrown.

The truth crashed over Kathryn like a tidal wave. Eden was running again! She'd only *pretended* to have changed. And now she stood over her mother, glaring, demanding to know where the truck keys were.

Kathryn jerked up, outraged, and it was then that she found that her hands had been bound—wrists and fingers, so she couldn't use them. And her ankles. Twine, the same she'd used on Eden, had bound her ankles to the bedpost.

"Tell me where the keys are!" Eden demanded again.

Kathryn stared at Eden's work, hardly daring to believe. She'd managed all of this without waking her. She'd planned it all along?

"What have you done?" she stammered.

"What I should have done a long time ago."

"You untie me this second, Eden Lowenstein! What in the depths of hell has possessed you?"

"*You* have," Eden bit off. "You've come out of hell and tormented me! Tell me where the keys are."

"Don't be a fool! You can't just drive out of here! Have you completely lost your mind?"

"I don't know, Mother, have I? You should know. You're the one who tried to break my leg."

"I had to! Don't you understand? I had to!"

"Of course you did. And if God—oh pardon me, *Zeke*—tells you to kill me I suppose you would do that too. But actually you won't, because I won't be around to kill."

"I would never . . ." Kathryn felt the first waves of a panic attack coming on as the full scope of Eden's intentions settled into her mind. It was getting light outside. The dogs would be tied off soon. Eden was going to drive out dressed up like her and she might very well make it. If she did . . .

Kathryn set her jaw and leveled her sternest warning.

"Now you listen to me, young woman. If you do this there will be hell to pay! Do you understand me? You will reap death if you sow death. An eye for an eye."

"I don't think you understand. I'm *leaving* hell. I'm going to drive the truck out of here and this time there's nothing you can do to stop me."

The hatred spilling out of her daughter could hardly be measured. What was this evil that had come over her? How dare she repay her mother with anger after all the years of loving kindness?

You, Kathryn. You're the evil.

She swallowed deep and pushed the thought out of her mind.

"I've looked everywhere for the keys and can't find them," Eden said. "So now you're going to tell me. And if you don't I'm going to break one of your fingers."

Kathryn couldn't comprehend those words. They weren't from her daughter. She had to remain strong and stand up to this demonstration of evil if she expected to save Eden.

"Never," she said.

There was no wavering in Eden's glare. Her daughter had learned to stay the course in the closet; that same resolve now directed her on a new path.

"Fine." Eden stepped up, jerked Kathryn's pinky finger from the binding, and tugged it back toward her wrist.

Kathryn gasped—a deep, guttural cry as much in shock that Eden could do such a thing to her own mother, as in pain.

"Tell me, Kathryn!" Eden said. "Or I'll break it."

"You're hurting me!"

"Tell me!"

This was her punishment, she thought. She was reaping what she'd sown. But that thought was immediately overridden by righteous rage.

"You're *hurting* me!" she cried.

"Have it your way." Eden applied more pressure and excruciating pain ripped up Kathryn's arm. Panic overtook her and she lost all bearings but those pointing to survival.

"Okay, okay, okay, let go!"

"Tell me!"

"In the shed!"

"Where in the shed?"

"By the lantern!"

"If you're lying to me . . ."

"I'm not, I'm not! For heaven's sake . . ."

Eden released her hand, stared at her with fixed inquisition, then crossed to the door, barely limping, and twisted back.

"If the key's where you say it is, the next time you see me will be with the police. If it's not there, I'm going to come back and break all of your fingers."

Eden turned and exited the room, leaving Kathryn breathing heavily, fighting back waves of dread. How dare Eden do this! How *dare* she!

It's what you taught her to do. An eye for an eye.

Kathryn let out a sob. Her mind wasn't working correctly. She couldn't seem to get enough air in her lungs. She had to stop Eden, she knew that much, but the horror of what was happening seemed to have turned her thoughts off.

If Eden got away . . . Dear God, she couldn't let that happen.

Then she remembered. *The cell phone.*

She had to get to the cell phone in her dresser across the room.

Sitting, Kathryn lunged for her feet, grabbed at the string that tied her to the bed, and dug at the knot. "Hurry, hurry, hurry . . ."

But she couldn't get her trembling, bound fingers to work properly on the knots. They were too tight!

She heard the front door slam shut. Eden was already out of the house, headed for the shed.

What if she finds the key? What if you can't get free?

But she already knew the answer to both questions. Driving by any onlooker, Eden would look like her mother and no one would stop her. She would reach the city. The police would come.

They would take Eden away from her.

The terrifying thought washed everything but itself from her mind.

Time seemed to slow.

They're going to take my daughter away again. They're going to take my baby away. They're going to take her away and hurt her. They're going to take my baby away from me again.

And then another thought came.

She's at the shed by now.

"Bobby!"

The house rang with her cry. She screamed his name again, this time at the top of her lungs.

"Bobby!" She took two heavy breaths. "Bobby!"

He barged through the doorway and pulled up, eyes wide, still half-filled with sleep. But he'd come. Thank God, he'd come . . .

"Listen to me, Bobby—"

"Are you hurt?"

"I need you to do something for me." It wouldn't take Eden long to discover that the truck keys weren't by the lantern. "I need you to help me."

"Why are you tied—"

"Not now, Bobby! Just do what I say. There's a phone in that dresser over there." She motioned with bound hands at the long dresser against the wall. "In the top drawer under my socks. I need you to get it for Mommy."

Bobby glanced over his shoulder into the hall. "Is Eden running away again?"

"No, Bobby. Eden's just running an errand for me. Now I need you to do something for your mother. Can you do that? I need you to get the phone out of my dresser."

He stared back, frightened.

"Why are you tied up?"

Eden was moving quickly—she could feel it in her bones. Maybe already at the shed . . . Maybe already coming back!

She couldn't afford to frighten Bobby, not now.

"I'm playing a game, darling. I'm practicing getting free so that I can protect you if anything ever comes to hurt us. You can help me by getting the phone. I need the phone. Hurry!"

His eyes brightened. "A game?"

"Yes. Yes, a game. Hurry, Bobby, please hurry!"

Now fully engrossed in the notion of a game, Bobby tore for the dresser, grabbed a drawer, and yanked it open.

"Not that one! The next one. Under my socks."

"This one?" He pulled the end drawer open, and peered inside.

"Yes. Under the socks. Do you see it?"

Bobby reached his hand in, fumbled around for just a moment, then jerked the small, black cell out and held it high.

"Got it!"

"Now bring it here." It was all taking too much time. "Hurry!"

Bobby rushed over and stuck the phone out. But she didn't think she had the dexterity to operate the phone herself.

"Open it."

"Me?"

"Yes, you. Open it and push the power button. Hurry!"

He flipped it open with his stubby fingers and dumbly stared at the keys. He'd never used a cell phone, had he? No. Neither of them had that she knew of.

"Hold the red button down."

"This one?" He showed her the phone.

"Yes! Push it. Hurry."

He did and the phone's small screen came to life. He grinned.

"Got it!"

The doorway was still empty, but Eden would be back. Any moment and she would be back.

"Now push the one button and then the call button. The green one at the bottom. Hurry!"

Once again he held the phone up to show her the one button. "This one?"

"Yes! And then the green button."

With great purpose, he pressed the one and then the green call button with his forefinger.

"I pushed it."

"Good! Now set the phone on the pillow."

He laid it down and she wriggled around so that she could press her ear against the receiver. It was ringing, she could hear that much. She wasn't sure what she was going to say when Zeke answered—the thought of confessing her failure again was as unnerving as having her finger broken, but she knew she had to face her own sin and confess.

"Mother!"

She whipped around to see Eden in the doorway, staring at her.

"I'm helping Mommy get free," Bobby said tentatively.

Eden's eyes shifted to him, then back at Kathryn, and then back to Bobby again.

She can't see the phone. It slipped off the pillow and my body's blocking her view.

"Go to your room, Bobby," Eden said.

"I'm helping Mom—"

"Go to your room!"

Bobby stared at his sister, dumbstruck. It was probably the first time he'd ever heard her anger directed at him. She had to stall them.

"No, Bobby," Kathryn said. "Stay with me. Stay with your mother."

He looked between them, confused.

"Bobby, you can't help Kathryn get free. I tied her up because Zeke ordered her to hurt me and she didn't want to disappoint him. She's not thinking straight right now and so we have to leave her tied up until someone can come to help us. Now go to your room and I'll come get you as soon as we're ready to go."

Kathryn blinked at the stunning rebuke. A small voice in the back of her mind told her that there was some truth to what Eden had just said. But that too was only the voice of temptation. She had to keep Bobby here—Eden wouldn't dare hurt her as long as he was here to watch.

"No, Bobby! You can't listen to Eden right now. She's under punishment. If you leave, she will hurt Mommy."

His eyes were wide, uncomprehending. "Eden won't hurt you, Mommy."

"Yes she will! She tied me up, didn't she?"

Eden walked into the room, eyes on Bobby. "Have I ever hurt you, Bobby?"

Kathryn scooted to keep the phone hidden but in doing so, felt it snap shut under her back. Which meant that she'd just cut the connection.

"No you would never hurt me, Eden," Bobby said.

"Have I ever lied to you?"

"No."

"And I'm not lying now. Go to your room and wait for me."

"No, Bobby!" Kathryn pleaded. "Please don't leave me! Please . . ."

Bobby was in a state of conflict, enough to keep him fixed to the floor, which was good. The longer the better.

But then he wasn't fixed, because he was suddenly turning and then running from the room, whimpering.

"Bobby!" Kathryn cried.

Before she could cry out again, Eden stepped up to the door and slammed it shut.

"How dare you use him!" she snapped, whirling back.

"How dare you tie me up! How dare you try to break my finger! You don't think God sees what you're doing? How in heaven's name can you possibly think you won't pay a terrible price for this rebellious behavior?"

"I'm only doing what you taught me to do, Mother! Isn't that what you do to daughters that stray? Break their wills and if that doesn't work, break their legs?"

"I'm the mother!" she screamed, face ripe and hot. "If I don't guide you, I will be judged, can't you see that? *God* is my judge!"

"Oh, I see," Eden bit off, heading around the bed. "You learned this trick from God, is that it? And you're only his instrument for torture on earth. It's your job to hate me so that God doesn't have to, is that it?"

"No, no, sweetheart! I don't hate you! I love you!"

"Of course you do." Her daughter's voice was thick with sarcasm. "That's why you're willing to see me hurt."

"Only if it's for your benefit."

"Because that's what God does, right?"

"Yes! That's what God does!"

"And if Zeke wanted to break my leg, you'd just stand by and let him do it!"

She saw her opportunity and dove for it.

"But I *didn't!* I didn't break your leg, Eden! He wanted me to, but I couldn't."

"But you would let him break it, wouldn't you?"

"Never!"

"You're lying."

"I would never let anyone break your leg! Never! Is that what I am to you? A monster?"

Eden glared, unimpressed.

What would Zeke do if he heard what she'd just said? It made her glad the phone had snapped shut.

She's right, isn't she, Kathryn? You're actually more concerned with Zeke's opinion than your own daughter's pain.

"No," she said out loud.

But Eden wasn't interested in her "no," which was just as good.

"You lied to me about the key," Eden said stepping up to the bed. "This time you're going to tell me."

It was as far as she got because the door suddenly swung open behind Eden. They both turned at the same time. They both saw Zeke's tall form filling the frame.

They both went still.

Zeke studied them with vacant eyes, took in the scene, then looked down at Eden's bandaged leg. For a long time he just stood there, and all Kathryn could think was, *He knows.*

He knows. Dear God, he knows.

When his eyes finally settled on Kathryn they were deep and dark, like two pits that had no bottom. And then she knew as well.

Knew what he was going to do.

"The next time I tell you to do something, you will do it." His voice was low and certain and had the edge of a razor to it. "That much I promise you."

He strode into the room, walked up to Eden, who was trembling where she stood, calmly took a fistful of her hair, and dragged her back toward the door.

"This time I'll do it for you."

Eden remained silent, jaw flexed with resolve. She shot Kathryn a glance, but there was no plea for help in her eyes—only bitter accusation.

Zeke pulled her through the door and shut it behind them, leaving Kathryn alone to consider her own anguish.

She knew what he was going to do. She knew it, and she knew that there was nothing she could do to stop him. She even knew it was the right thing, because he was Zeke and Zeke always did the right thing.

But she didn't know how to react to the terror now sweeping

through her. Or to the voice that wept for mercy in the face of punishment. Or the soft voice that suggested she was wrong.

No. No, she couldn't listen to those lies. Abraham hadn't and she couldn't afford to either.

She heard Eden's door slamming shut.

Yea, though I walk through the valley of death I will fear no evil.

Kathryn settled on the pillow and closed her eyes, still tied hand and foot, breathing as deliberately as she could, attempting to shut her mind down. It was the only way.

It was . . . She knew this too, but it wasn't working.

What have I done? Dear God, what have I done?

What happened next came in small chunks that Kathryn tried not to comprehend.

A long period of impossible silence.

A soft blow and a crunch.

A bloodcurdling scream.

Eden's.

The shepherd had broken the leg of the lamb who would otherwise lead them all off a cliff.

Dear God, what have I done?

"WELL, WELL . . . Now you're in a pickle, aren't you?"

"Yes."

"Tell me what happened."

The voice belonged to Outlaw, though I couldn't see him. It's like we were two souls on the edge of a great dark void and we were looking down into empty space, reflecting on the tragedy that my life had become.

I felt strangely disconnected from my body, which I couldn't see or feel. But I could remember what had happened easily enough. So I told him.

"Zeke broke my leg."

"My, my. A tear in the costume."

"He didn't tear my clothes. He broke my leg."

"Like I said. Your costume seems to be broken. Did it hurt?"

"Yes."

"How bad?"

"Very bad." Saying that, I felt a throbbing ache in my right leg, the first sensation I'd felt in some time. "It hurts right now."

"And how long has it hurt?"

"I don't know. How long have I been asleep?"

"That's for you to tell me. A couple days, I would guess."

"How could I sleep a couple days?"

"Perhaps because you refuse to wake up and face the pain."

And with those words, self-pity swept in and swallowed me whole. It was too much to hold and I began to cry. I don't think I was just *dreaming* that I was crying . . . I really was crying, like a little girl who'd run totally out of hope.

I was lying on my bed, silently crying in my sleep. I'd been there for two or three days, refusing to wake because I wanted it all to be over. Sleeping forever was far more attractive to me than waking to spend even one more hour in that living hell my mother forced me to call home.

Or maybe Zeke had given me some drugs.

"Why do you cry for yourself, Eden?"

"What do you mean? I've been hurt!"

"Is that really why you're crying? Because you were hurt?"

"Of course that's why I'm crying. Zeke dropped his knees on my leg with all his weight and I felt my leg snap." A shiver ran through my bones at the thought of it. "How could anyone do such a thing?"

"You're not crying because your leg is broken," he said. "You're crying because you think your leg is part of who you are, and so you think you've been attacked and you're feeling sorry for yourself."

"Well, don't you?" I demanded.

"Don't I what?"

"Feel sorry for me?"

"I have compassion for you because you're crying. But there's nothing wrong with you, so I don't feel sorry for you."

"Of course there's something wrong. My leg's been broken!"

"Your leg? Well, that's only your costume. And as long as you hold onto the belief you are somehow your leg and have therefore been hurt, you will see yourself as a victim and continue to feel sorry for yourself."

I hated him saying that, I really did. I thought it was cold and inconsiderate and I didn't want to listen to him anymore, so I turned away and tried not to listen.

"Do you want to walk on water, Eden?"

I didn't answer.

"When you do, I'll be waiting to show you how."

"You already showed me how! And now I have a broken leg."

"Then maybe you weren't listening. When you're ready to listen, I'll be in the boat. Maybe this time you'll actually hear me. If so, you'll be able to walk on water."

"I already *did* walk on water!"

"And why aren't you doing it now?"

The questions stumped me because I knew by water he meant trouble, and he was right—I was drowning in all of my troubles.

"Meet me in the boat, Eden. I'll show you how to walk on water."

But I didn't want to talk to him or think about it anymore. So I retreated into the darkness of a more comforting dream that was immediately and entirely forgettable.

Sometime later I woke up and opened my eyes to see that my mother was at my window with her back to me, staring out. There were fresh bandages on my leg. She'd set it?

I quickly sealed my eyelids and lay perfectly still, not wanting her to know I was awake.

I could imagine the pain that she must be in, seeing her broken daughter lying helplessly on the bed. Or maybe that was wishful thinking. I hoped she was so sickened by her own cruelty that she couldn't bear herself. I hoped it gave her an ulcer and kept her awake for weeks. Whatever pain she felt, she had it coming because she was right: we do reap what we sow. Now it was her turn to do a little reaping of her own.

She must have given me some drugs and set my leg when I was under, because I had no recollection of having my leg set, and I still felt groggy. Maybe she kept giving me drugs to keep me asleep; that way I could never run, what with a broken leg and being asleep.

Dream, Eden. Go back to sleep and dream. Dream of walking on water.

Find the narrow way that so few find. The way to be saved from all of your troubles.

The thoughts were mine, coming from me, like a long-lost memory calling to me. The words weren't Outlaw's; they were actually my own. It's like I was calling to myself.

Go to the boat, Eden. You were born to walk on water.

And then I was asleep because the next thing I knew, I was lying at the bottom of the boat in a dream that felt far too real to be a dream.

I gasped and scrambled to my knees, then pushed my head up to peer around. The boat was in the middle of the lake, as before. And the moment I stared out at the water, the wind began to gust and I knew that a storm was gathering.

Fear welled inside me as the boat began to roll with surging waves whipped by the strengthening wind. I searched the distant shore but there was no sign of Outlaw, and I thought, *Oh no! I'm going to drown this time. Oh no!*

A soft chuckle startled me, and I spun around.

Outlaw sat on the rear bench, leaning back on the boat's stern, smiling.

"Hello, Eden," he said.

I stared at him, both relieved at his presence on my boat and slightly put off that he was so nonchalant while there was a storm building.

"Are you ready to step out of this boat that seems to keep you safe from a sea that seems to boil with trouble? On your own this time?"

So here we were again.

"I don't want to walk on water," I said.

"Why not?" He was still leaning back, arms hooked over the side of the boat, legs stretched out before him, as if he didn't have a care in the world even though the waves were now foaming and the wind starting to whistle.

"I could drown," I said.

"Well then, you seem to have a problem," he said. "Because the only way back to shore is over those waves."

"We can row the boat."

"Not without oars, we can't. Besides, the wind would only push the boat back, no matter how hard you rowed. Eventually, the water will splash over the side and the boat will sink and yes, you will drown." He shook his head and *ts*ked. "Such a problem to have."

"Then you can save me," I said, thinking of the last time. The waves were slapping the hull with anger now, tipping us like a cork on a raging sea. "You can lead me."

"But I am, Eden. I am."

He drilled me with kind eyes, smiling mischievously, and it was only then that I noticed his hair. It was long and should be whipped about by the wind, but it wasn't. In fact, the storm wasn't having any effect on him.

"You're wondering why I don't feel the effects of the storm," he said. "It's because this is your storm. You see the threats and so they're real."

A larger wave slammed into the boat and sent me reeling. I grabbed the bench in front of me and hung on for dear life.

"Help me!" I cried, twisting round to see that the waves were growing larger by the minute. "Help me!"

"I am helping you," he said.

I whipped around and faced him. "Stop the waves!"

His smile faded and he stared straight at me with such intensity and certainty that for a moment I thought he was angry. But only for a moment because when he spoke, there was only kindness in his voice.

"You stop them, Eden."

"How?"

"I told you how last time."

Panic crowded my throat and I searched my mind, but I couldn't remember what it was that I was supposed to do.

"Tell me again!"

"Let go of the offense these waves cause you," he said. "Forgive the water."

"Forgive it? That's impossible! Forgive it for what? There's nothing to pardon!"

He unhooked his arms from the hull and stood, undaunted by the storm.

"I didn't say pardon. I said forgive. When I say forgive, I mean to see no fault or offense in the troubled sea. Let go of even the thought that it threatens you or has offended you. See it as innocent. Offer it no blame or defense. Stand tall and offer it, instead, your other cheek, no longer offended."

I didn't see how that was possible. We were wasting time! I quickly scanned the horizon and saw only an endless stretch of bucking waves, all flowing toward the boat.

"Help me!" I cried again, now completely desperate.

"Look at me, Eden."

I spun back to him and locked on to his eyes.

"Keep your eyes on me. Don't look at the water. Can you do that?"

I was struck by my intense desire to check the waves again, just to make sure they hadn't grown even more threatening. I had to protect myself from them, you see? I was terrified that a large wave would swamp the boat and leave me flailing in the water.

"Can you focus on me?" he cried above the wind.

"I am!"

"Your eyes are on me, and yet your mind is on the danger presented by the waves," he said. "You still see threat on all sides. As long as you feel the need to protect yourself from that danger, you know that you *haven't* let go of it. Forgive the sea and put your mind on my word. Hear me!"

"I am! Hurry!"

"I can't hurry, Eden. Only you can. I'm not the one with the problem, you are. The problem will only go away when you decide to let go. There are very few people on this earth who know what it means to truly forgive and even fewer who walk the path of forgiveness. But the power of that forgiveness is staggering. And I do mean staggering."

I saw that I was out of options, because he was intent on leading me to let go of whatever I had to let go of to survive.

"Then tell me how to do it!" I started to look away.

"Keep your eyes on me, Eden!"

I fixed my stare and tried to calm the trembling in my limbs.

"As long as you feel the need to defend yourself against that water, you see it as a threat."

"That's crazy!"

"Then your master was insane as well!"

"What master?"

"Jesus, the first water walker, of course. Why do you suppose he taught never to resist the evil man who comes against you? Why did he say we must turn the other cheek and love our enemies? Because he knew! Hear me, Eden and hear me well: Only in not defending are you ever truly safe. Every time you resist or defend against any perceived threat from the water, you give it power to fulfill that very perceived threat and it will crush you. But there's another way!" His voice rose with intensity. "There's a narrow way that few find but if anyone can find it, it's you!"

"They're right there!" I shoved my finger at the tumultuous waves. "Would you also suggest that I put my hand in a fire to prove it can't burn me?"

"Touché!" He spread both hands and leaned forward. "Dead man walking; now you're talking! Yes! There *is* a way not to be burned by the fire." He jabbed his finger at the air to accentuate the word *is*. "There *is* a way to walk on water. There *is* a way to move a mountain. There *is* a way to part the sea. There *is* a way to be healed of any disease. There *is* a way to abide in perfect safety and love. And only *one* way!"

He was talking about Jesus and his miracles, a subject I was altogether too familiar with, though I couldn't remember him walking in fire.

Dear God . . . how many nights had I spent in prayer, begging for him to make my way straight?

"I do believe!" I yelled. "I believe and look where that's gotten me!"

"Ah yes, they believe what all devils believe. But they don't *trust.* They have no faith! If you want to be saved from this troubled sea, you must surrender your mad belief in the danger it poses, and put your trust in that which truly keeps you safe instead. Forgive this world and all of its mad threats. Let go! See no harm in that which comes to destroy you because only your costume can be hurt. The real you is always safe in your Father's arms. Always! You are his daughter!"

Spray from the waves was now soaking me, head to foot—I could hardly deny the reality of that water threatening to swamp the boat. But one thing he'd said blared through my mind.

Only in not defending are you ever truly safe.

Could it be? Something about those words struck a chord deep in my bones. His ideas suddenly seemed a little less absurd. For the first time, they tempted me with a kind of deep certainty that I hadn't yet felt. I say tempted because I only saw a glimmer of truth and then only in a single thought:

What would it be like to not take any offense at what was done to me, ever? I would never be upset. Ever. What kind of power would such a person have? They couldn't be hurt! They would be invulnerable, like their master.

Outlaw must have seen something on my face because he flashed a smile.

"Yes, you see, don't you? Imagine the power you would have in this life, abiding in this truth alone."

"But . . . how can you not take offense when someone hurts you?" I asked.

"Well, you have to change your thinking entirely, don't you? *Metanoia.* Repentance, remember? A whole new operating system to transform the way you think and see the world. Being transformed by the renewing of your mind. And that takes faith, Eden. A complete letting go of what you think you know and trusting in what doesn't necessarily make sense at first. Faith."

His words arrested me. What if it was true? It seemed utterly careless and reckless, but what if he was right?

And suddenly I understood even more. These troubled waters around the boat were like the troubles I had with Mother. If I forgave her, she couldn't hurt me. And by forgive, he meant seeing no offense . . .

A twinkle came to his eyes, as if he could read my thoughts.

"Ah, yes, now you are seeing. Forgive. See no fault, even as your Father sees no fault in you. Surrender to this knowledge and nothing can harm you. No storm, no misguided mother, not even a broken leg!"

The simplicity of his words fell into my mind like rays of light that quickened a dormant set of laws deep in my soul, patiently waiting to be brought back to life.

"Step out of the boat, Eden!" he cried, eyes fired. "If you can do it here, in your dream, you will be able to do it when you wake!" He pointed to his right. "Take a leap of faith and see that these troubled waters have no power over you unless you give that power to them, and even then they lie."

I took his outstretched hand to mean I could look at the water, so I did. Fear battered me and I lost my train of thought. All I could see were angry waves.

"Everything in you cries out to remain in the safety you believe the boat offers you, doesn't it? Of course it does! The boat is your defense against the water! But the very defense is what empowers the water to trouble you. Let go of this understanding. Faith, Eden. Faith!"

He thundered the word above the storm and I felt a surge of confidence rise through me—just enough to give me the strength to take a step forward and grasp the hull with my right hand.

But the threat of those waves looked utterly real to me. And the last time I'd stepped out, I'd gone under! And this time he wasn't there to catch me!

"I can't!"

"Well then . . . you'll only drown here in your boat, won't you? You will lie there in your bed with a broken leg, seething with anger and bitterness and you will live in terrible suffering, all because you can't bring yourself to let go of your offense."

He'd said it all matter-of-factly, but he now jumped up next to me and yelled above the story, eyes wild.

"No, Eden! No! You will not take the path the rest of the world takes. You will find the narrow path because it's your destiny! Stepping off the edge may feel like death, but trust me, letting that old self die is no loss."

"I'm afraid!"

"And yet perfect love casts out fear."

"I don't feel perfect love!"

"Nothing can separate you from that love. Nothing! It's already inside of you, only forgotten."

He thrust his hand out to the waves.

"Now step out!"

"You're pressuring me!"

He withdrew his hand and stepped back as if reprimanded.

"I'm simply passionate about showing you the only way you can be saved from these troubled waters. I didn't make this stuff up. I'm only sharing it with you."

"Then who did make it up?"

"It's always been this way. You were raised in a monastery, didn't they teach you?"

I was?

Like a blossoming fireworks display, some of the memories so long suppressed by my mind suddenly erupted to life. By that light, I suddenly saw.

My many prayers and invocations.

The simple faith I'd had as a child a long time ago.

A field of flowers under a bright, blue sky, swaying lazily in a peaceful breeze.

And in that vision I suddenly knew that everything Outlaw had said was true. Our Master had made it so. Not the vengeful God that Kathryn had shown me, but the one who'd calmed the storm and walked on water.

Oh ye of little faith. Peace be still.

Outlaw started to speak, but I was suddenly moving, fixated on the simplicity of the path I saw in my heart, illuminated by even this thinnest sliver of light.

I didn't crawl over the side as I had before. I gripped the hull with both hands, jerked my right foot up and onto the bench-seat to give me a launching point, and, before I could reconsider, I shoved off my right leg and leaped over the side.

I was midflight before my fear vanished completely and I realized what was happening.

Oh, I thought, *Outlaw's right. There never was a storm. I only thought there was.*

I didn't see the change at first because my eyes were closed, but I felt it when my feet landed in the water. I felt it because I didn't sink.

And then I saw it, because I opened my eyes and saw a crystal-clean surface stretching out in all directions. There were no clouds, no wind, no waves—only water perhaps an inch deep, before turning spongy solid, holding together in a way that prevented me from sinking.

I stared in amazement, stunned. The glossy surface under my feet bowed slightly as I applied pressure.

"Stephen!" I cried, spinning back, expecting to see him in the boat.

But there was no boat. Stephen stood on the water where it had been, arms crossed, smiling wide.

"Now you're talking," he said.

I was so relieved, so excited, so overwhelmed with this turn of events that I let out a squeal.

Outlaw raised his brow. "Indeed."

I walked to my right, testing each footfall, and then marched back.

"I'm walking on water!" I exclaimed.

"You're walking on water."

"Can I run on it?"

"You can dance on it if you like. Do you know how to dance?"

"I don't know. Do I?"

"Well . . . you aren't operating under the old laws anymore. You can probably do anything."

I turned in a circle, still flabbergasted by the miraculous shift that had transformed my world. But even in that, I was wrong wasn't I? The world hadn't changed—I had. Or, more accurately, my perception of the world had changed.

I had forgiven—let go of—the old offense and saw none of the threat that had once promised to drown me. And I'd done it by stepping out of a boat I was sure would save me from all of that trouble.

"So now you know," Stephen said.

"Now I know." I faced him, curious. "But I'm dreaming, right?"

"It doesn't matter. If you think about it, your reality is only as real as you perceive it to be in any given moment, wouldn't you say?"

I got his meaning immediately. "And so all of my troubles are only as real as I believe they are."

He dipped his head. "Bravo, my dear. Now you see."

"Now I see," I said grinning wide. "Nothing can hurt me unless I say so."

His smile softened. "Always remember . . . You have been given the power to forgive any offense, and in so doing, remove it from your awareness as far as the east is from the west. True vision is his gift, allowing you to see no blame; forgiveness is your truest purpose in this life. Seventy times seven, always, leaving the old self in a watery grave and rising to find no fault. That's grace, that's true baptism, and that's good news, wouldn't you say?"

My mind spun. A lump formed in my throat.

"It's fantastic . . ."

"Fantastic." He winked at me.

"Far better than the watery grave my mother baptizes me into each week!"

He nodded. "So then, take care not to forget just how good this news is when your eyes open in your mother's house."

And with that, Outlaw unfolded his arms, clapped his hands together, and vanished.

But then so did I. So did everything.

I snapped my eyes wide.

It was dark.

I was lying in my bed.

And every inch of my body was soaked.

IT WAS dark, and every inch of my body was wet. I thought, *Dear God, was that real?*

I didn't necessarily mean it as a prayer, but that's how it came out, and immediately I knew the answer, as if a voice deep in my soul had answered.

Yes, Eden. More real than anything you have ever experienced.

I closed my eyes, and a gentle portion of the staggering truth I'd just observed washed through me. My body began to shake, from my head to my feet, and my breathing came in deep, heavy pulls.

I didn't dare move because I was smothered by a knowing of good news so profound that I could barely grasp it, and at the same time so outlandishly contrary to the beliefs my mother had drilled into me that I was afraid I might forget the goodness of that news.

In reality, I was invulnerable, and nothing—no power on earth or in heaven or under the earth or under the heavens—could separate me from the infinite love that held me secure, right then, as I lay trembling in bed.

Not Kathryn; no, she was only a lost soul trying to find her own way.

Not Zeke; no, he was only a spoiled child who did what he thought to be right in his own eyes.

Not the loss of my childhood; no, that was only a story of the past.

Not my captivity, nor my broken leg, nor anything that happened to this body because Eden was only my costume.

I was lying on my back in the darkness, I knew that, but it seemed like I was also above my body, watching what wasn't myself at all. The form below me was only a shell in which I temporarily resided. A sled on which to slide down the snowy hill. A car on a roller coaster in which to take the ride.

A boat on the stormy seas of life, to be stepped out of because I was a water walker, unaffected by the storm unless I clung to that boat.

There are no words to express how I felt in that moment as the truth raced through me, not on rails of reason, but on rails of a far deeper, infinite knowingness flowing with a bottomless peace that passed any understanding I had ever sought, much less embraced.

I think the awareness of that truth affected me more profoundly as I lay awake than it had in my dream. Every cell in my body vibrated with certainty, all in perfect symmetry and union. I had never felt so whole and complete as I felt at that moment in that house, which was also just a temporary holding place, like my body, like the roller-coaster car, like the boat I'd clung to with all of my strength.

I was free. I never had been a captive. I was whole! Nothing could hurt me. All of the threats had been of my own making because I'd mistaken my body for the real me, and my place as Kathryn's suffering daughter for far more than it was—just a temporary role.

All of this came to me in the space of one breath and I couldn't contain the gratitude that welled up in me. Tears began to flow from my eyes, and once they started, there was no stopping them.

Great sobs silently wracked my quivering body. I was gripped in the embrace of peace and love, a drug so powerful that even a hint of disappointment or an ounce of grievance could not be known in its presence. And without the slightest disappointment or grievance, only intoxicating love remained.

I could feel slight, throbbing pain my right leg, gently reminding me that it was broken, but I didn't care, you see? I wasn't disappointed by the condition of that right appendage down there. What could it possibly matter? In fact, I was so lost in gratitude and peace that I couldn't remember why a broken leg had ever mattered more than a broken blade of grass underfoot. Both would soon heal. Or not.

I don't know how long I lay awake because each moment felt like an eternity to me. Time didn't seem to exist in that place of being. It was ticking away, naturally, but I would only notice this in retrospect without being able to quantify those ticks with labels, like seconds or minutes or hours.

So I don't know how long it was before I heard the whisper from my dreams, reminding me of my purpose. Outlaw had said it on the lake, but now I heard it come from me, spoken by a gentle, prodding, female voice.

You have been given the power to forgive sin . . .

Yes.

And how staggering is that power.

"Yes," I said aloud, eyes still closed. Then again, weeping with it. "Yes . . ."

True vision is his gift, allowing you to see beyond all blame.

"Yes . . ."

Forgiveness is your only true function in this life.

"Yes . . . yes."

Seventy times seven, always, leaving the old self in a watery grave and rising to find no fault.

And then I couldn't speak because in that moment I knew the course before me with such clarity that it robbed me of breath. So I said it with all of my mind and all of my heart.

Yes! Yes, I will! I will, I will, I will . . . I lay in bed with tears streaming down my face, repeating the same words over and over in my mind, embracing them, loving them.

I will, I will, I will, I will . . .

"What's wrong?"

The voice came from the door and it confused me, because nothing was wrong.

"Eden?"

I let my eyes flutter open and I saw that morning was coming.

"Why are you all wet?"

I slowly turned my head and looked at the door. There, dressed in a pale-blue, flowered nightgown, stood my mother, arms at her sides, eyes wide like a deer caught in headlights.

This was Kathryn, my birth mother, who'd subjected Eden to countless challenges to her self-worth. There stood the woman who had drowned the me I used to know in the waters of condemnation and guilt every week, every month, every year, determined to purge me of my endless failure. There was the one who'd attempted to break my leg and then blessed the man who had.

But that's not what I saw.

I saw a woman who was blinded in her own suffering.

I saw a mother confused by a role that she'd tried desperately to fulfill.

I saw an innocent child who felt abandoned by love and worth because she didn't understand either.

I saw an astoundingly noble being, loved without blame by her Father and not knowing it, and therefore utterly lost.

I saw . . . I saw myself.

I saw all these things and an aching knot coiled in my throat. I knew—even as my mouth parted in a soft groan of compassion, even as tears gushed from my eyes—that she wouldn't be able to comprehend what she was seeing. But I couldn't seem to contain the emotions bubbling out of me.

She might interpret the sight of me crying on the bed as a sign of trouble, but there was more in that room than just a mother and her broken daughter. There was a connection between us that I can't possibly begin to describe.

I was looking at her, you see, and I was feeling nothing but endless love for her. No, not just feeling . . . Offering. Giving. And I think this, more than my crying, confused her.

"What's wrong?" She glanced about the room, searching for any sign of trouble, maybe half expecting to see Zeke sitting in the corner. But there was only me. And her.

She walked in slowly, dumbstruck, the stopped a few feet from the bed and looked at my body.

"What happened? You're wet . . ."

I tried to speak, but only raspy breath came out, and, judging by the wrinkling of her brow, this confused Kathryn even more.

Alarmed, she sat on the bed and quickly placed her palm on my forehead. "What's wrong, sweetheart? You're frightening me! What happened?"

I took the hand on my forehead in my own and tenderly pressed it against my cheek.

Immediately tears sprang to her eyes. It was then that I realized we were already communicating. Our hearts had somehow found each other's.

I stared into her eyes and offered her only love with all of my heart. I couldn't remember anything but her innocence, and in that place I saw her as a precious and perfect child who could not possibly disappoint me, much less her Father.

My only problem was that the more I offered her love, the more I cried. And the more she received my love and saw my tears, the more she cried. At first perhaps misunderstanding the reason for my demonstration of love, maybe thinking I had finally come to my senses and was once again on the correct path. But she'd never seen this kind of outpouring from me, and I could see the question in her eyes.

Tell her, Eden. Speak to her.

"I forgive you, Mother." The words came out strained. I kissed her hand and said it again. "I forgive you."

She blinked, struck by these simple words. Then meaning fell into her mind, and her face knotted in anguish.

"I love you," I said.

And she could take it no longer. She closed her eyes and began to sob, then lowered her head to my belly and wept into my already wet pajamas. She didn't offer any words, only those tears of remorse and guilt.

But I didn't want her to feel any guilt because that wasn't my intention or business. I only wanted to love her and find her blameless, and as she began to come apart, I found that my own strength returned and my own crying began to settle.

You would think that it would take more than a few words to shatter my mother's hardened shell after living so many years under her burden of guilt, and you would be right. Far more than a few words. Something with far more power than mere words.

A true expression of love borne of the heart, not the mouth. In the space of that love, no words are required. My mother was being deeply impacted by something I could hardly understand myself and still, I gave it with all of my heart.

I saw myself as a tree, administering healing over a wounded spirit who had come to me for love. She was my mother and I was only too willing to stroke her head and give her as much love as she could possibly drink in. And to offer her a few words as well.

"I love you, Mother. It's all going to be okay."

"I'm sorry." She sobbed into my pajama top. "I'm so sorry."

"It's okay, Mother . . ."

"I didn't know what to do. I'm so confused. I'm so sorry."

I had always wondered something about the crucifixion scene—the part where Jesus says, "Forgive them for they know not what they do."

It had confused me because I'd thought, *Well of course they know what they are doing. They're treating him with cruelty. They're pounding nails into him and hanging him up on a cross. Every cruel person always knows that they're being cruel.*

But in that moment with my mother begging on my belly, I understood perfectly. She, like those who'd crucified Jesus, had justified what she'd done and made it permissible in her own mind. And so goes the whole human race.

They should have known better, and there was plenty of cause for blame, and yet blamelessness had been offered. That was grace and that was me, ministering forgiveness to my mother by offering her no blame.

I drew a deep breath and said what was in my spirit to say.

"I forgive you, Mother. You've done nothing wrong to me."

The moment I said it, a tingling spread over my scalp.

Mother's crying eased and her body stilled.

"Nothing, Mother," I said. As if following specifically routed electric circuits, the tingling sensation rode down my arms and spine. "You did nothing wrong to me."

She sat up and stared at me with red eyes. "How can you say that?" she cried. "How can you even say that!?"

I'm sure there are ways I could have psychoanalyzed her angry response, but my mind wasn't interested. It was captivated by the power flowing through my body, from head to foot. The current buzzed through my bones for a moment, and then it was gone, out the bottom of my feet.

Overcome by her own failures as a mother, Kathryn covered her face with both hands and wept. And I let her, silent now, still captivated by the lingering balm of that energy that had swept through my body. For a long while, we remained like that, me prone on my back, her sitting, basking in a power greater than both of us.

Something had happened to me, hadn't it? Something about me had changed.

"What did you do to me, Mother?" I asked.

She shook her head in shame.

"Tell me what you did to me," I said.

"You don't understand, Eden. I had to. I can't disobey. I just can't go against him. I can't . . ."

"Tell me, Mother. Tell me what you did to me."

"I hurt you!" she blurted, pulling her hands from her face. "I took my little daughter and I . . ." She looked away, choked up by terrible guilt.

"You forced me under the water and made me stay in my closet and starved me?" I asked.

"Yes!" she sobbed. "Yes!"

"And tell me how Zeke hurt me."

"He broke your leg!" she screamed, standing. "He commanded me to break it and when I didn't he broke it!"

"He hurt your daughter," I said.

"Yes! Yes, he hurt my daughter!" She was livid.

I let a beat pass.

"But don't you see, Mother . . . I'm not hurt." I sat up in bed and stared at her. "I don't feel any of the wounds that were in my heart only yesterday." I leaned over and began to unravel the bandages on my right leg. "I'm a water walker, Mother. Water walkers don't assign blame. Only their costumes can be hurt, and costumes come and go."

I continued to unwrap my leg.

"What are you doing?"

Zeke had opted not to put a cast on my leg so that walking was out of the question. But he'd never broken a water walker's leg before, had he?

"I'm showing you how unhurt I am," I said, and pulled the last of the bandage free.

My mother took a step back, eyes fixed on my right leg, which was smooth and white and showed not a single bruise, much less swelling, from any break.

"Sweet Jesus," Mother breathed. "Oh dear, sweet baby Jesus."

I swung my legs off the bed and pushed myself to my feet, still weak from the exhausting emotional journey I'd taken through the night. Then I walked to the window, parted the curtain so that I could see out, and stared in the direction of the lake.

"Sweet baby Jesus," my mother said yet again. "You . . . What happened?"

I turned back to face her. "Forgiveness happened," I said. "Just the way it's supposed to happen."

"You . . . Your leg isn't broken."

I looked down at my body. "No, it's not."

"But how?"

"I went for a walk on the lake last night," I said.

"The lake? That's why you're wet? How . . . I . . . I don't understand."

"You don't need to, Mother. I'm not sure I do either." I approached her slowly, heart bursting with compassion. "There's only one thing you need to know right now."

Her eyes searched mine, stricken with apprehension. This was new territory for both of us.

"I'm your daughter," I said, reaching for her hand. "You're my mother and I love you with all of my heart. And if I love you that way, your Father loves you far more, just the way you are. You can't possibly impress him or upset him, he's not that small. Everything you've done, you've only done because you were lost, but today you are found by your daughter and your Father."

Overwhelmed in ways that I couldn't possibly fully grasp, Mother sank to her knees, took me into her arms, and wept. I held her and stroked her hair, feeling beautiful and whole and overflowing with gratefulness.

I had finally found my mother and I found her only by finding myself.

For a long time we held each other. I didn't know what effect this might have on my mother, or her strict religious code, and honestly, I didn't care. I felt utterly loved and invulnerable, both in my mother's arms and apart from them.

Honestly, I felt as though I might be able to walk up to a bathtub and make the water float in the air if I wanted to, because in my mind's eyes, the very water that had once been my grave was now life.

When the tears had subsided and Kathryn had run out of ways to express her remorse, she stood and paced, but even then new tears came. She couldn't keep from looking at my leg.

"I don't understand, Eden." She sniffed and wiped the tears seeping from her eyes. "I just don't know what to think."

"There's nothing to think, Mother. What's done is done and there's no harm."

"You keep saying that, but all I can see is harm." Guilt seemed to have a strangle hold on her, but that was her journey to take. "I didn't mean to hurt you, sweetheart. You have to believe me."

"You can't hurt me."

"Of course I can! I did!" She stared at me with red eyes. "I don't know why I didn't see it before . . . I . . ."

"It's okay, neither did I. But we see now, right?"

She stared at my leg. "I see it but it's still hard to believe. How could your leg just . . . heal?"

"I don't know how, really. I just let go. My old beliefs about how the world worked had to die. I had to see that the troubled sea posed no threat to me."

Her face wrinkled with sorrow again.

"That's what I've put you in, isn't it? A troubled sea."

"No, Mother. It was and is my choice to see or not see trouble in the sea. It's all so plain now. I had to confront my troubles to learn they were only of my own making. I had to take that journey. It's like walking through the valley of death to learn that death is only a shadow, even there. Yea though I walk through the valley of the shadow of death . . ."

"I will fear no evil," she said, finishing one of her favorite psalms.

But she was still gripped by worry. Not the same kind of fear that had held her captive for so long, but anxiety nonetheless.

It was Zeke, I thought. She had to figure out what to do about Zeke.

"Now what?" she said.

"Now we are free, Mother," I said. "If you want to be."

"Free from what? I can't just . . ."

She was getting hung up. And no wonder—she had four decades of bad thinking habits to unlearn and she hadn't had the benefit of growing up in a monastery as I had. Nor had she met an Outlaw yet.

Well, there was me. I guess I was an Outlaw too now.

"Free from whatever you think keeps you safe," I said. "You get to step out of your own boat." Not having been on the lake, she might not fully grasp that analogy so I used more familiar language. "It's up to you to walk into the valley of death and find only a shadow."

She stopped her pacing and looked at me for a long time. Then looked down at my leg. When she lifted her head, I knew she'd made a decision—I had learned to read my mother's resolve from a hundred paces.

"What are we going to do about Zeke?" she asked.

"I'm not going to do anything about Zeke," I said.

She set her jaw and gave a curt nod.

"Well, I am," she said.

KATHRYN HAD spent two hours swinging wildly from states of great peace to places of terribly anxiety. The battle in her mind refused to give her any final emotional resolution. It was amazing how moments of complete clarity could so quickly fog into moments of confusion and fear.

But Eden's leg isn't broken. How's that possible?

And then she'd remember.

She paced, and she tried to make herself busy around the house without truly knowing what she was doing, and she listened to Eden telling Bobby how beautiful he was while she played blocks with him in his room, seemingly oblivious to the war raging in her mother's mind.

But surely Eden knew as well as she did what had to be done. Kathryn had to *undo* everything she'd done, of course.

The problem was, she kept teetering on the brink of exactly what *did* have to be done. Was undoing *everything* really the wisest thing?

Yes, of course it was. She'd subjected her own daughter to a life of expectations she herself couldn't possibly satisfy. And she'd been courting that realization for days now without realizing it. For months, even. Maybe even since the first time she'd baptized Eden.

Once having taken that step years earlier, she'd silenced all her reservations and refused to look back for fear that doing so was only a demonstration of weakness in her own flesh.

How she'd come to see her guilt so clearly in Eden's room, she wasn't sure. But the moment Eden had suggested she'd done nothing wrong, the floodgates had opened and Kathryn had seen just how much she *had* done wrong.

In truth, she'd been a monster deserving of her own drowning. The fact that Eden didn't see it that way only filled her with more guilt, and following that guilt, a terrible need to right all she'd done wrong, even if Eden didn't think of it as wrong.

Eden, whose leg was no longer broken.

So she had to undo what she'd done, and that meant freeing them from Zeke's control.

But was that *really* the wisest thing to do?

She couldn't just confront him. What if he lost his mind and killed them all? She couldn't just run to the police, could she? Zeke would never be so careless to allow it. He no longer trusted her. He'd already taken the cell and cut all the telephone lines. He would undoubtedly have a guard in place, or the road blocked.

Even if she did get past him and made it to the authorities, what then? She would go to prison and leave Eden without a mother to care for her. Was that fair?

She could hold back and look for an opportunity, but it was only a matter of time, maybe today, before Zeke discovered that Eden's leg was no longer broken. Then what?

It doesn't matter, Kathryn. She threw the dishtowel she'd been dragging around for no particular reason onto the table and set her jaw.

It doesn't matter what then. Eden's right. Only your own fear is keeping you from facing the truth.

There was only one way to step into the valley of death, and that was to step into that valley. There was no skirting it or finding a better way around or running away from it.

She had to do this, as much for herself as for Eden.

And she had to do it now, on her own, before she lost the courage.

Kathryn walked to the door, snatched the keys off the nail on the wall, turned the handle, and stepped out into the sunlight.

The sound of the insects in the swamp stopped her cold, there in the doorway. For a moment she became Eden. A young girl who'd awakened five years ago to the same sounds. This was the sound of her prison, reminding her in every waking moment that she was trapped in swampland with no way out.

Kathryn swallowed hard. It was her prison too, wasn't it? It always had been.

She had to undo what she'd done. Yes, she had to.

Walk, Kathryn. Just walk.

She closed the door behind her, stepped down from the porch, and headed to the truck, refusing to lift her eyes to scan the perimeter. Was there a guard there? She didn't care. She just had to walk.

Walk, Kathryn.

Problem was, she *did* care. She cared enough to be terrified because she knew that Zeke owned her and was waiting.

Yea though I walk into the valley of the shadow of death, I will slay that vile beast and make the path right . . .

No. No, that wasn't right. I will fear no evil. I will walk and I will fear no evil. Just like Eden. Just like my daughter.

So she walked. But she still felt fear.

She felt fear when she opened the truck's door and climbed inside and she sat there for a full minute, rehearsing what might or might not happen.

She felt fear when she started the truck, put it into gear, and headed down the driveway because now she was moving, and moving meant closing the distance between her and Zeke.

She felt mind-swooning fear as she guided the truck down the long gravel road, driving far too slow because fast meant sooner, and she wasn't that brave yet.

She felt a chilling spike of fear when she saw Claude's white truck parked on the side of the road past Zeke's house. She was right; Zeke wasn't taking any chances. The only way in or out was through him.

By the time she made the turn and pulled into Zeke's driveway, her fear was so acute that her vision blurred. She brought the truck to a stop, turned off the motor, and tried her best to gather herself.

Yea though I walk, yea though I walk, yea though I walk . . .

She whispered the mantra, hoping to gain strength, but barely heard the words much less found any power in them.

I will fear no evil, I will fear no evil, I will fear no evil . . .

But she did. So much that she considered turning back to rethink a better plan because the one she had in mind was doomed to fail.

At any moment, Zeke would come out, wondering why she'd come and even more, why she was sitting in his driveway like a dead duck. She had to get to his phone and she had to do it now. Just get to the phone in his office, which was the only one she knew of, and make the call to the authorities, and that was all. Just that.

Taking a deep breath, Kathryn opened the door and stepped out. See, now it was too late to turn back. And, surprisingly, that simple thought gave her a moment's courage.

She smoothed her dress, cleared her throat, and headed to the steps. Then climbed them, one at a time. Then she was there, facing the door.

Then knocking on it, thinking, *Yea though I walk, yea though I walk,* over and over despite the fact that she drew no encouragement from the thought.

It's not supposed to feel good, Kathryn. You're only reaping what you sowed. It's supposed to feel like death because . . .

The opening door cut her thought short and she found herself face to face with Zeke, in the flesh, wearing dark pants and a white button-up shirt with a starched collar.

She felt like a schoolgirl caught red-handed, and she hated herself for feeling like that.

"Good morning, Zeke."

In answer he cocked his brow—that condescending look that said, *What now, Kathryn?*

"Nothing," she said, as if answering his unspoken question. "I just . . . Do you mind if I come in?"

"Nothing?"

"No . . . Not really . . . I just . . ."

She stopped herself there, struck by her own words. *Nothing?* Was her experience with her daughter earlier nothing? Was the well-being of her daughter nothing? Was the privilege to be Eden's mother nothing?

Was Eden *nothing?*

Something deep inside of her seemed to flip over, and a surge of anger replaced the fear sucking at her life. Not just anger . . . rage. In fact, for the briefest moment she imagined tearing into the monster before her and ripping his tongue out. *Now tell us what to do!*

But she immediately recognized the danger of showing any emotion similar to rage. If she failed, Zeke might go to the furthest extremes to protect himself.

"Actually, it is something," she said. "May I come in?"

He gave her a shallow grin and swept his hand into the house. "Be my guest."

"Thank you." She stepped past him and scanned the room. "Is your wife here?"

He closed the door and walked past her without answering. This was his way, always keeping her off balance. She'd known it all these years, but had never thought of his manipulation as anything more than a shepherd's steady rod.

"Spit it out, Kathryn. I don't have all day."

"No . . . no, I suppose you don't."

He slipped his hands into his pockets and faced her. "No need to suppose. Just know. Know that I have little patience left for your ineptitude and failures. Know that you're lucky I didn't break *your* leg. Know that I'm still considering it."

She felt her heart pound. Anger felt far better than fear, but she had to let him think it was fear. Easy enough, because at least half of it was.

"Yes, Zeke. Of course. You won't need to do that. I swear you—"

"Don't tell me what I won't need to do. Just tell me why you're here so early in the day."

"It's almost ten o'clock."

"Now you think I'm too stupid to read a clock?"

"No, Zeke. I'm sorry."

"For what? Hmmm? Sorry for what? For mocking me? I give you one simple task, easily accomplished by anyone half your strength using a few basic tools and you can't even do that for me, the one you owe your very life to? Is that it, Kathryn?"

She stared at him, stunned by his coldness.

"Or is there something else you're sorry about now?"

Had he always been this way and she not able to see it?

"I'm sorry . . . I was just sorry for suggesting that you were too stupid to—"

"Do you know how deeply I hate you every time you use those words, Kathryn? *I'm sorry* only reminds me of your failure. You come in here and tell me about your sin, and I'm not above God. I too hate sin. So don't tell me *I'm sorry* and, for the love of God, stop doing whatever it is you're sorry for. Both he and I could use a break, wouldn't you agree?"

Her head was spinning.

"Yes."

"Good. So be a good woman and just lay what you have on the table. Trust me."

She had to remember her purpose. She had to distract him and get to the phone in his office. The only way to distract him was to first earn a measure of *his* trust—he was far too cagey to let his guard down unless she proved herself.

"I'm concerned about Eden."

"Is that so? I broke her leg, didn't I?"

"Yes."

"She can't stand on it, much less walk, right?"

"That's right."

"There's no telephone, no boat, no way to swim through a lake infested with alligators, no wings to fly out on . . . That about covers all of our bases, don't you think?"

"Yes. But that's not my concern. I'm worried about *her.*"

"What's there to worry about? I told you we'd put a cast on soon enough. So she walks with a limp the rest of her life—every garden of Eden has its rotten fruit."

His indifference was bone deep.

"What if she dies?" Kathryn said.

That put a dent in his armor, she thought, as he hesitated.

"Well, that depends on when she dies," he said, stepping over to the kitchen center island to his right. He reached for a cup of coffee next to a frying pan. By all appearances, she'd interrupted his breakfast preparation. Which meant that his wife wasn't around or she likely would've made it for him earlier. "If she dies after the money's transferred we have nothing to worry about."

He took a sip from his cup and set it back down.

"If she dies in the next twenty days, we'd have a problem. The thirty-day cure requires she accept the money when it's transferred. So, technically anyway, she needs to be alive. What makes you think this is a concern?"

She knew most of what he said, but she hadn't realized just how little regard he had for Eden's life. A hum went off somewhere in her head; the room seemed to narrow.

"I think her leg might be getting infected," she heard herself say.

"Oh? What makes you say that?"

"She woke with a fever. Her leg's swollen pretty bad."

"So you're saying that you *don't* trust me."

"No."

Zeke approached her and stopped within arm's reach. She dared not avert her eyes from his.

"If you trusted me, you wouldn't be here to tell me what I already know, now would you? But the truth is, you think I'm too stupid to have thought about infection. You probably think the penicillin shot I gave her when I broke her leg was just for grins?"

The revelation surprised her. She had no idea he'd given her a shot.

"I just thought—"

"Don't. *Think*," he snapped.

"Yes, Zeke. I'm sorry, I just—"

He slapped her face with an open hand, hard enough to make her stagger. She gave up a soft grunt, knowing better than to cry out in his presence.

"I told you not to speak that word," he said, turning his back on her. "You both sicken me."

For two hours, Kathryn had contemplated a dozen scenarios as to how she might accomplish the simple task of getting to the phone, knowing that only in doing so could she undo what she'd done before Zeke learned more than he knew and made any undoing impossible.

She'd left no option unconsidered. She'd thought about using seduction and quickly abandoned the notion. She'd toyed with the idea of using force and turned her attention elsewhere with even more haste. She'd considered wit, lies, speed, stealth, screams, blackmail, explosions, poison, and even more seduction, and in the end landed on using any and all means, depending on what presented itself, because walking into the valley of death didn't come with a plan any more than walking on water did.

But none of her scenarios had anticipated the blind rage that darkened her world when Zeke said those four words.

You. Both. Sicken. Me.

She was moving before any conscious thought told her to move. Pushed by indignation so deep that her very cells forgot their need for survival, she lunged for the counter, scooped up the frying pan, and blindly swung the cast iron weapon with all of her strength as she turned his direction.

To her surprise, the back of his head was there, in the skillet's pathway. His skull stopped the pan's momentum with a loud, hollow *thunk*.

He didn't cry out. He didn't have time to mount a defense. He didn't even try to turn.

He simply dropped to his knees, swayed there for a second, then toppled over, face down, unmoving.

Kathryn stood over him, breathing hard, at a complete loss. She'd hit him. She'd hit Zeke. She'd knocked him out.

This simple realization was quickly followed by another one.

He's going to punish me for this. He's going to kill me.

Her hands were trembling and she dropped the skillet without meaning to. It landed on his leg and clattered to the wooden floor.

Oh my God, oh my God, what have I done? He's going to kill us all!

But Zeke wasn't getting up to kill them all. He was just lying there. He was still alive—she could see his lungs expanding with each breath—but he wasn't moving his legs or arms, and as long as he couldn't move those, he couldn't punish or kill anyone.

All of these thoughts trained by so many years under Zeke's guidance flew through her mind before a far more obvious one took root.

He's unconscious. Which means I can call 911 without him knowing.

Kathryn spun and took two steps toward his office before another thought pulled her up short.

What if he woke up? He'd come after her! She had to tie him up!

She spun back and stared at his large frame on the floor, expecting movement even as she looked. She had to hurry before he did wake, but for that she needed rope, and there was no rope here that she could see. Maybe outside or in the shed, but what if he woke while she was out looking for something to tie him up with?

No, she couldn't risk it. She had to tie him up right now, while he was still unconscious, and she had to tie him up good because he was a bull. There was only one way to do that.

Kathryn grabbed the hem of her skirt with both hands and ripped as hard as she could. The cotton fabric resisted at the hem, but then tore past, leaving a long split up her thigh.

Working in frenzy, begging that form on the floor to remain still, she shredded the bottom of her dress, tearing off four strips before deciding she could wait no longer.

Dropping to her knees, Kathryn straddled Zeke's thighs and reached for his right arm to pull it back. It was then that he groaned and tried to lift his head off the floor.

The change came so unexpectedly that Kathryn cried out, jumped back, tripped on her heels, and went sprawling to her seat beyond his feet.

Zeke grunted and shook his head. Started to push himself up.

No! No, no, no . . .

Blinded once again by panic, Kathryn dove for the fallen frying pan, grabbed its handle, scrambled to her knees, and, with all her might, brought the skillet back down on his head from behind.

Zeke dropped to his face like a bull that had just received a million-volt surge of electric current.

Thump.

She sat back on her heels, panting. There. There, he was down. Still breathing but down.

She had to hurry.

Straddling him, Kathryn started with his hands once again, pulling them behind his back. This time he stayed out.

She wound a strip of cloth around both wrists and tugged the tie tight. Then wound a second strip overlapping the first, this time using her heels for leverage as she cinched the knot as snug as she could.

She quickly did the same at his ankles. And then, to be absolutely sure, she tore off another two strips and bound one around his arms at his elbows, and the second around his knees.

That made six bindings, but that wasn't good enough either, was it? She tore off a seventh strip of cloth and bound it around his mouth so he couldn't yell out and alert Claude or anyone else posted outside.

She stood up and stared at her handiwork. Zeke lay facedown on the wooden floor, bound and gagged like a hog. Not by the strongest ropes, but without any leverage he would be hard-pressed to break any of the bonds.

I've stopped him, she thought. *I've tied Zeke up.*

It took a moment for this thought to become real for her because the very idea still struck her as somehow impossible. Nothing could stop Zeke. That's just the way it was.

And yet there he was, out cold, like a side of beef.

So why was she just staring at him? She had to make a call, so why was she just standing here if he was bound up like a dead bull?

She'd done that?

Slowly the significance of her accomplishment settled into her mind, and with each breath her resolve to do what she'd come to do grew.

This is what it means to walk through the valley of the shadow of death, she thought. Eden claimed to be a water walker. Maybe this meant that she too was a water walker.

Somehow she doubted that.

Didn't matter. She was going to save that water walker.

"Don't move," she said, jaw firm. Then she turned her back on Zeke, walked into his office, crossed to the desk, and lifted the phone.

"This is for you, Eden," she whispered, and with her forefinger she pressed the number 9, then 1 and another 1.

A female operator answered after the second ring.

"Thank you for calling 911, please state the nature of your emergency."

"Yes . . ." She lost track of what words to use.

"Ma'am, please state the nature of your emergency."

"Yes . . . I . . ."

"It's okay, honey. Tell me what's wrong."

Kathryn drew a deep breath.

"I would like to report a kidnapping," she said.

A hesitation.

"Who's been kidnapped, ma'am?"

"Alice Ringwald, daughter of the late senator James Ringwald, was taken from her home in Greenville, South Carolina, five years ago. She is being held at 2090 Rosecrans Road south of Interstate 10 out of Lafayette, Louisiana. Please inform the FBI, I'm sure they have a file."

"Are you sure about this, ma'am?"

"Of course I'm sure. I have the man who kidnapped her bound up on the floor in the next room."

"And do you have his name?"

"His name is Zeke Gunner and he's the devil."

Another short pause.

"And how do you know that Zeke Gunner kidnapped Alice Ringwald, ma'am?"

"Because I helped him do it," she said. "Please hurry."

Then she dropped the receiver in its cradle and walked back into the living room.

There, she thought. *There. I've undone it.*

Now what? But as soon as the question presented itself, she knew exactly what now.

Now she would wait and let the chips fall where they would fall.

Kathryn walked to Zeke's preferred high-backed, upholstered chair in the corner of the living room, poured two fingers of his preferred Scotch into a crystal glass on the side table, and sat down.

Zeke's body remained where she'd left it, back slowly rising and falling as he breathed in darkness. Not so much now, was he? No, not at all.

She leaned back, crossed one leg over, and swirled the Scotch in her glass. Eden wouldn't do it this way, she was sure of that. She would probably just walk on down the street, having no worry. After all, she could heal her own leg.

No, Eden wouldn't do it this way, but then Eden probably wouldn't do it at all. And either way, she wasn't Eden.

She was Eden's mother. And as her mother, she wasn't going to let anyone hurt her again. Ever. Not Claude, not Zeke, not herself.

"They're going to lock you up and throw away the key, you stupid pig."

She didn't hear Zeke speak the words with her ears, but she could hear him nonetheless, speaking from her own mind.

"Shut up, Zeke," she said.

She threw back the Scotch as she'd seen him do so many times, swallowed it in one gulp, and slapped the empty glass back down on the lamp table.

"Just shut up."

Two Days Later

WE SAT in our living room—Mother, Wyatt, myself, and Olivia, the FBI agent who'd worked my case since that first night when Wyatt took me from my home in Greenville, South Carolina. They were talking about the law and about the consequences of their actions, but my mind was on something else. On someone else.

On Stephen Carter, the Outlaw.

He was coming, you see? He was a real person and Olivia knew him, and he was coming today.

I can't tell you how that made me feel. Butterflies were doing aerial loops in my stomach. My heart had been beating like a drum since Olivia had told me an hour earlier.

Why was I excited? Because Stephen seemed to know more about me than I knew about myself. And because he'd shown me all the meaning that my life had for me—all in a dream that was as real as sitting on the couch while Olivia explained the law to Kathryn and Wyatt.

"You have to understand that the law is the law," Olivia was saying. "I understand the situation has changed, but turning yourself in doesn't negate the fact that you kidnapped Alice five years ago. Kidnapping is a serious offense. There's no statute of limitation, you understand? My hands are tied."

Her words bothered me, and I didn't like that, so I put her speaking out of my mind and watched her as she continued.

I was fascinated to learn the extent of the effort she'd expended on my behalf. It made me feel quite special, in an old sort of way. I say "old sort of way" because in the new me, *everything* felt rather special, so it was strange to think of one thing being more special than another. Or threatening, for that matter. But that's hard to explain without stepping out of the boat, so to speak, so unless you've gone to that place where there really is no difference between the water and the sand, you'll have to take my word for it.

Still, I fell in love with Olivia from the moment she climbed out of the black FBI car and walked up to me wearing a tentative smile. She held out her hand.

"My name is Olivia," she said. "I'm with the FBI. And you must be Alice."

I took her hand. "My name is Eden."

She nodded. "Okay. Eden. Are you okay?"

"I always have been," I said. "I just didn't know it."

She searched my eyes, clearly not understanding, then she took me into her arms and held me tight enough to squeeze half the air out of my lungs.

"It is so good to finally see you," she breathed.

She didn't need to hear more about what I meant when I said that I'd always been okay—she simply knew that it was true, even if it made no sense. Something about my presence told her that. There's a way that we speak to each other without words or looks, that's how it works. I can't explain it, I can only report it.

But let me back up a minute.

When I first woke from walking on the lake two days earlier and forgave my mother the way Outlaw had shown me, I wasn't the only one who'd changed. Kathryn had as well. I know that such profound change may sound far too simple, but when you let go of *everything*, it really is simple because there's nothing left to figure out, and nothing to change because letting go of this world completely is the only change you need. Letting go of even the need to understand and trusting your Father.

And that is miraculous, you see?

But just to be clear, letting go is something you *do*, not just talk about. Talking about forgiving changes nothing.

Doing it changes everything, not just in you, but somehow in those around you. We are not healed alone. Don't ask me to explain.

So when I shifted my perception and embraced love instead of blame and threats, something also shifted in my mother. At the very least she was looking at things differently. Sure, seeing my unbroken leg didn't hurt, but she was seeing more than a healed leg.

She was seeing a new kind of love. The only real kind, actually. And the physical power of real love is staggering, because real forgiveness is staggering.

I later learned that while I was spending time with Bobby, whom I loved in whole new way, she'd gone down to Zeke's house, hit him on the head with a cast-iron frying pan, tied him up, and called the police.

I didn't know she had it in her.

It's weird, I know, but part of me had compassion for Zeke. He always was a miserable wretch, not because he was any less loved than I ever was, but because he was blind to that love, just like I had been.

You could say that Zeke was in a kind of hell. Still is. Someone needs to rescue him.

Twenty minutes after Mother made the call, a whole troop of cars with flashing lights swarmed the place. They'd taken Zeke and Claude away in handcuffs on bootlegging charges and then rounded up a bunch of others, none that I knew because I only really knew Kathryn, Bobby, and Wyatt.

As for Paul, Zeke had sent him away with his mother following his beating. I hope to see him soon.

They didn't take my mother away because she'd made the call and there was some confusion about her role in a whole mess of things that would probably take weeks to figure out, beginning with these kidnapping charges that Olivia was now discussing with them.

I didn't know what was going to happen to my mother, but none of that worried me. Kathryn had returned from Zeke's house beaming. She'd run to me and hugged me off my feet, kissing my neck and face. She'd walked though her own small valley and found out that death was only a shadow.

As for my trust account, the money was mine to do with as I pleased, and I had no idea what pleased me as of yet. Maybe I'd just give it all to my mother. Maybe I'd give it to Stephen. Maybe I'd buy a big house and a fast truck for Bobby.

So there I sat on the couch, only half listening to Olivia talk about the case and kidnapping and prison, because I didn't want to think about prisons.

Besides, Stephen was coming to see me.

"There's no way the law is just going to turn a blind eye to such a blatant offense," Olivia was saying. "What you did was wrong. There are consequences. Punishment. Surely you understand that."

"Excuse me," I said, bothered again by what I was hearing.

Kathryn, Wyatt, and Olivia all turned to me as one. They'd treated me like some kind of angel the last two days, not that I blamed them. After all, I was the one who'd walked on water, so to speak. And there seemed to be some speculation that my walking was more than just *so to speak*.

But hearing Olivia talk about how badly I'd been treated and how unfair it would be for Mother not to be punished, only made me feel like sinking again.

I stood up. "I'd like to go check on Bobby, if that's okay."

"Of course, sweetheart!" Kathryn said. "I think he's down by the lake."

"Okay. If Outlaw comes . . ."

"We'll send him right down," Olivia said.

"He'll be here soon?"

"Should be any minute."

"Okay."

I headed for the door and was halfway there when I thought better of it. I turned back and looked at Olivia.

"Can I say something?" I asked.

"Of course, honey."

"I would like to stay here with my mother and father, if that's okay. We have a lot to catch up on."

Olivia exchanged a look with Mother, who smiled proudly.

"Well, sweetheart, I think that's very kind of you. But there may be some complications—"

"I don't want her to go to prison. Wyatt either. I don't think prison will be a good place for them."

"I understand. But we have laws for a reason. The courts can't just overlook a charge in view of a full admission of guilt."

"What charge?" I asked.

"The kidnapping charges."

"I don't want to press any charges."

That made her blink.

"You were underage, sweetheart. And, it's the state that presses charges in these cases."

"I don't think either the orphanage or John and Louise would want you to press charges," I said. "And I don't want you to either."

"They do want me to."

"But they can change their minds. And so can you, right?"

"Well . . . yes . . . But . . ."

"Then please change your mind. Then we won't have a problem."

"Maybe, but that's assuming quite a bit, sweetheart."

"Assuming you'll drown is why you drown," I said. But I immediately knew that she wouldn't understand that, so I put things more in her way of understanding.

"I'd like to assume you and they will hear the heart of a daughter who wants to spend some more time with her mother before she goes off into the world. I'm sure you can all understand."

"That's very loving of you, Eden, but that's not the way we do things under the law."

I thought about that for a second and then looked at Mother, who was watching me with fascination. Strange how all of my grievances against her were no more, as if they'd never been.

I turned back to Olivia.

"Don't you think I've suffered enough already?"

"Yes, of course. I . . ."

"Then why are you trying to put me back into a prison, just when I've found my way to freedom?"

She blinked. "I'm not, dear. I'm only . . ."

"By putting my mother in prison, you only tempt me to think that she offended me, which might put me in my own prison, don't you see? I've let that go. We've had enough offense and punishment in this family to last a lifetime. Please, don't try to make us suffer any more."

She stared at me in silence, and I think the truth of my words finally connected with her because her face slowly softened. In truth, only I had the key to any prison in my mind, but I didn't want to see my mother suffer.

My mother was beaming proudly. There was no way I could let her go to prison. It seemed absurd to me.

I smiled at her. "I'm going to find Bobby."

I left them sitting in silence and made my way toward the lake to look for Bobby.

Funny how the swamps looked so different to me the last two days.

I had lived in fear of them—they were a part of my prison. But now I saw that it was my fear of the swamps, not the actual swamps, that had fortified that prison. There's always something to fear if you think fear will keep you safe. Fire. Swamps. Alligators . . .

Water.

I'm here to say that you can't make the troubled waters of life go away by defending yourself against them. You can only walk over those troubled waters if you offer peace to them and leave the safety of your boat.

Or so it was once written, and I have found Jesus' teaching to be true.

I was walking on the ground without shoes—the first time I'd done so since coming to Louisiana, and I must say, the grass felt glorious under my feet. I wore a tank top, another first outside, and the sun was caressing my skin like a warm, loving hand.

Even the insects in the swamp were singing for joy at my rebirth.

All of this had so distracted me as I made my way down to the lake that at first I didn't even notice there was a man squatting beside Bobby on the shore ahead.

I pulled up and felt my heart rise into my throat. I had been expecting Stephen, rehearsing every vivid detail of his visits in my dreams, but seeing him in the flesh without warning took me completely off guard.

Their backs were to me—they hadn't seen me yet. Stephen had a small flat stone in his hand as did Bobby, who was cocking his arm to throw it.

"Like this?" He gave it a hurl and it skipped once before diving under the surface.

"Perfect!" Stephen said. "Just like that! Now try two skips. Just a little lower to the water."

He handed Bobby the stone in his hand, and Bobby cocked his arm in his own ungainly way, and hurled the stone with all of his might.

This time the flat stone sailed low, skipped once, twice, then three times before plopping into the water.

Bobby bounced up and down, arms in the air, hooting his great accomplishment while Stephen chuckled.

"What did I tell you, boy? Each throw is perfect because . . ."

Bobby finished: "Because practice *is* perfect!"

Stephen gave him a soft punch in his shoulder. "That's right. There's no trying, there's only doing, and each doing is . . ."

Again Bobby finished: "Its own perfect."

They gave each other a high five. "That's right," Stephen said.

I wondered how long he'd been here, waxing philosophical with Bobby. Even in this I loved the Outlaw, I thought. He treated Bobby with no less affection than he did me, taking time for him when he could just as easily have come straight to the house. How he'd come upon Bobby, I didn't know, but it didn't matter. I was glad he had.

I started down the path and got halfway to them before Bobby turned.

His face lit up. "Eden!"

"Hi, Bobby."

Stephen stood, hooked one thumb over his belt, and faced me wearing a gentle grin.

"Watch this, Eden!" Bobby scrambled around searching for a smooth stone. "Watch this!"

Outlaw winked at me.

I smiled wide, face flushed.

"Watch this!" Bobby said a third time, scooping up a stone. He whirled and threw it without aiming. In that split second I knew that the stone could take any number of paths, one of which was sailing true, skipping off the surface, not once but many times all the way to the far side. And I knew, in that instant, that its path could be determined by a choice.

I wasn't sure exactly how, logically, but I knew without a shred of doubt that it could.

The stone skipped twice and plunged beneath the surface.

"See?" Bobby cried. "I can make stones fly."

"Yes, Bobby," I said, walking up to them, eyes on Outlaw now. "Yes you can."

Stephen stepped up to meet me, never breaking his gaze. He stopped a pace from me and for a few moments we stood still, as if acclimating to our roles on this shore in the flesh for the first time.

The wind seemed to stall, the lake stilled, the crickets thought to be silent for the magical moment passing between two who know more than they.

Outlaw offered me both of his hands in invitation. "Eden," he said.

I placed both of my hands on his, palm to palm. "Hello, Stephen. It's good to see you."

He lifted my right hand and kissed my knuckles. "The pleasure is all mine," he said, flashing an intoxicating grin. "I've waited a *very* long time to meet you. We have so much to talk about."

"So much," I said, grinning.

"And you have such a beautiful costume."

I heard myself giggle once—a tiny, girlish offering of delight. But I couldn't help it. I felt as if I was floating in his presence. .

"I was raised in a monastery?" I asked.

"Yes. It was called Project Showdown. Along with thirty-five other orphans. Only a few remember. All of you are truly special. In time, I will draw the rest."

My mind spun with questions.

"Where did you come from?"

"I grew up in a jungle, far away. That's where I became Outlaw. It's all in a book; I'll share it with you soon."

"That's where you learned to walk on water?"

"Yes."

"Which jungle?"

He gave my hands a gentle squeeze. "All in good time."

Then Stephen Carter, the Outlaw, took me into his arms and held me close. "I am so proud of you," he whispered, and kissed my hair. "So very, very proud, my precious Eden."

A lump rose in my throat. "Thank you," I said.

Tears filled my eyes, unbidden. I wasn't sure why I suddenly felt such overwhelming emotions; I wasn't even sure how to define them. I can only say that my tears came from a very deep well, and I seemed to have no power over them.

My shoulders began to shake. I pressed my face into his shoulder, weeping silently and with growing intensity beyond my control.

"The angels kneel in honor to one as beautiful as you, my dear."

With those words, I lost myself completely. Why? Because I'm human. Beyond that I don't know.

"The world weeps with gratitude."

All that I can say is that a lifetime of suppressed relief and longing and joy and sorrow and love and peace, all rolled into one unspoken emotion, bubbled out of me.

It felt like a new kind of baptism.

"Welcome home, my dear water walker," he whispered in my ear. "Welcome home."

And I was. There, in his arms. There, in Louisiana. There, on the earth, in a girl named Eden . . .

I was home.

ACKNOWLEDGMENTS

A massive shout-out to my friend and partner in crime, Kevin Kaiser, without whom I would be lost. Together we take a journey into all things spiritual, together we concoct wild scenarios that find their way into these stories, and together we imagine and commune with the tribe of Outlaws who gather in the world of story both on paper and in cyberspace.

I can't adequately convey my gratitude for your partnership, so I'll just go with thank you. *Water Walker* would not be what it is without you. Neither would my life. Thank you, from the bottom of my heart, thank you.

ABOUT THE AUTHOR

Ted Dekker is a *New York Times* best-selling author with more than five million books in print. Heralded as a "master of suspense" by *Library Journal,* Dekker has sold millions worldwide. Dekker's upbringing as the child of missionaries who lived among the headhunter tribes of Indonesia gives him a unique perspective outside the cultural bubble, enabling him to craft provocative insights, unforgettable characters, and adrenaline-laced plots in his fiction. Two of his thirty-plus novels, *Thr3e* and *House,* have been made into movies, with more in production.

Dekker resides in Austin, Texas, with his wife and children. You can find him at Teddekker.com and Facebook.com/teddekker.

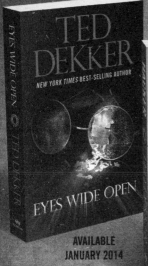
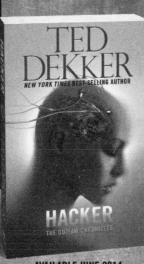
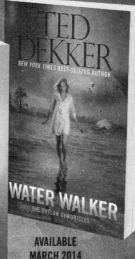

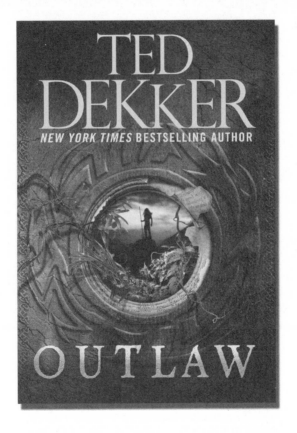

WORTHY

P U B L I S H I N G

If you enjoyed this book, will you consider
sharing the message with others?

- Mention the book in a Facebook post, Twitter update, Pinterest pin, or blog post.

- Recommend this book to those in your small group, book club, workplace, and classes.

- Head over to www.facebook.com/TedDekker, "LIKE" the page, and post a comment as to what you enjoyed the most..

- Tweet "I recommend reading #WaterWalker by @TedDekker // @worthypub"

- Pick up a copy for someone you know who would be challenged and encouraged by this message.

- Write a book review online.

You can subscribe to Worthy Publishing's newsletter at worthypublishing.com

WORTHY PUBLISHING
FACEBOOK PAGE

WORTHY PUBLISHING
WEBSITE